THUNDER CITY

OTHER SCHOLASTIC BOOKS
BY PHILIP REEVE

PHILIP REEVE

THUNDER CITY

Scholastic Press
New York

Library of Congress Cataloging in publication number: 2024012280

ISBN 978-1-5461-3823-5

10 9 8 7 6 5 4 3 2 1   24 25 26 27 28

Printed in Italy   183
First edition, November 2024

Book design by Steve Scott

*For Jeremy Levett, long-time friend of the WOME,
explorer of the Great Southern Continent,
and architect of the Zebra Crossing.*

CONTENTS

1   Tamzin Pook   1
2   Revenant Engines   7
3   Trouble Comes to Thorbury   11
4   Strega   17
5   Bad to the Bone   23
6   Rescue   31
7   Airships   38
8   The Man in the Bouncy Castle   48
9   Paris   52
10 Groundscraper   59
11 Jailbreak   65
12 The Daunt   69
13 Putting Out the Trash   75
14 Out-Country   81
15 In Thunder City   88
16 The Scavenger Town   93
17 Such a Pretty City   99
18 The Hercules   104
19 Bad Luftgarten   107
20 The Soldier of Fortune   115
21 The Thing with Eve Vespertine   122
22 A Spot of Art   128
23 An Early Bath   131
24 The Air B&B   141
25 Fire in the Sky   148
26 The Swimming Pool   153
27 Squid Squad   160
28 Rock of Ages   168
29 Kush Tundurbai   174

30	Worm Runner	179
31	Down on Base Tier	183
32	Missing Tamzin	186
33	The Prodigal Star	193
34	Maximum Confusion	200
35	Surviving Contact with Reality	209
36	In the Dead Corner	216
37	Troubled Waters	229
38	Six Against a City	235
39	The Lava Fields	241
40	Shilpit	248
41	The Architect Entertains	256
42	The Dismantling Yards	263
43	A Slight Awkwardness at Dinner	269
44	Boogie Wonderland	274
45	The Pudding Course	283
46	The Hideout	287
47	Small Cat	292
48	Stop the City!	297
49	Scrap Metal	303
50	Surrender	309
51	The Gates of the Sunless Country	313
52	Home	319

1

TAMZIN POOK

The sea was calm that evening, and the raft town of Margate lay at anchor just off the rugged western coast of the Great Hunting Ground, surrounded by a slowly spreading slick of sewage and chip wrappers.

What portion of the Hunting Ground that was, with its stern cliffs and stony beaches, Tamzin Pook was not sure. She caught only a glimpse of it as she went with the rest of the team and their guards along the walkway that led to the stage door of the Amusement Arcade. The walkway was mostly enclosed, but outside the stage door there was a section called "the paddock," walled with wire mesh, where keen fans and gamblers gathered to watch the players pass. The other players waved at the onlookers, or showed off their muscles, or blew kisses. They were all much more glamorous than Tamzin. Tamzin was a girl you wouldn't look at twice: short and wiry, her black hair cut short, her blunt, tan face set in a semipermanent scowl. While the others went in for colorful costumes and flashy bits of armor, Tamzin always wore the same plain, close-fitting tunic and leggings in which she trained. But it was Tamzin the fans were waiting for. As soon as they caught sight of her, the usual shouts began.

"Tamzin!"

"Over here!"

"Tamzin Pook!"

"Good luck, Tamzin!"

"Should have been you, Pook!"

"Vengeance for Eve Vespertine!"

Hooting like a lot of monkeys, Tamzin thought, ignoring them. *It ought to be them inside this cage, not us.* She looked out through the wire again toward that anonymous shore. Two small motorized towns had stopped on the tide line. Airships and passenger balloons filled the sky above them, drawn like moths to the lights of Margate and its infamous Amusements.

Then the stage door swung open, and Tamzin passed through it with her fellow fighters into the backstage area, where the stagehands were waiting to hand them their weapons.

There were four boys with her that night, and three other girls. All of them were bigger and stronger than Tamzin. Some showed their nervousness; others tried to hide it. They talked and laughed together, but not to Tamzin. They were still mistrustful after what had happened last season with Eve Vespertine, she thought. Their side-eye glances made her feel guilty. She wanted to tell them she had their backs and would keep them safe if she could, but she wasn't the sort of person who was good at saying things like that. If she tried, she would only end up mumbling and stumbling and making everyone embarrassed and more nervy still.

The stagehands were handing out the gear: axes, chain-swords, serrated cleavers. From a gantry overhead, minders with guns kept

2

watch in case any players got the bright idea of trying to fight their way to freedom rather than face another show.

A stagehand gave Tamzin her knife. Its smooth rubber handle was stained black with her sweat. An armored cable trailed from it, plugged into a battery pack that fit onto her belt. She checked the battery herself, as she did always, making sure it had been fully charged. When she looked up, one of the new boys caught her eye and smiled.

"This waiting is the worst," he said. "Wonder what Mortmain's got lined up for us tonight?"

Tamzin didn't answer. She guessed he wanted to talk to calm his nerves. Maybe he thought if he got friendly with her she could save him from whatever was waiting for them. But the best thing he could do for all of them was let her concentrate. He was cute, that boy, and he had performed well in his first few shows, but she didn't even bother to learn her new teammates' names anymore. It hurt less that way when a show went bad.

She turned away from him and stared at the door that led into the Arcade. It was a big door, squarish and twice as tall as Tamzin. Its timbers were bound and studded with iron.

"Two minutes, people!" shouted the stage manager.

One of the new girls was sobbing with fear. The others moved away from her, afraid she'd bring bad luck. From beyond the door came the eager voices of the crowd, blurred into one huge, ominous wash of noise that sounded like a stormy sea. Tamzin did not hear it. She was concentrating on the ironbound door. She had learned that if she concentrated hard enough, even her thoughts fell quiet. Then there was only Tamzin, and the door, and the unknown thing that was waiting beyond the door to kill her.

"OK, people!" chirped the stage manager. "Big smiles, everybody! Break a leg! You're going to knock 'em dead tonight!"

The bolts were drawn back. A burly stagehand grasped the lever that worked the door. Tamzin heard the voice of Dr. Mortmain, Margate's Master of Amusements, telling the crowd something that made them go quiet, then laugh, then cheer.

The door slid upward on greasy chains. Tamzin's team ran past her, and she gripped her knife and followed them out into the arena.

The big space was in darkness, as it always was when a show began, the house lights dimmed, the small, high windows shuttered to make the blackout complete. Then spotlights mounted in the high dome of the roof were turned on and began to sweep to and fro, following the players as they scattered and took up their fighting positions.

"Let there be light!" commanded Mortmain, from up in his private box, and the technicians switched on more lamps until the oval pit in which the players stood was bathed in it. The floor had been spread with fresh sawdust, pinkish in places where the blood from the warm-up acts was soaking through. Around the edge ran a high timber wall, marked with the scars and stains and scorch marks of previous shows. From the steeply raked seats above, five hundred eager faces stared down at Tamzin and her comrades.

The players were barely aware of the audience. Their eyes were on the far end of the arena, where more chains were rattling as another massive door heaved upward. In the dark behind the door, a Revenant Engine raised its armored head.

The spotlights swept away from the players to form a cone with the Revenant pinned at the point of it. As the reflections blazed from its armor, Tamzin saw that it was lizard-shaped. A high spine

4

of metal plates; a long, segmented tail with a bundle of ferocious spikes at the end. It looked as if Mortmain had dug up a dinosaur from some deep tar pit and armored it in steel and chrome. But its small eyes glowed a ghostly green, as the eyes of Revenant Engines always did.

Inside the Revenant's armored skull, a dead brain was nested, jolted back into a sort of life by weird old electrical machines left over from before the Sixty Minute War. The brain was not human, because strict laws forbade the building of Revenants with human brains or human bodies. Perhaps it was the brain of a crocodile in there, Tamzin thought, looking at the lizardy length of the new engine, its spines and sharpnesses. But the Revenants' bodies did not always reflect what sort of beast their brains had once belonged to — it might just as easily be the brain of a monkey, or a dog, or some wild creature Tamzin had never heard of. All she knew for certain was this: It hated her. Hate was what drove the Revenant Engines. Maybe Mortmain trained them to hate, or maybe it was natural for dead things to hate living ones, but Tamzin had never met a Revenant yet that did not want to murder her.

There were gasps from the crowd, and a scream or two, as the latest Revenant stalked out into the arena. Those rubes from the towns parked on the coast had likely never seen a Revenant Engine before. Mixed with the gasps, Tamzin heard a few disappointed groans: Those would be from serious gamblers who watched every show and had bet on the Revenant winning tonight. Mortmain had built dinos before, and Tamzin knew how to deal with them. She glanced left and right and saw something like relief on the faces of the others. The cute new boy — his name was Sergio; she couldn't help but hear his fans chanting it — glanced back at her and actually grinned.

But Tamzin knew overconfidence could be as dangerous as panic, or despair, or any of the other emotions that tugged at players in the Arcade. It couldn't be just another dino, she thought. She risked a glance at Mortmain, up in his private box. Mortmain, with his fussy lilac beard and gigantic silver lamé turban, and a faint smirk playing about his lips as he watched the fight developing below him. He had some surprise in store for them, Tamzin guessed, and she would have to work out what it was and warn the others before it was too late. She must not fail them as she had failed Eve Vespertine.

So think, Pook, think. What looks like a dinosaur but is even more dangerous?

"It's a dragon!" she shouted.

The players reacted just in time. The Revenant Engine cranked its steel jaws open and a plume of oily orange fire poured out. The sawdust floor flashed briefly into flame; the dampened timber of the arena walls steamed. The crowd roared. The game had begun.

2

REVENANT ENGINES

At least no one was dead, thought Tamzin. Not yet. The Revenant coughed up another fireball and the arena walls flickered like a zoetrope with the shadows of her teammates running out of range. The boy called Sergio had not dodged quickly enough: He stumbled around shrieking, trailing smoke and a stink of burnt pomade as he beat frantically at his burning hair. Skip Recap ducked in under the dragon's jaw and started flailing with his chain-sword at the armored hydraulic cables on its legs. Another boy ran in close with an axe, but the tail lashed around and a scarlet fountain jetted into the spotlight beams as he fell. The crowd liked that. The crowd went *ooh*. The crowd went *aah*. The crowd boomed and sighed like a steep sea.

And Tamzin Pook kept herself out of the dragon's way and kept her wits about her and kept doing what she was supposed to: watching the way the Revenant fought.

This one had a thick hose under its lower jaw, armored in steel mesh. Up that, Tamzin reckoned, gas or paraffin must be pumped from an internal tank, and set on fire by a flame in the back of the dragon's maw. She ran to the nearest player, the bad-luck blonde girl who had been crying earlier, and who was crying still, frozen in panic and waiting to be killed. Tamzin grabbed her, shouted, pointed to the hose, and gave her a shove to send her stumbling into the melee that was developing around the dragon. She caught another player's eye and motioned for him to give Bad-luck girl cover. If they could cut that fuel line, it might save a few lives; if they couldn't, it might still distract the Revenant and give Tamzin time to do what Tamzin did best.

❋

What Tamzin did best was killing Revenants. She had arrived on Margate as a small child, part of a job lot of slaves who had been captured when the static settlement of Mayda was devoured by predator rafts. She had not been an obvious choice for an Arcade slave; she was too small, not a good runner, not built to wield the heavy power tools that the others used to hack the deadly machines apart. But Mortmain's trainers had seen something in her, and developed it. She could keep calm in the face of the Revenants, and while the others whaled on them she would watch until she felt she understood them, until she could sense the patterns in their moves and was able to find a weakness, an opening . . .

This dragon, for example. Beneath its baroque blades and razor-edged flanges, it was only another Revenant. Its head swayed one way, then the other. If someone moved in front of it, it let rip with the flamethrower. (It belched its fire again, just missing bad-luck girl as she scampered in under its head.) If they moved to either side, the tail lashed around. (It lashed around now, wounding the boy Tamzin had told to run interference.) But the others had seized the idea and they were rallying, darting in and out around the dragon's legs, trying to distract it from what was going on beneath its chin.

Tamzin began to move. She moved like a dancer, guided by the rhythm of the fight. The crowd, who had been waiting for this, let out a murmur of excitement, which rose and grew and turned into her name, chanted.

The Revenant dimly sensed danger. Its head swung to track her, its eyes flaring with that eerie marsh-gas light. But just as it opened its jaws, the hose beneath them parted under the teeth of Bad-luck girl's chain-sword. Tamzin danced nearer, leaning back hard as the bladed tail swept past her, ducking beneath it as it swung back. She ran in under the dragon's flank, reached up, fit her fingers between the armor plates on its side, and started to climb. The metal under her hands was hot. It was so shiny she could see her own reflection in it.

"Tamzin! Tamzin! Tamzin!" the crowd was shouting, until the sound seemed to fill the whole world.

Mortmain always put the brain in the Revenant Engine's head. Maybe it had to go there for the Revenant to think and behave like a living creature, or maybe he wanted to give his players a fair chance. One day, Tamzin thought, he would surprise her, hide it in the engine's spine or up its bum. But today was not that day. The dragon bucked, trying to shake her off. She clung on hard and edged up its neck, writhing her way past the lethal spines. The rest of the team was attacking it below, whooping and hollering, swinging axes, chain-swords. Their noise and movement kept drawing its attention away from Tamzin. She almost felt sorry for it. The stink of spilled gas from the severed fuel line made her head reel, so she tried to hold her breath as she crept the last few feet to the dragon's head. She grabbed hold of a horn and regretted it, for it sliced her left hand open, but the pain helped to counteract the effect of the fumes. Everything grew very clear.

"Tamzin! Tamzin!" went the crowd.

Tamzin drew her knife. The handle ended in a metal claw, which she used to pry open one of the hatches on the back of the dragon's head. Inside were tubes, wires, things for which she didn't know the names. The dragon reared up, tipping her backward. She grabbed the horn again and shouted with pain as it cut her to the bone. With the other hand, she drove her knife as deep as she could into the dragon's brain.

Sparks flew out at her, then a gout of thick fluid. She pressed the switch on the knife's handle. The dragon shuddered. It spasmed. It toppled sideways like a demolished building, with players skipping clear as it came down. Tamzin rolled out of its wreck, cursing her sliced-open hand. She saw Bad-luck girl laughing in amazement to find herself still alive. She saw a wounded boy being dragged off, dying maybe, and Sergio with his burnt hair smoldering. She saw the others, spattered with oil and gore, starting their victory chant.

"Death to the Dead! Death to the Dead!"

She saw Mortmain rising to his feet. His dark eyes were fixed on her. Mortmain the inventor was furious that she had defeated his new Revenant with such speed. But Mortmain the showman was happy. He raised his hand. Stagehands waiting up in the Arcade's high roof let his microphone down to him on its long cable. His voice boomed out of the speakers like the words of a cheerful god.

"Ladies and gentlemen! Are we not amused?"

3

TROUBLE COMES TO THORBURY

Miss Torpenhow had just reached the Diet of Ulp when she began to realize that her city had eaten something that disagreed with it.

All afternoon, Thorbury had been chasing a shabby, twin-tiered merchant town through a desolate portion of the central Hunting Ground. The movement of the city, as it crawled over the larger hills in its path and barged its way through the smaller ones, caused the room to sway and the windows to rattle, and set the ceiling lights swinging like pendulums. Miss Torpenhow, who had lived all of her fifty-seven years aboard Traction Cities, barely noticed. But she was annoyed at the way the chase distracted her pupil.

She was coaching the mayor's daughter, Helen Angmering, whose final school exams were now less than three months away. Today's lesson was on the history of the Wheeled Wars (480–520 TE). Miss Torpenhow had always found it a most rewarding period, but Helen seemed far more interested in how the chase was going. She kept getting up from her desk to open the window and listen to what people were saying in the square outside.

"I wonder if there will be any nice dresses aboard the town when we capture it?" she mused, while Miss Torpenhow was writing out a list of important dates for her to memorize. "I expect not. It sounds a rather dull little place. It's been absolutely ages since we ate a town with any decent shops."

It was not the girl's fault, Miss Torpenhow reflected. Even aboard a city as cultured and genteel as Thorbury, women were not thought to really need an education. The only career to which Helen Angmering could look forward was as the wife of some wealthy gentleman. It had been the same for Miss Torpenhow, when she was young. She had not been a mayor's daughter like Helen, of course — her late father, who had encouraged her interest in learning, had been a member of London's Guild of Historians. But the Guild did not accept female members, so she had moved to Paris to study, and then to Thorbury to tutor the children of its mayor and councillors.

Watching Helen Angmering lean out of the window again to ask the passersby if they had noticed any shops aboard the chase, Miss Torpenhow wondered if she had been wasting her time.

All in all, it came as rather a relief when the people in the square started cheering and one of the servants looked in to say that the hunted town had seen reason and accepted that it could not outrun Thorbury any longer. It had stopped and was raising flags of surrender.

"Now here we see a living example of the things I have been explaining to you, Helen," Miss Torpenhow said. "When mobile towns and cities were a new invention, the big ones ate up the little ones without any regard for the damage done or the lives lost. But in 520 TE all the great cities gathered at the Diet of Ulp . . ."

"Diet?" asked Helen, who was very conscious of her figure.

"A sort of conference," explained Miss Torpenhow. "All the great cities came together, and laid down the laws that govern Municipal Darwinism to this day . . ."

As she spoke, in accordance with those very laws, Thorbury slowed to a halt a quarter-mile from its prey, opened its jaws, and allowed the captured town the dignity of driving up the ramps into the city under its own steam. But as she went on, reminding Helen of the splendid resolutions contained in the Treaty of Ulp, strange and ominous noises started to emerge from Thorbury's Gut.

Miss Torpenhow was well used to the sounds made by the dismantling engines down there, and to the vibrations that rippled through the city's metal frame whenever its giant saws and angle-grinders started chewing through the deckplates of a captured town. But what were these dull booms? These shudderings? These quick, sharp cracklings, which sounded almost like . . .

"Gunfire!" said Helen, running to the window again. When she opened it, the sounds came in much more clearly.

"It cannot be," said Miss Torpenhow. "People on civilized towns and cities do not shoot at one another. It is true that wicked pirate suburbs will sometimes use guns to disable their prey before they eat it, but the town Thorbury is eating was no pirate. It surrendered in the proper manner, and came aboard peaceably . . ."

And yet the sounds went on, and gradually all the other noises of the city were stilled. Miss Torpenhow imagined the people in the streets and parks all standing in silence like her and Helen, listening and wondering.

It did *sound* a little like gunfire.

"What does it mean, Miss T?" asked Helen.

"Come," said Miss Torpenhow. "We shall see what your father makes of this."

She went briskly to the door and out into the hallway. Helen hurried after her. The schoolroom was in the starboard wing of Thorbury's ornate town hall, and there were many yards of wood-paneled corridor to walk along before they reached the lobby, where the grand sweep of the twin staircases rose to the mayor's quarters on the second floor. But, rather than start up the stairs, Miss Torpenhow hung back, for a great crowd of gentlemen was coming down. There were Defense Corps officers in braid-encrusted uniforms, wearing plumed hats of startling size. There were councillors, looking very wise and dignified in their black official robes. There were clerks, clutching maps and plans, and Her Grace the High Priestess of Peripatetia with her wheeled staff of office and her bevy of attendants. There was a man carrying a small portable writing desk in case anyone needed to dash off a message. And amid them all, in the full splendor of his purple dress uniform, came the Mayor of Thorbury himself, Amadeus Angmering III.

Normally at such a time, Mayor Angmering would have been waiting in the town hall's grand reception room to welcome aboard the mayor and dignitaries of the captured town. But the councillors who had gone down to the Gut to escort the new arrivals had not returned, and these alarming noises kept going on and on, so he had lost patience and decided to see for himself what the trouble was.

He glanced at his daughter as he passed, but did not smile, or acknowledge her, or give any sign at all that he had noticed her.

He has much on his mind, of course, thought Miss Torpenhow. Amadeus had been a cold fish when she arrived in Thorbury to tutor him nearly thirty years ago, and the responsibilities of power had done nothing to thaw him out. She could not help feeling sorry for Helen, and glad that she and her brother, Max, had inherited the warmer and sunnier nature of their late mother.

She took the girl's hand and said, "Come, my dear. Your father will soon get to the bottom of it all."

They funneled out through the big front doors with the rest of the crowd, making for the elevator station. This topmost tier of Thorbury was known as the Command Deck, or *Befehlsebene*, a name that dated back to the city's earliest beginnings as a nomad traction fortress. But the hairy warriors who had traveled aboard it then would not have recognized this new Command Deck, where lovely buildings in the Motorized Gothic style were arranged in a ring around a circular park with the low, domed terminus of the Spinal Elevator at its center.

The sun had set by that time. The spires and turrets of the town hall and the other buildings stood out sharply against the afterglow, like silhouettes cut from black card. A flock of starlings swirled across the western sky, making ready to settle for the night on their usual roosts in the trees of Bellevue Park, down on Tier Two, where Miss Torpenhow had her own apartment. It felt just like any other evening in early spring. The sounds that had caused all the alarm had faded. A pungent, bluish smoke hung in the air, but smoke and bad smells often issued from the Gut when the city was eating, and it seemed natural that the vapors would hang about on a still night like this, rather than blowing away across the Out-Country.

As she trotted after Mayor Angmering and his retinue along the gravel pathways toward the elevator station, Miss Torpenhow started to think that there was no emergency after all. But at the

15

foot of the steps that led up into the station the procession came to a halt, so suddenly that several councillors tripped over their robes and the man with the portable writing desk dropped his inkwell.

"Aha, the elevator is coming up!" said a sandy-haired man standing close to Miss Torpenhow and Helen. "That must be the delegation from the captured town at last. I wonder what caused the delay? An explosion or tier collapse perhaps. Let's hope no one has been hurt."

The big gilded arrow above the station entrance was slowly turning, marking the elevator's passage up from the Base Tier Terminus, through the lower, middle, and upper residential tiers, until it reached the Command Deck. A bell chimed as it arrived, the clear sound echoing from the watching buildings. In the tiled interior of the station, the elevator doors opened. The attendants who stood waiting to slide the outer concertina gate aside fell back in confusion, and someone inside the elevator reached out and opened it instead.

The elevator car looked crowded, but most of its occupants made no move to leave. Only one man emerged, striding out into the twilight to stand at the top of the station steps, staring down the crowd.

"Oh!" said Miss Torpenhow. "Gabriel Strega has come back!"

4

STREGA

He was a small man, neatly dressed in black. He had a pale face, with a high forehead and a trimmed black beard. His eyes were very large and dark, and they glinted with what seemed like mischief as he surveyed the startled faces of Mayor Angmering and his councillors.

"Who is he?" asked Helen.

"Gabriel Strega," said Miss Torpenhow, trying to calm the tremor that crept into her voice. "He was Thorbury's Chief Planning Officer when you were just a little girl. A very brilliant young man, but his suggestions were unsound. He made a bit of a scene at a council meeting, and was dismissed. He left the city in a huff. I never thought we would see him again. I suppose he must have come aboard with that town we just ate. Perhaps he wants his old job back?"

The man in black came down the steps of the station. He was smiling a reassuring smile. Somehow, no one in the crowd felt reassured.

"Mayor Angmering," he said. "We meet again. Do you remember me?"

The mayor stepped forward then. He was not a particularly noble-looking man, nor a particularly good mayor, but he was an Angmering, and that alone made him an impressive figure. His long-ago ancestor Lothar Angmering had persuaded a small Anglish-speaking traction town called Steeple Plumbury to combine with a small German-speaking traction town called Thorburg, creating the city that became Thorbury. Lothar's descendants had guided it safely through the horrors of the Wheeled Wars and the Zagwan Deluge into this peaceable Golden Age of Traction. Now, in the year 882 TE, it was big enough and prosperous enough to run smoothly without much help from mayors, but the electors still liked to keep an Angmering in the town hall for old times' sake.

"Gabriel Strega," said the mayor. "I thought the council had expelled you from our city?" He spoke in a firm if slightly peevish voice, which echoed back at him from the grand facades of the town hall, the Civic Library, the Planning Department, and the Temple of Peripatetia. From their pediments and balustrades the gilded statues of his gods and ancestors looked down approvingly, as if they felt he was taking exactly the right tone with this interloper. "I do not recall pardoning you, Strega. Why have you returned?"

"Some years ago, Mayor Angmering," said Strega pleasantly, "I offered you a way of making Thorbury great. You threw me out. Now I have come back to eat your city."

There was a little murmur of surprise at that, but only from those people standing near the front of the crowd: Strega was not so used to public speaking as the mayor. Many of the onlookers could not hear him.

Mayor Angmering snorted. "One man alone cannot eat a city!"

"Oh, indeed he can," said Strega cheerfully. "He can if he eats it from *within*, the way a maggot eats an apple. And, anyway, I am not alone."

He raised his hand and snapped his fingers. The men who had been waiting mostly forgotten in the elevator car came hurrying out to form up on the steps behind him. There were so many of them that they must have been packed in like sardines for their journey up from the Gut, completely ignoring the elevator's safety regulations. But these did not look like men who ever paid much heed to safety regulations. They wore the scruffy clothes of Out-Country scavengers, augmented with rusty breastplates and other scraps of armor. Many had steel helmets on their heads, and swords at their sides, and bandoliers of bullets draped across their chests. Most seemed to have about them somewhere a white badge in the shape of a leering cartoon skull. All carried guns.

"Allow me to introduce the Boethius Brigade," said Strega. "They will be taking over security from now on. Their comrades down below have already seized your Dismantling Yards and engine rooms on Base Tier. They are nomad mercenaries from the borders of the Ice Wastes, and rather a bloodthirsty bunch, I'm afraid. They boarded that town you ate this afternoon, killed everyone, and used the place as bait. Bait that your greedy little city ate up as eagerly as I had expected. Now they will kill everyone aboard Thorbury too, unless you obey my instructions to the letter."

Another murmur of alarm went rippling through the crowd, much louder this time. Several of the military men drew their swords, but small popping sounds echoed across the park, and Miss Torpenhow realized, as the crowd reeled backward, carrying her with it like a tide, that Strega's mercenaries were shooting into the air.

"Stay!" shouted Strega, raising his hand again. The guns fell silent. Glass tinkled from broken windows high in the town hall. Miss Torpenhow looked around for Helen, who had been separated from her in the panic.

"If you think you can fight us," said Strega, "you would be well advised to think again. Your city is mine."

"This is an outrage, sir!" declared Mayor Angmering. "It is against all the rules of Municipal Darwinism!"

"Well, rules are made to be broken, I always think," said Strega lightly. He took from his pocket a small silvery thing, which he held out as if to show to the mayor. There was a quick, sharp noise, a puff of smoke. Mayor Angmering took a step backward, looked indignantly at Strega, and collapsed.

For a moment, Miss Torpenhow did not quite understand that the silvery thing had been a gun, and the quick, sharp noise a gunshot. Nor did anyone else in the crowd, it seemed, for there was an awful silence while the echo faded. Then one of the High Priestess's women screamed, and suddenly everyone else was screaming too, or shouting, or running, or doing some combination of those things.

Miss Torpenhow had no idea what she should do. It was a horrible feeling, for she prided herself on being a sensible and decisive sort of person, and was seldom at a loss for long. But violence was something so very far outside her experience that she simply froze, like a terrified animal. It was only when she heard, amid the uproar, the thin, high voice of Helen Angmering wailing, "Father!" that she remembered she had a duty to her pupil.

She waded through the panicked crowd. One of Strega's nomads loomed up in front of her, grinning and looking very pleased with himself for all the chaos he was causing.

"Out of my way, you oaf!" snapped Miss Torpenhow, pushing past him, and there beyond him was Helen, kneeling on the wet grass, in great danger of being trampled in the stampede. Mayor Angmering's aides had dragged him away, but there was a great puddle of blood soaking into the lawn where he had fallen.

Miss Torpenhow seized Helen by the hand, pulled her to her feet, and began walking swiftly across the park toward the stairway beside the fountains on the forward side. A lot of her fellow citizens were heading in the same direction, all eager to return to their nice, quiet houses on the tiers below and wait for the unpleasantness to end. But as those at the front of the crowd reached the stairhead they wavered, and drew back, and moved aside. Up the stairs came hurrying another group of Strega's nomad friends. Behind them, moving with a jerky, mechanical gait, came figures too large to be quite human, armored in dark metal, with a green light shining through the slits and eyeholes of their visors.

"The aft stairs, perhaps," said Miss Torpenhow, turning Helen briskly around, and they walked very quickly back through the darkening park and along a narrow street between the town hall and the Temple of Peripatetia.

"What were they?" sobbed Helen. "What were those things?"

"Those are Stalkers, my dear," said Miss Torpenhow. She was glad of the question, because she found that talking calmed her nerves. "The technomancers of the old Nomad Empires devised a way of reanimating dead warriors to fight their wars. They are also known as 'Jaegers' and 'Revenants.' I have heard that a few of them still exist, but I had never expected to meet any, least of all aboard our own dear city. They must be very old, for it would be illegal to construct them nowadays. Although the raft town of Margate has a ghastly tourist attraction where slaves are forced to do battle with such things . . ."

But the Revenants Strega had brought with him had been built for battle, not just butchering hapless slaves.

If *Strega has Stalkers with him*, thought Miss Torpenhow as she hurried Helen toward the aft stairs, *then who can stand against him? Our poor, lovely city is lost. And it is my fault! It is my fault! If it were not for me, we should never even have heard of Gabriel Strega . . .*

5

BAD TO THE BONE

The aft stairs were old, and very little used these days. To Miss Torpenhow's relief, Strega's nomads did not seem to have found them yet. Helping the half-fainting girl down them, she reached the Upper Residential Tier, and soon arrived at her own apartment, on the ground floor of a pleasant block on Circular Street. Once she was inside and the door was shut, it felt as though none of the unpleasantness had ever happened. Or it would have, had it not been for poor Helen, who had been sobbing so long and so steadily that she had given herself the hiccups.

Miss Torpenhow led her into the living room and sat her down in the armchair by the window, then went into the little kitchen to make tea. She believed very firmly that there was no problem that could not be made at least slightly better by a nice cup of tea. Besides, there was something calming about the normality of filling the kettle, boiling the water, warming the pot, carefully scooping two spoonfuls of Weerasinghe's Best Indian Breakfast Blend into the infuser, fetching the cups from the dresser, pouring milk into the jug . . .

"My father is dead," said Helen Angmering in a small, flat

23

voice. She seemed to have run out of tears. She sat trembling, curled in upon herself, watching Miss Torpenhow pour steaming amber tea into two cups.

"I am afraid so, my dear," said Miss Torpenhow.

"But how could Mr. Strega do such a thing? Why? Father had done him no harm."

"I am so very sorry. Now do try and drink a little tea. It will help to calm you."

"I don't want to be calm! How can I be calm? I shall never be calm again," said Helen angrily. But she took the cup that Miss Torpenhow passed her, and after a little while, in a lower voice, she asked, "What will become of us, Miss Torpenhow?"

"My friends call me Hilly," said Miss Torpenhow. This was not entirely true, because Miss Torpenhow was a shy and reserved person who had no friends, but she always thought that, if she had, she would have liked them to call her Hilly. In this terrible new situation, she wanted poor Helen to think of her as a friend, not just a tutor.

"Hilly," said Helen uneasily, as if trying the name out. "What will become of our city? Is Gabriel Strega really in charge now?"

"I fear he is, my dear. It is most desperately unfair, but if his mercenaries and their Stalkers have captured Base Tier and the Command Deck, then the tiers in between will be theirs soon enough. Our soldiers are no match for such vicious desperadoes, especially with General Kleinhammer away on his annual holidays — no doubt that is why Strega chose this moment to strike."

"But the councillors, the Planning Department . . ."

Miss Torpenhow shook her head. "I daresay Strega's men will

round them up and throw them all in jail, or worse. That is how it was usually done, in the bad old days."

"But why? What does he want with our city?"

Miss Torpenhow sighed. She wished she did not know what Gabriel Strega wanted, or anything else about him. But she did. She pinched the bridge of her nose between her thumb and forefinger and squeezed her tired eyes shut, remembering conversations she'd had with him. Some of them had taken place in this very room.

"Strega believes that our modern Traction Cities are doomed," she said. "He has convinced himself that there is not enough fuel to keep them all moving for much longer, and not enough prey to keep them all growing. He claims that the great cities of the Hunting Ground will turn to hunting one another."

"What an appalling idea!" said Helen.

"It does not appall Strega. He is excited by it. He intends to give Thorbury more powerful engines, and bigger jaws, so that it may become the apex predator of the brutal new age he sees approaching. And he means to strip away all the old traditions that make our city what it is. Strega does not see the past as something we can be inspired by and learn from, but rather as something to be blotted out and forgotten so the future can be built . . ."

She stopped, realizing that to Strega this sad, shocked girl might be something to be blotted out too. With her father dead, and her brother far away aboard Paris, Helen was the last of the Angmerings on Thorbury. A man as thorough and calculating as Gabriel Strega would not want that loose end left hanging . . .

"Come, my dear," she said, standing up quickly and setting down her teacup.

"Where are we going?"

"I shall take you to stay with some neighbors, Mr. and Mrs. Werner. If Strega's thugs are looking for you, they are sure to come here."

Helen just sat staring at her, trembling, too exhausted by her grief to move. As she helped the girl to her feet, Miss Torpenhow recalled again how Strega himself had once sat in that very chair, and how he had looked almost as scared and vulnerable as Helen.

✹

The first time she'd seen him had been in a bookshop near the elevator station on Middle Residential. She had been leafing through a newly published novel when a tremendous commotion broke out. The bookseller had caught a boy trying to leave with an illustrated edition of Memling's Historia Tractionis stuffed inside his tunic. He was holding the thief by his collar, and shouting loudly for the police.

If she had been in any other sort of shop — if the boy had been helping himself to sweets, or jewelry, or pastries — Miss Torpenhow would have run to find a constable herself, for she did not approve of thieves. But the fact that he was stealing a book moved her. The Historia Tractionis had been a favorite of hers too, when she was young. And although the boy was ragged and grimy, there was an intelligent look in his big, dark eyes. So she paid for the book herself, and persuaded the bookseller not to press charges.

The man was reluctant at first. "Don't let him fool you, Miss Torpenhow," he said. "He's bad to the bone, that one." But Miss Torpenhow was a good customer, and she did not believe that anyone was bad to the bone, especially not anyone who read books. After all, she said, a child should not be punished for trying to educate himself.

She took the boy for something to eat at a café, and listened to his story. His name was Gabriel Strega. He thought he was maybe fourteen years old. He had no family. He had been an engine room slave in a little barge town that Thorbury had eaten a few months earlier, and he did much the same work in Thorbury, although he was free now, and paid a little for his labor. He lived in workers' barracks down on Base Tier. No, it wasn't too bad; the older men were kind to him, and he had ear defenders to block out the noise. Yes, he loved books. He read himself to sleep most nights.

"What drew you to the Historia Tractionis, Gabriel?"

"History's important, ain't it, miss? If I can find out where everyfink came from, maybe I can start to see where it's all going."

It seemed tragic to Miss Torpenhow that such a bright, inquiring mind should be buried down there on Base Tier. So she took the boy to the public library and introduced him to the librarians, who agreed he should be allowed to borrow books and work there whenever he needed to. And she encouraged him to apply for the Civic Planning Department examinations that autumn.

He passed easily, as she had known he would.

Over the next ten years or so she had watched with a certain pride as Gabriel Strega rose through the ranks of the department to become Deputy Chief Planning Officer. He was said to be devising all sorts of plans for altering and improving the city. Some of the younger men in Planning admired him — they called him "the Architect" and began to copy his manners and his severe black clothes. But Mayor Angmering and the City Council were not impressed. Thorbury was not a city that liked change. Things worked very well just as they were, and they saw no reason to go making improvements.

Miss Torpenhow could see their point. She too liked Thorbury as it was. Reading reports of the angry meeting where Strega had tried to push his plans through, and urged his supporters to revolt when they were rejected, she began to feel slightly uneasy about her part in his rise. And although she felt sorry when he was banished from the city, she could not help feeling it was for the best.

But now he was back, and causing more trouble than anyone could possibly have imagined, and Miss Torpenhow could not keep from blaming herself. She kept recalling the gleam of intelligence in Strega's eyes, which had seemed so encouraging when she first knew him, and so sinister later. Had he deliberately allowed the bookseller to catch him on that long-ago day? Had he seen Miss Torpenhow browsing there and guessed that she was just the sort of naive, good-hearted person who would come to his rescue? She supposed that a man of Strega's dreadful brilliance would have found his way to power eventually without any help from Miss Lavinia Torpenhow, but she could not deny that she *had* helped him. Which meant that the dreadful things unfolding aboard this city were her responsibility . . .

❄

The outer streets of Upper Residential were deserted, but faint and disturbing sounds came from deeper in the city. Somewhere, fierce voices were shouting or chanting, too far off to make out the words or even the language, and there were echoing bangs, and rumblings, and still, now and then, the quick, urgent pecking of gunfire.

The Werners lived only a few yards from her apartment. Mr. Werner was a retired mechanic who had spent his working life down on Base Tier. The other residents of Circular Street thought him and his wife terribly common, but Miss Torpenhow had no time for snobbery of that sort.

"The Werners are kindly people," she explained as she hurried Helen toward their house. "They gave most generously when I was collecting for the Stray Cats' Home last year."

Helen did not reply. She had the look of a sleepwalker, trapped in a nightmare. Miss Torpenhow was glad to hand her into the care of Mrs. Werner, who she was certain would be much better than her at consoling the poor girl.

"We'll take care of her," said Mr. Werner, standing in the doorway of his narrow little house while his wife led Helen gently inside. "This devil Strega . . . I don't know what the world has come to. But we'll hide her if he comes a-hunting, and if things get too hot we'll send her down to Base Tier. My brother-in-law's a section foreman down there. He'll know places where all the mercenaries of the Frost Barrens couldn't find her, not if they looked for a year."

"Let us hope it will not come to that," said Miss Torpenhow, thinking how out of place poor, delicate Helen would be among the oily warrens of the engine district.

But perhaps she was underestimating the girl's resilience? Helen had dried her tears when Miss Torpenhow went to bid her good-bye, and she seemed surprisingly calm and clearheaded for one so young, who had seen such dreadful things.

"We cannot let Strega win," she said as they parted. "We must take our city back."

"We must," agreed Miss Torpenhow. "We shall!"

There was steel in the Angmerings still, she thought as she hurried homeward. It showed itself in times like these. And she thought suddenly of Helen's brother, Max, away in Paris. Poor Max, who could not know yet that his father was dead and his city stolen.

Max! she thought. *Yes, Max is the answer! If he were here, everyone would support him. Everyone would say he is the rightful mayor, not Strega. And Max is a fighter; he was forever skipping his lessons to train with the Defense Corps, and he looked so splendid in his uniform when they had parades. He is still very young, of course, but that will only make him even more inspiring. And while it is true that he was always rather lazy, and a little spoiled, he has been away in Paris for almost a year, so no doubt he will have matured . . .*

As she stopped outside her front door to rummage for her keys, she felt, for the first time that night, a flutter of hope. It was like the first stirrings of a breeze that will rise and blow a dismal fog away. There was a way out of this pickle after all. It only needed someone to go to Paris and fetch Max Angmering.

It was not until she was indoors that she realized, with a dawning sense of shock, who that someone would have to be.

6

RESCUE

The news from Thorbury spread slowly across the Great Hunting Ground, carried by air-traders and wandering towns. It caused quite a sensation aboard the other cities for a week or two. But Gabriel Strega's coup had been so swift and complete that the story seemed already ended, and it was soon overtaken by other news. The old world kept on turning, the cities crept across its face, and one evening in May, six weeks after Strega's return to Thorbury, Tamzin Pook fought in Margate's Amusement Arcade for the forty-ninth time.

The Revenant Engine that day was a spikily armored apelike thing, daringly manlike in its shape and movements, as if Mortmain were mocking the laws that stopped him from making human Revenants. It fought fiercely, maiming three players before Tamzin outguessed it. Afterward, there was the white-tiled medical bay, the bitter taste of painkillers, Mortmain's surgeon stitching up her flesh wounds. The sounds of the excited crowd came dimly through the metal bulkheads, fading as the spectators went off to spend their winnings or drown their sorrows in the sternward bars.

The uninjured players would be celebrating down in the

barracks they shared. But Tamzin had not been welcome at those after-show parties since the thing with Eve Vespertine. She did not care. There was always a hysterical edge to the celebrations, and pretty soon it would turn maudlin as they started mourning lost comrades. She was happier on her own, in the private apartment she had won for herself as the longest-surviving player. It was a cool white room with a little balcony overlooking the town's starboard paddle wheel and the sea beyond. There she would sit, and carefully drive all thoughts of the evening's show out of her mind until she had no thoughts at all. Then, perhaps, she might be able to sleep.

But when she got home Mortmain was there, rising from his seat on her little sofa as she entered, towering over her in his stupid silver turban. It was like getting a house call from a giant toadstool. A big man, Mortmain: built like a fighter himself. He was fiftyish, but still handsome, and he knew it, shining his white smile around like a flashlight, designed to dazzle. It almost blinded Tamzin when she walked in on him.

"Tamzin Pook! What a show tonight! What a spectacle! You are wrecking my Revenants faster than I can build them. You get better and better."

"Is it true when I've fought fifty shows you're going to give me my freedom?" Tamzin asked.

"Freedom?" A brief look of annoyance flashed across Mortmain's face. "Why would you want freedom, Tamzin? You are a star. You are an icon. Without you, the Amusement Arcade would lose half its glamour. And without the Amusements, what would you be? Just a girl, not very pretty or unusually clever, not very well educated. All that makes you special is your knack for killing off

32

my Revenants, and that's hardly a transferable skill. Who would want you?"

Tamzin nodded, but her eyes went to the shelf over her bunk. There she kept her most treasured possession: the brass disk that had been hanging on a cord around her neck when the slave traders first brought her to Margate. On one side it was stamped with the image of a smiling sun. On the other were the words *Tamzin Pook*. Someone had scratched them there so that, wherever she ended up, Tamzin would at least know her own name. But who would have cared so much about her? And what had become of them? It made her wonder if she had a family out there in the world. What if, somewhere, someone was wondering what had become of little Tamzin?

Mortmain's big hand landed on her shoulder, fatherly. "You stay here with us, Tamzin my dear. Stay where you are known and needed. I have all manner of ideas for Revenants that will challenge even you next season."

"And if one of them kills me?" asked Tamzin.

Mortmain's smile flickered, replaced for an instant by some expression Tamzin did not understand. Then he was smiling again. "That may never happen. You could survive for years. I expect you'll end up as a trainer, teaching your secrets to the next generation of Arcade stars. We will make sure you are comfortable. I've been thinking we should move you to a larger room . . ."

"I like this one."

"Well, what about a pet? Eve Vespertine once asked me for a cat, I recall. The unfortunate incident occurred before we could get her one, but we would have been happy to provide it. Would you like a cat, Tamzin?"

Tamzin shrugged. She had no feelings about cats.

"Now," said Mortmain, "I know you need your rest, but there is someone I would like you to meet. A journalist from the Traction City of London. Planning a book about the Arcade, apparently, and wants to hear our star player's thoughts."

"I don't have any thoughts," said Tamzin. She only wanted to sit on her balcony and forget tonight and fall asleep. But Mortmain was not the sort of man who listened to what girls like Tamzin wanted. He was already at the door, calling for the journalist to come in.

The journalist turned out to be a woman. She was the wrong side of fifty, with gray crinkly hair like wire wool and a long, stern, disapproving face. She wore a gray knit jacket over a high-collared white blouse and an ankle-length skirt of dark wool. Tamzin recalled seeing her in Mortmain's box at that night's show, making brisk little notes in a spiral-bound notebook. She had the notebook with her still. Mortmain fussed about, finding her a seat, then stood by the door with his arms folded, waiting for the interview to begin.

There was something fluttery about the journalist, thought Tamzin. She was the way some of the players got before a game, stretching some kind of fake calm over a lot of fear. But what did she have to be frightened of? She couldn't be frightened of Tamzin, surely? She ought to know Arcade players only hurt Revenants, not actual people.

"My name is Lavinia Torpenhow," said the journalist. "I write for the London Evening Palimpsest. I am sure my readers will be fascinated to hear your own account of your experiences, Miss Pook. After all, they tell me you have survived longer than any Arcade slave in Margate's history —"

"We call our competitors 'players,' Miss Torpenhow," said Mortmain good-humoredly. "'Slaves' is such a dehumanizing term."

"And yet Tamzin is a slave," Miss Torpenhow insisted, checking her notes. "I gather she was brought here by traders after Mayda fell —"

"I don't remember any of that," said Tamzin truthfully. "I've always been at the Arcade."

"We treat our athletes almost as part of the family," said Mortmain silkily.

"Of course . . . Oh!" Miss Torpenhow reached into a pocket of her jacket and took out a small cardboard tube. "I quite forgot! I brought these to eat during the show this evening, but the performance was so . . . diverting, they quite slipped my mind. Do have one. They are from Paris."

The tube contained pastel-colored macarons. Tamzin waved them away — she did not like macarons — but Miss Torpenhow took one, and then Mortmain, who had a sweet tooth, helped himself to two. As Miss Torpenhow put the tube away, Tamzin noticed that her hands were shaking.

"Now, Miss Pook," the journalist said. "What I want to know is . . . how do you do it? How do you outwit, out-think, outmaneuver those terrible machines?"

Tamzin did not want to answer, not with Mortmain standing there. But answering seemed the quickest way to get rid of the journalist so she said, "We are very well trained. Dr. Mortmain makes sure of that."

"But you all receive the same training, so what is it that makes Tamzin Pook better than the others?"

Tamzin glanced at Mortmain to see what he wanted her to say. But Mortmain, oddly, did not seem to be listening. He stifled a

35

yawn, and Tamzin said, "I can just . . . see what the Revenants are thinking, somehow. They don't think much, so it isn't hard."

"Extraordinary," said Miss Torpenhow, not bothering to write anything in her notebook. Tamzin thought she seemed to be waiting for something.

"I'm not feeling too . . ." said Mortmain suddenly, and toppled sideways, demolishing a small table.

"Splendid!" said Miss Torpenhow brightly, springing up from the sofa.

Tamzin ran to where Mortmain lay. She was afraid he was dead. At the same time, she hoped he was dead. It was hard to be sure what she felt.

"He's been drugged, my dear," said the journalist, sounding rather pleased about it. "By me! It was the macarons. Well, one particular macaron, the second one down. Don't worry; I got the sleeping potion from a very reputable pharmacist in Paris. Dr. Mortmain will wake up in a few hours. So will the gentlemen who guard the exit to this building: I left some macarons with them too. I'm here to rescue you, my dear."

Tamzin knelt beside Mortmain. He was snoring. She looked up. "But what if I don't want to be rescued?" she said.

"I'm afraid I really must insist," said Miss Torpenhow. She took a firm hold of Tamzin's hand and started leading her toward the door. "Here," she said, taking her own long gray cloak from the hook in the vestibule and wrapping it around Tamzin's shoulders. "Pull up the hood, in case someone recognizes you on the way to the air harbor. You're quite the celebrity on this town."

She went ahead of Tamzin to the main door, opened it, checked the walkway outside, and glanced back to make sure that Tamzin was still following.

Tamzin hesitated, waiting for the knowledge of what to do to come to her the way it did in the Arcade. But Miss Torpenhow was harder to read than a Revenant Engine. Tamzin snatched her sun pendant from its shelf.

"Where are we going?" she heard herself ask.

"To Paris," said Miss Torpenhow.

"Why Paris?"

"There is something I am hoping you can help me with there."

"What something?"

"I'll explain once we are aboard the airship."

7

AIRSHIPS

Tamzin did not know if she had ever been aboard an airship before. Some slaver's vessel must have carried her to Margate as a child, but she had no memory of it, and whether it had arrived by sky or sea she did not know. She had seen airships often enough, coming and going from the town's skydock, or casting their fat shadows over the exercise yard outside the players' barracks. But, big as they looked when they were in the air, she was still somehow unprepared for the size of them as Miss Torpenhow led her up the skydock stairs.

Even then, she could not really believe that she was leaving, that she would be allowed to leave. All the way from the Arcade she had been waiting to be stopped by Mortmain's men, or recognized by passersby. But as they exited the Arcade — past a guard post where the men on duty were snoring just as peacefully as their master, with pastel macaron crumbs in their beards — Miss Torpenhow had reached into her pockets again and handed Tamzin a white mask, like the disguises carnival revelers wore. It was not carnival time, but such outfits were not uncommon on the top decks of Margate in any season. When the mask was in place and the cloak's hood pulled up, there was nothing to draw anyone's attention to Tamzin as she went beside Miss Torpenhow along the busy promenades.

It is going to work, she thought as they neared the skydock and the men on duty at the entrance recognized Miss Torpenhow and waved them through. *I am escaping. I am leaving Margate. I am leaving the Arcade.* And she was not sure how she felt about that, because Margate and the Arcade were all she knew, and although she had tried so hard not to grow friendly with her fellow players they were still the nearest thing to friends she had.

"I cannot leave them behind," she said. "The others — they need me . . ."

Miss Torpenhow put a hand on her shoulder, not unkindly, but very firmly, propelling her up the metal stairs to where the airships waited. "I know, my dear. But I cannot free them all. I am taking a big enough risk by spiriting you away."

The tethered airships looked like a herd of huge beasts slumbering. The night wind boomed softly against their flanks. Miss Torpenhow led the way to one of the largest. Men were busy behind the lit windows of the little gondola that jutted from its belly, and passengers clutching toy Revenant Engines and boxes of Margate fudge were climbing a spindly aluminum ladder to go through a hatchway in its flank.

Tamzin reached the ladder's foot, and froze. She was more afraid than she had ever been backstage at the Arcade, waiting for a show to start. She was afraid of leaving Margate. It was true that life there had involved a fight to the death against killing machines every week, but it was the only life she knew. What Miss Torpenhow had planned for her, she could not even guess. She almost turned and ran.

Miss Torpenhow mistook her fear of freedom for a fear of flying. "It is quite all right, my dear," she said. "I was afraid myself, when I left my home in Thorbury, but airships are really quite safe these days, and this one is operated by a very reputable firm."

"I thought you said you came from Paris?" muttered Tamzin.

"I said we are *going* to Paris," Miss Torpenhow corrected her. "I came from Thorbury, that unhappy city. Let's get ourselves settled in our cabin, and I shall tell you everything."

❖

Airships had still been something of a novelty when Miss Torpenhow was a girl. They had proved themselves useful in hauling cargo between cities, especially at a time when the Hunting Ground was beginning to be so scored and scarred by track marks that land barges could no longer operate, but she had often heard grown-ups grumble that they would never catch on. She still recalled how, as a child of five or six, she had seen the sky-clipper *Daisy Darling* go down off London's stern, blazing like a great airborne brazier, with its passengers and crew roasting like chestnuts inside it. She had resolved then and there that she would never venture aboard such a dangerous contraption. When, as a young woman, she had traveled from London to Paris, and then from Paris to Thorbury, she had made the journeys aboard respectable trading towns. It was a slower way to travel, but far less liable to end in fiery death.

But there had been no respectable trading town to carry her away from Thorbury. She had known the air harbor was her only hope, and she had made her way there, carrying a change of clothes in a carpetbag, and 800 Thormarks in small gold pieces sewn into the lining of her skirt.

She had expected to find crowds of people at the air harbor, all clamoring for flights. But the citizens of Thorbury were so used to peace that they did not seem to understand yet what had happened. They were hoping the rumors of the mayor's assassination were untrue, and that all the unpleasantness would soon blow over. The only obstacle Miss Torpenhow encountered was a pair of Strega's nomad henchmen who stood guard at the entrance to the docks. They looked most alarming, with their body armor and bandoliers, but they were no older than a lot of the boys she had tutored for the Municipal Exams. So rather than obeying when they yelled at her to halt she kept walking, head up, shoulders back, and said, "I am here on Mr. Strega's orders. I am surprised he did not inform you."

The two louts looked at each other, then shrugged and stepped aside. What harm could it do to let her pass, one middle-aged lady carrying a carpetbag? It had annoyed Miss Torpenhow in the past, the way that everyone ignored women of her age and thought them good only for gossip and housework, but she was glad of it that night.

There was an airship newly docked at the main quay. The leering skull of the Boethius Brigade was painted on its envelope, and its nomad crew was offloading what appeared to be some kind of cannon. The other quays were mostly empty. Air-traders had a keen sense for trouble, so the ships that had been docked there had scattered like starlings at the first sounds of gunfire. The only one left was a shabby Ventvogel called the *Gutterby Spar*, and she was making ready to leave too, her captain yelling at his crew to hurry as they rolled heavy barrels of Thorbury's famous brandy up her gangplanks.

"My business is cargo, not passengers," he grumbled when Miss Torpenhow interrupted him. But his wife, a practical woman, took the gold coin Miss Torpenhow proffered, bit it to check it was genuine, stuffed it inside her bodice, and led the way up creaking metal ladders inside the ship's envelope to a tiny cabin. It was positioned between two huge gasbags that bulged like giant lungs, and which Miss Torpenhow suspected would explode at the merest suggestion of a spark.

She wondered, as the Gutterby Spar pulled away into the night, whether she might not have been safer staying aboard Thorbury. But she was not trying to keep herself safe; she was trying to do her duty. Someone had to tell poor Max Angmering about his father's death, and persuade him to come back and help restore order. And a man like Strega was capable of anything . . . For all she knew, he might send someone to Paris to murder Max too. Yes, someone had to make this dreadful voyage. It was one of the strange tricks of history that the task should fall to Lavinia Torpenhow.

In later years, as the air trade developed, cities would install beacons, and airships like the Gutterby Spar would carry radio sets to home in on their signals. But such conveniences were still decades away when Miss Torpenhow began her journey, and the air-traders of her time found their way from one wandering city to the next mostly by luck. A week out from Thorbury, she disembarked aboard a town called Dynamo Tashbin. From there another airship carried her to a trading cluster on the edge of the Shatterlands. There she met a third air-trader who claimed to be bound for Paris, and, just as importantly, to know where Paris was. His ship was even more ramshackle than the first two, but by then Miss Torpenhow felt herself to be an experienced aviatrix. Not only could she cope with the cold, the noise, and the endless low-level fear of life aloft, she had even begun to enjoy the clean chill of the open sky. Below her, when there were gaps to look through in the plains of cloud, the Golden Age of Traction kept playing out its small dramas: motorized hamlets fled from hungry villages, predator suburbs tracked herds of merchant towns, while the great cities went to and fro about their business, trailing long scarves of smoke behind them like the wakes of mighty ships.

A mere month after leaving Thorbury, Miss Torpenhow arrived on Paris. A few hours after that, she was knocking on the door of Patrice LeClerc, the chief of the Parisian Bureau de Navigation. He was an old acquaintance from her student days who was now quite high up in the city's ruling council. She was sure he could tell her where to find Max Angmering.

"And indeed he could," she told Tamzin Pook. "But there was a problem."

They were eating breakfast in their cabin aboard the skyliner *Anna Karina*. Outside the cabin window, the high, white clouds went by. Somewhere below, spring hawthorn rolled like surf in the overgrown track marks of the Hunting Ground. Somewhere behind lay Margate, but a brisk west wind was helping the liner swiftly on her way, and the sea was already lost in the haze astern.

"What sort of problem?" asked Tamzin. She had only half listened to Miss Torpenhow's long account of the fall of Thorbury. Now she sensed another rigmarole beginning. What had any of this to do with her? "Do you think I can fight Strega's nomad Revenants for you?" she added. "Because I can't. The Revenants Mortmain makes are designed to be killable. Those olden-days

Stalkers were designed *not* to be. What I do in the Arcade would just be play-fighting to things like them."

"No, no," said Miss Torpenhow, impatient at having her story interrupted. "I would not ask you to do that. It will take well-trained men and heavy weapons to defeat those creatures."

"Then what do you need me for?"

"That is what I am trying to tell you, my dear. When I reached Paris, my friend Monsieur LeClerc informed me that poor Max Angmering is in prison! 'For his own safety,' they say. It seems Strega had requested the Parisians deliver Max to him. To my disgust, some of the city council actually wished to do so! They said it is no business of theirs who rules Thorbury, and they should recognize Strega as its mayor. But others rightly suspect poor Max would be murdered if they sent him home. So, rather than make a decision one way or the other, the Mayor of Paris decided on a compromise. Max is languishing in the Oubliette Prison, at the very bottom of the city.

"'Can't you use your influence to have him released?' I asked Monsieur LeClerc, but he told me it cannot be done. He says there are men more powerful than him on the council who insist that Max remains locked up.

"'Then I shall help him to break out,' I declared. 'I am not sure how such things are arranged, but I shall smuggle a file to him hidden in a fruitcake, or bribe his jailers . . .' But Monsieur LeClerc shook his head and said that could not be done either. You see, the Oubliette is in the very depths of Paris, and it is considered escape proof. The human jailers might be bribed, but there is another, who stands guard unsleepingly outside the cell where Max is being held . . ."

"A Revenant?" asked Tamzin, finally starting to see where she might fit into all this.

"A Revenant. Designed by your Dr. Mortmain himself. It seems the machines he tests against you and your teammates in the Arcade are then improved and sold on to cities all over the Hunting Ground. A horrible trade. Anyway, to free poor Max, I must first disable this mechanical monster. 'It cannot be done,' said LeClerc, and at first I was inclined to agree. Then I recalled the Amusement Arcade — I donate sometimes to a charitable organization called End the Arcade Games. And I thought, I shall go there, and find myself an expert who knows how to kill a Revenant."

"So you want me to fight this thing?" said Tamzin.

"I can think of no one better."

Tamzin shook her head. "Well, think again. I thought you were rescuing me. Isn't that what you said? But you're just using me. You're no different from Mortmain."

"Oh, my dear child, that is hardly fair! Mortmain wants only to make money. I am trying to free an innocent young man, and liberate my city from a tyrant. If you help me, you will be a hero in Thorbury . . ."

"And if I don't?" asked Tamzin bluntly.

"Well," said Miss Torpenhow, "then you will be free to go your way when we reach Paris, and I shall have to deal with the Revenant myself."

Tamzin fell silent, fingering the sun pendant on its string around her neck. She was unused to being offered choices. The thought of having to make her own way in the world worried her. Where would she live? How would she eat? How did other people manage such things? She wondered if she should just make her way back to Margate and ask for Mortmain's forgiveness. At least life in the Arcade had been simple.

"May I see your pendant?" asked Miss Torpenhow.

Tamzin, startled from her thoughts, slipped the string over her head and passed the pendant to her. "I've had it always," she said. "Someone wrote my name on it. My mum or dad, I reckon. I suppose it was in case we got separated. And we did, so this is all I have of them."

Miss Torpenhow turned the pendant toward the window, letting the light play over the embossed rays that surrounded the calmly smiling face of the sun. She handled it carefully, as if she understood that this cheap bit of brass was the most valuable thing in Tamzin's world.

"It is a token of the sun god Apollo," she said as she handed it back. "He was worshipped in Ancient America, I believe, and he is still, aboard some of the raft cities of the Caribbean. Rather unusual in our part of the world, though. Your parents must have been great travelers, my dear. And I am sure they would be proud of you."

Tamzin snorted. "I doubt that." But when she put the pendant back on she knew that something had changed between her and Miss Torpenhow. She liked this woman, she realized, and that felt dangerous. Her time in the Arcade had taught her that it was not worth liking people, because they got killed too easily. And if Miss Torpenhow tried to free Max Angmering from his prison without Tamzin's help, she was definitely getting killed. Tamzin was the only one who could stop that happening.

"So all I need to do is fight this one Revenant?" she asked.

"That is all. Then you may you go wherever you wish."

Tamzin nodded cautiously. It sounded like a plan. It sounded like a deal. One last fight against one last Revenant, and then a new life.

"All right, Miss Torpenhow," she said.

Miss Torpenhow smiled. "My friends call me 'Hilly.'"

"Why?"

A gloved hand tapped on the cabin door. A steward's voice said, "Thirty minutes to docking."

"Come," said Miss Torpenhow. "We should get you out of those pajamas. In the cupboard there you will find a skirt and blouse of mine — the skirt will be a little long on you, I think, but I can tack up the hem if we are quick. And then we shall go to the observation lounge. It is not every day a girl gets her first glimpse of Paris."

8

THE MAN IN THE BOUNCY CASTLE

Fog hung low over the Anglish Sea. Margate rode at anchor on the greasy swell. The Arcade and all the cafés and Amusements were shut up and silent, and so were most other things. Margate was a town that slept late. But Mortmain was awake. He had woken just after midnight on the floor of Tamzin's quarters, groggy with the aftereffects of the drugged macaron. He had spent the small hours drinking strong coffee, and making statements to the town police, and then the press, about the escape of Tamzin Pook.

Dr. Mortmain had arrived on Margate nineteen years earlier. No one on the raft town knew where he had come from, and he seemed disinclined to tell them. Some said he was a disgraced professor from Heidelberg, dismissed for conducting vile experiments. Others claimed he was merely a freak-show proprietor from a nomad carnival in the Frost Barrens. One story cast him as an escapee from a prison for the criminally insane. The truth was that the machines he devised for the Amusement Arcade had brought so many paying visitors to Margate that he could have been all those things and no one would have cared. The town had grown rich, and Mortmain had grown rich with it.

His mansion stood higher than the town hall now, on a raised section of Margate's upper deck. It was called the Bouncy Castle, and it had been constructed to Mortmain's own design by craftsmen who usually specialized in airships. Its multicolored inflatable turrets were just for show, but among them was nestled the suite of elegant wood-paneled rooms where Mortmain lived. The rooms were firmly bolted to the deckplates below, but the passages and stairways that led between them were not, so Mortmain could always tell when he had visitors by the way the battlements and towers began to wobble in time to their approaching footsteps. Most people who came to see him at his home were unsettled and a little seasick by the time they reached his inner sanctum. Mortmain liked his visitors unsettled.

But the men who arrived as the sun was starting to break through the mist that morning seemed to have coped pretty well with the wobbling passageways through which Mortmain's butler had led them. There were two of them, and their names were Mr. Coldharbour and Mr. Lint.

Mr. Coldharbour was tall and running to fat, with cheerful eyes that vanished into the folds of flesh above his rosy cheeks whenever he smiled, which he did often. Mr. Lint was short and scrawny and had the look of an undertaker who has just heard bad news. Mortmain knew them both to be extremely dangerous. They were the men he called upon when he needed things done quietly, quickly, and with no regard for anyone who got in the way. Recently, for instance, he had learned that the archaeologists of Magnitogorsk University had unearthed some very ancient and sophisticated Stalker brains from the Ice Wastes. He had sent Mr. Coldharbour and Mr. Lint to see if the archaeologists were willing to sell the brains. The archaeologists had not been willing. But somehow — Mortmain did not care to know the details — the university had burned down, the archaeologists had all died, and the Stalker brains were now safely in Mortmain's laboratory, waiting to be embedded in suitably impressive bodies. Mr. Coldharbour and Mr. Lint could always be relied upon.

Mortmain received them in his private study. He did not rise from his chair as they entered, nor did he invite them to sit down.

"I am sure you can guess why I have called you here, gentlemen."

Mr. Coldharbour smiled. "Of course," he said. "The girl," he added. "Your errant star . . ."

"And the woman who helped her to escape," said Mr. Lint.

"A valuable girl. You'll want her back. And the woman punished."

"Or maybe both of them should be punished," said Mr. Lint, and quickly licked his lips.

Mortmain fetched out a cardboard folder containing a few sheets of paper. "These are all the details we have," he said. "The woman called herself Lavinia Torpenhow. She left aboard a skyliner, the *Anna Karina*, bound for Paris."

"Ah, Paris!" said Mr. Coldharbour.

"We'll track 'em down," said Mr. Lint.

"Gay Paree! The cherry blossom in bloom on *le Premier Étage* . . . The girls in their summer dresses . . ." said Mr. Coldharbour.

"We'll sniff 'em out," said Mr. Lint. "We'll make 'em suffer."

"You understand that Tamzin Pook is of great value to me, and to the Arcade, and to Margate," said Mortmain, looking at Mr. Lint with distaste. "I have plans for her, and I do not wish those plans to be disrupted. I will give you written instructions regarding her retrieval. As for her accomplice, or kidnapper, or whatever this Torpenhow person turns out to be, you may punish her in whatever way you see fit."

"Oh, I'm sure we'll think of something, won't we, Mr. Lint?" said Mr. Coldharbour cheerfully.

"Oh, I'm sure we will, Mr. Coldharbour," said Mr. Lint.

9

PARIS

Paris in the springtime! Paris in the morning sunlight! Paris, city of love, city of light, city of art, city of fashion! Paris, trundling on its stately way over the scarred plains of the Hunting Ground with a crowd of smaller towns hurrying alongside, all hoping to trade with the gigantic ville mobile, or snacking on the refuse it threw overboard, or simply praying that its looming presence would be enough to keep them safe from predators.

Tamzin had seen Traction Cities before, or thought she had — lumbering two- or three-tier behemoths had regularly parked up on the shore so their citizens could visit Margate. But Paris was another kind of beast entirely. Its lower tiers were the same dark industrial levels you would find on any Traction City, with a forest of giant exhaust chimneys sprouting from the stern. But rising at the forward end was an off-center stack of oval deckplates supported by prettily painted iron columns, and on these plates stood beautiful buildings, ringed by the green of parkland and the sheen of ornamental lakes. On top of it all, soaring above the rooftops of the Premier Étage, rose the city's famous mooring tower.

"It is beautiful," said Tamzin, mostly to herself, as she looked out at it through the slanting celluloid windows of the *Anna Karina*'s observation lounge.

"Paris is the finest city of the age," agreed Miss Torpenhow. "It has been wandering for four hundred years. It has used the stuff of the countless smaller towns it has devoured to make itself ever more immense and beautiful. It was only the second city to mobilize, you know. People sometimes say it was merely a copy of London, which was the first, but the builders of Paris were able to learn from London's mistakes, and their architecture and engineering were far superior."

Escorted by a Girondelle gunship in the royal-blue livery of the Hussars Aëronautiques, the skyliner sank slowly toward one of the quays that jutted from the sides of the huge tower.

"As soon as we dock," said Miss Torpenhow, "we shall pay a call on my friend Monsieur LeClerc. He promised to find out all he can about the Oubliette, and to procure the tools we shall need to break Max Angmering out."

Tamzin's pleasure at the city's beauty faded slightly. She was not here to see the sights and have Miss Torpenhow give her history lessons. She was here to fight.

She remained quiet as Miss Torpenhow shepherded her through the Parisian customs office and into the elevator. She had never imagined a city could grow this big. She stared out of the elevator windows with a mixture of wonder and unease. But Miss Torpenhow was too happy to notice. Ignoring the other passengers, she moved from window to window, pointing out the grand buildings that could be seen below as the car descended through the tower's steel basketwork. There were the law courts, and the offices of the city's council; there was the mayoral palace. There was the famous Louvre Museum, with its unrivaled collection of

Ancient slatted doors. When the elevator reached the base of the tower, she led the way along the winding paths of the Tuileries Garden, over ornamental bridges, and through blizzards of wind-blown cherry blossom to the grand offices of the Bureau de Navigation.

The buildings were so huge and important-looking that Tamzin thought it was impossible that she could actually go inside: This was no place for someone like her. But Miss Torpenhow seemed to think they both had a perfect right to be there. She strode up the wide front steps with such confidence that Tamzin could only follow, and none of the gorgeously uniformed men who sat at the long mahogany reception desk in the lobby had the nerve to ask them what their business was when Miss Torpenhow announced that they were there to see Monsieur LeClerc. One of the men scribbled a message on a pink slip, another placed it in a brass cylinder, and a third put the cylinder into a vacuum tube, which sucked it with a *whoosh* up through the ceiling and off into the maze of offices above. Two minutes later, a reply came back: Monsieur LeClerc would meet Mademoiselle Torpenhow for lunch at the Baguette Pneumatique at 12:30 p.m.

"Excellent," said Miss Torpenhow. "That gives us just enough time to do some shopping. That outfit is not quite the thing for the Baguette Pneumatique, my dear."

✸

The Baguette Pneumatique was one of Paris's most popular restaurants in those years. It was a small airborne building, supported by a large gasbag that had been designed to resemble a long loaf of fresh-baked bread. It trailed on hawsers from the stern of the Premier Étage, and diners reached it by means of a cable car.

When Tamzin and Miss Torpenhow arrived, Monsieur LeClerc

was already waiting for them, sitting at a table on the broad veranda, screened by potted ferns from the gaze of the other diners. He stood up when his guests approached, bowed low, took Miss Torpenhow's hand and kissed it. Then he took Tamzin's hand and kissed that, much to her embarrassment — she felt conspicuous enough already in the new blue trouser suit Miss Torpenhow had just bought her in a shop that had looked like the temple to a god with expensive tastes.

LeClerc was a small, plump, pink sort of man, with a neat white beard, and mustaches teased into sharp points. He seemed silly at first, but his smile was so genuine and his eyes gleamed with such good humor that it was impossible not to like him.

"My dear Mademoiselle Torpenhow!" he said, inviting them to sit, then beckoning a waiter and sitting himself. "And so this is the famous Tamzin Pook, the killer of Revenants? But, pardon me, my dear, I had expected someone taller, stronger . . ."

"Strength doesn't help much when you go up against a Revenant," said Tamzin. "Nobody's stronger than they are. You can be faster, though. And cleverer."

Monsieur LeClerc nodded solemnly. "And I am sure you are both fast and clever, Mademoiselle Pook. I am glad you agreed to honor us with your presence. When I told Mademoiselle Torpenhow there was a Revenant guarding her Max Angmering, she said, 'I shall fetch Tamzin Pook, who is the expert in such things.' I said, 'You will never get her away from Margate,' and yet here you are. Mademoiselle Torpenhow has a habit of getting her way. I am sure you will defeat the creature that guards Max Angmering."

"What have you been able to learn about this prison he is kept in?" asked Miss Torpenhow, but LeClerc shushed her. A waiter was approaching, looking scornfully at the newcomers. LeClerc ordered food and wine, and the man snorted disgustedly, scribbled something on his notepad, and stalked away, shaking his head. It seemed to Tamzin that he despised them, but Miss Torpenhow was pleased.

"Parisian waiters are famed for their rudeness," she explained. "The better the restaurant, the more rude the staff."

"The Baguette Pneumatique has the rudest waiters in the entire city," said Monsieur LeClerc proudly. "It is one of the reasons I chose it for our little tête-a-tête. I must remember to tip him well."

Tamzin scowled. Everything about this strange city seemed wrong to her. But the food when it came was good. She ate in silence, while Miss Torpenhow and LeClerc talked of Paris: what had changed since her time there, and what had not. Only when the waiter sneeringly came to remove their plates did LeClerc look around to make sure no one was listening to them. No one was. At a nearby table, some men and women with the shabby, disreputable look of writers were arguing about art and politics and eking out a single bottle of wine between them. The waiter lounged against the veranda rail and smoked a cigarette.

"This arrived for you," said Monsieur LeClerc, bringing a rather crumpled-looking envelope out of his inner pocket.

Miss Torpenhow tore it open and unfolded the letter inside. "Oh my," she said, frowning as she read. "Oh my. It is from my friends the Werners, in Thorbury. Things are worse there than I feared. They say that Strega has strengthened his grip on the city. His nomad mercenaries are in complete control . . . They have seven of those dreadful old Stalkers — 'the Scrap Metal Seven,' they call them — and everyone is terrified of them. Oh, he has demolished the temple of Peripatetia, that lovely old building! And, oh dear, he is still searching for Helen! Oh, poor Helen . . . And oh, my poor, poor city."

She folded the letter away and looked up. There were tears in her eyes. Tamzin, watching her, wondered how it must feel to have a place and people you cared about so much.

Monsieur LeClerc passed Miss Torpenhow his handkerchief so she could dry her eyes. "The Council here has voted to recognize Strega as Mayor of Thorbury," he said. "That is another reason for meeting here, rather than in my office — I don't know who I can trust. Some of my fellow councillors feel we have a duty to protect Max Angmering, and plan to keep him locked away until this all blows over. But there are others who think Strega could be a useful ally. A few may even be in Strega's pay. I fear they will murder Max if they get a chance."

"Then the more quickly we can free the poor young man and spirit him off your city, the better," said Miss Torpenhow. "Have you worked out how we can get inside this Oubliette?"

LeClerc nodded. His round, cheerful face was not made for looking serious, but now it looked very serious indeed. Taking a pencil from his pocket, he started to make a drawing on his napkin.

"The Oubliette is situated at the very base of Paris," he told them. "It is a small building in the engine district, but it is bigger than it looks, for the larger part of it hangs down below the Base Tier, between the city's tracks. It is shaped like a drum, with cells arranged on three levels. Max Angmering is being housed on the lowest level. I gather he is being well treated. During the daytime, food and drink are carried down to him. But there is no way for us to get inside then: the only entrance is at the top, and it is too busy, too well-guarded. At night, there is only a skeleton staff on duty, so we might be able to slip in, and slip Max out. But at night the Revenant is released. The creature prowls the prison until it is lured back into its cage at dawn."

"What sort is it?" asked Tamzin. "Does it use blades? Fire? How many legs? Is it fast?"

Monsieur LeClerc shook his head. "I am sorry. I only know that it is called 'the Daunt,' and it is very deadly. There have been accidents; several jailers were killed. The council hushed up their deaths, of course. There would be a great scandal if anyone knew Paris employed a Revenant."

Miss Torpenhow turned the napkin around and studied the diagram LeClerc had drawn. "So how do we get inside?" she asked.

"You will be disguised as engine-district workers — I have overalls for you both. After 11 p.m., there will only be two guards on duty in the upper building — the authorities feel there is no need for more, with the creature loose below. I thought you could hold them at gunpoint while Miss Pook goes down, deals with the Revenant, and frees Max Angmering. Then you can run with him to the air dock and be away before the alarm is raised."

"I don't have a gun," Miss Torpenhow objected. "And the guards certainly will, and they will shoot me."

"I have a gun for you, and I have also had a technician in the low city make an electric knife, of the sort Miss Pook is accustomed to using in the Arcade. But you must act as soon as possible. Strega will be frustrated that the Parisian council did not kill young Angmering for him. He may find a way of sending his own assassins into the Oubliette."

Miss Torpenhow agreed. "There is no time like the present, and no point waiting around, letting ourselves get nervous. You must fetch us these overalls and the weapons, Monsieur LeClerc. We shall break into the Oubliette tonight."

10

GROUNDSCRAPER

M ax Angmering had been with his friends in the Café Frederique when they came to tell him that his world had ended. The Frederique was in the heart of Montmartre, an area of twisting narrow streets and zigzag stairways deep in the shadowy center of Paris's second tier. It was the haunt of an artistic, bohemian crowd — painters, poets, actors, and other, less-savory characters. To Max and his friends — the sons of senior officials from Paris or other Traction Cities, studying to follow in their fathers' respectable footsteps — it was all unimaginably thrilling.

They liked best to sit at the tables outside the café, watching the street life of the city go past like an endless parade. The Café Frederique stood in a busy square opposite the Montmartre elevator station. Constant streams of people came up and down the station steps and flowed around the statue in the center of the square. The statue was of the city's gods, a huge fat one carrying a gigantic teardrop-shaped stone upon his back, and a smaller one leading the way. There was a little dog running beside them, and although the statues were dull and tarnished, the dog's nose gleamed like gold where passersby had reached up to rub it for good luck.

Max had done the same that day as he crossed the square to join his friends at their usual table. But it did not bring him good luck, because when his turn came to order another pot of coffee and a plate of pastries the waiter looked stony-faced and shook his head.

This was a surprise, for the Café Frederique was not the sort of place that could afford the rudest waiters, and most of its staff were almost pleasant. But not today. The man refused to take Max's order unless he paid in cash, which was unheard of — and also impossible, since Max had gone through his allowance like water that month. Embarrassed at being humiliated in front of his friends, Max said, "Look here, don't you know who I am?"

"I do," said the waiter.

"I do also," agreed the café's owner, coming out to see what the disturbance was. "You are the son of the former Mayor of Thorbury . . ."

"Exactly! I'll pay my bill at the end of the month, when my regular allowance from my old man comes through with the mail from home. Wait, what do you mean, *former* mayor?"

Max's friends were already leaning away from him, as if they were afraid of being infected by his misfortune. The grim, crag-like face of Madame Frederique looked for a moment almost sympathetic.

"Ah, mon pauvre garçon," she said, shaking her head. "You have not heard the news from Thorbury, then? There will be no more allowance for you. And no more credit at my café."

Max had just enough spare change in his pockets to buy a third-class elevator ticket and that morning's copy of the *Paris Flaneur*. He read the report from Thorbury while the elevator was carrying him back to the Premier Étage.

He emerged from the elevator stunned, dropped the paper into

60

a recycling chute, and stumbled through the Tuileries Garden like a sleepwalker. Paris was chasing a scavenger town, the whole city rocking with the movement, and everyone else was hurrying toward the observation terraces to watch the catch. Max barely noticed them. His father was dead. This Gabriel Strega was calling himself Mayor of Thorbury, and the mayors of at least a dozen other great cities seemed happy to accept him.

And where did that leave Max?

He had never been close to his father, but now odd, long-forgotten memories surfaced of a time when the old man had not been so stern and reserved, when he had wrestled with little Max on the parlor carpet, and tossed him up, laughing, high above his head.

I must light a hundred candles for him at the Temple of Peripatetia, Max thought. *Enough to light his way, so he can find Mother again, down in the Sunless Country.*

And what about Helen? His little sister was such a silly goose — she could not possibly cope alone. What might the brute Strega do to her?

A righteous anger began to build in him. How dare Strega do what he had done! How dare he think he could just barge in and take the city Max's family had founded! He would go to Thorbury himself, this very day, and challenge Strega to a duel . . .

And then it occurred to him that he could not afford an airship fare. He could not even afford the candles for his father. He was not only an orphan — he was a penniless one.

Max had never had to think about money before. What did poor folk do for money? Must he find himself a job? He supposed he would have to leave the university, for he could not possibly afford its fees. But that would mean giving up his rooms. So where was he to live?

The last question was soon answered. When he reached his college, he found two officials of the city government waiting for him. They were polite, but very firm. It had been decided that Max would be taken into custody — for his own protection, of course, and in the interests of good relations between Paris and the new regime in Thorbury. The council would reach out to Gabriel Strega and arrange a compromise that would allow Max to return home, but it would take time, and he must be patient. Yes, yes, they would inquire after his sister, Helen, and make sure that she was safe. But, in the meantime, if Monsieur Angmering would just pack a few belongings and accompany them . . .

They made it all sound so reasonable that it was not until the door of the Oubliette closed upon him that Max understood he was a prisoner.

❀

The Oubliette was a kind of upside-down tower of a type known as a groundscraper: a three-story steel stalactite sticking down out of the city's belly. Max's cell was a circular chamber at the bottom of the tower, partitioned to form a living area, a bed space, and a small bathroom. In truth, it was not too bad. He had books to read, his own clothes to wear, the Flaneur delivered daily with his midday meal by jailers who were not unfriendly. He was their only prisoner, they said; the Oubliette was used only for the most important captives. He felt rather proud of that.

Once a day, he was allowed to walk with two guards on a narrow balcony that ran around the outside of the prison. From there he could look down at the mud and torn earth passing between the enormous tracks, or up at the underside of the rusty, battered baseplate on which the whole of Paris stood. Other structures hung down from it: a rusty steel blister that sometimes leaked sulfurous smells, and a clump of tenement blocks where the poorest of the city's poor were housed. It was like an upside-down city of its own. The pigeons that roosted in the clefts and crannies of the vast axle assemblies flew between the groundscrapers in grubby flocks, and laundry fluttered on long lines stretched between the balconies.

A pretty girl lived in one of the lower flats, and if Max was lucky, she would sometimes be standing at her window when he was exercising. He waved once, and she waved back. The guards did not seem to care. He wondered about calling out to the girl to ask her name. Perhaps she would take pity on him, and help him to escape. He had imagined, before he came to Paris, that he would fall in love here, but he had been too shy to speak to many girls. Maybe this dark-haired damsel of the groundscrapers was the one?

But the noise beneath the city was so loud — the boom of engines, the squeal of axles, the tidal snarl of stones and soil churning under the tracks — she would not hear him if he called to her.

Anyway, he was not sure he wanted to escape. He still grew furious sometimes when he thought of Strega, and imagined all sorts of ways to avenge his father. But increasingly he could see that his plans were no more than foolish fantasies. Better to wait. Surely Paris would not keep him kicking his heels here for ever. Life was dull inside the Oubliette, but at least it was safe.

Only at night did he really feel like a prisoner. Then the guards went away, and the doors were locked, and sometimes in the silence he would hear something they called the Daunt going stealthily about in the corridor outside the entrance to his quarters.

It was a Stalker, the jailers had told him, un Revenant, one of those armored robot-zombie creatures the mad Ancients had devised. It longed only for blood, they said, and could never have enough of it. It would be happy to slaughter Max if he found a way out of his rooms.

Listening to the stairs creak under its weight, Max believed them.

So there he stayed, while a week became a month, and a second month stretched out toward a third. He dreamed up wilder and wilder escape plans, which he knew he would never even try to put into action. The girl on the groundscraper balcony waved sometimes. And then, one night, while he lay half sleeping, dreaming of the starlings swirling above the roofs of home, he heard movement outside — small, sinister noises — the scrape and chink of metal.

He was awake instantly and on his feet, poised to run, but with nowhere to run to. Whatever it was out there sounded closer than he had ever heard it before. It seemed to be fumbling with the lock of his cell door. The electric lamps set into the ceiling had been dimmed for the night, but they gave him light enough to see the door handle slowly turning.

11

JAILBREAK

It had been almost midnight when Tamzin and Miss Torpenhow arrived in the engine district, and there had been few people in the tunnel-like streets. None of them paid any attention to two workers in corduroy caps and blue serge overalls, one carrying a large toolbox, who made their way along Rue Tamburlaine toward the bunker-like guardhouse of the Oubliette.

Miss Torpenhow rang the bell on the heavy steel door. She had to ring twice before there was an answer, which made Tamzin hope that the guards really might be as lazy as LeClerc had promised. Or was it only that they had not heard their doorbell above the ever-present grumble of the engines?

At last, the door opened. A man with a blue uniform and a doleful mustache looked out at them, saw the maintenance-crew insignia on the breasts of their overalls, and asked if there was a problem.

"There is no problem," said Miss Torpenhow. She took a gun from her pocket and pointed it at the man. The gun was only a small-caliber pistol, meant for target shooting, but it looked as if it would do damage at close range. The guard cried out and started to shut the door, but Tamzin grabbed it and pulled it wider and with a rush they were all inside, Miss Torpenhow busy explaining that they meant no harm while jabbing the guard with her gun as if to warn him that actually they might.

They were in a dingy, low-roofed room with a metal table in the middle. Another man, who had been sitting at the table, sprang up and made to reach for a gun of his own, which hung in a holster on the coat stand, but the man with Miss Torpenhow's gun sticking into his ribs shouted at him not to be a fool, and he stopped and raised his hands.

"We shall not detain you long, gentlemen," said Miss Torpenhow. "I would be obliged if you could give us the keys to your prison."

The first man, the one who had opened the door, seemed more biddable than his friend. He unhooked a set of keys from his belt and held it out for Tamzin to take.

"Thank you," said Miss Torpenhow. "Now, in which cell would we find Mr. Angmering?"

"Trois," said the man, holding up three fingers. "The very bottom."

The other glowered and said, "You don't know what's down there, Madame. Le Revenant. Le Chien Diabolique. It will tear you limb from limb."

"Thank you for your concern," said Miss Torpenhow politely. She gestured with the gun for them both to step into the broom cupboard, and locked the door behind them. Her face was flushed when she turned back to Tamzin, her eyes shining. "So far, so good," she said. "It's rather fun, don't you think?"

Tamzin ignored her. She pocketed the keys and opened the toolbox, which held Miss Torpenhow's carpetbag and the electric knife. The knife buzzed encouragingly when she tested it. She hung the power pack on her belt, and went through a door into a circular room whose floor was mostly taken up by a heavy hatch cover.

"Do take care . . ." said Miss Torpenhow nervously.

Tamzin ignored her. She always took care.

A tug on a lever caused the hatch to crank slowly open, revealing a short flight of stairs leading down to another metal door. She ran down, fit a key into the lock, and set her shoulder against the door. It opened onto a narrow corridor that curved away out of sight in either direction. The metal floor was pierced with small holes, as floors often were on cities' lower levels, to save weight. Through these, Tamzin could see that she was on a landing, and that there was another below her, and that a flight of metal stairs led down to the lower one. It was dark down there, a cat's cradle of complicated shadows, the only light coming from low-wattage bulbs set in wire cages on the wall. She could see nothing moving.

She went fast and quietly along the corridor, past the door of what she assumed was cell number one (it had a large 1 stenciled on it). The stairs were old and rusty and they grated as she went down. Flakes of paint broke off them and fell fluttering through the glow of the wall lamps. She stopped halfway and listened, but there was no sound except the steady background noise of the city.

Perhaps there is no Revenant, she thought, going quickly down to the second landing, passing cell number two. *Perhaps this Daunt thing is just a rumor the jailers put out to keep their prisoners quiet* . . .

She did not see the shadow unfolding itself from the shadows high above her, or the two points of green light that appeared in the dark up there and swung to focus on her.

After the unfortunate incidents with the jailers, the thing that guarded the Oubliette had been given strict new instructions. It was to attack only when people came out of cell number three, and only if more came out than had gone in. It crept to a better vantage point and crouched there, watching hopefully, while Tamzin hurried down the third flight of stairs and began fumbling with her keys.

12

THE DAUNT

As the cell door started to swing slowly open, Max hurled himself at it, using all his weight to slam it shut again. From outside came a muffled curse.

"Who's there?" called Max.

"Max Angmering?" said the voice. "I'm here to rescue you."

It was a girl's voice. For one soaring moment, Max imagined the girl from the neighboring groundscraper must have come to help him. Then he wondered if the Parisians were playing a trick, luring him outside where their Revenant would kill him.

"What about the thing out there? What about the Daunt?" he asked.

"I don't think there is a Daunt," said the girl on the other side of the door. "I reckon it's just a story. Now let me in, you fool. We have to go."

Max stepped back and watched as the door opened again. It was not the girl from the groundscraper who stood in the shadows outside, but another girl: short, plain, and angry. She had a strange knife in her hand, attached by a flex to a box on her belt.

"Who — ?" he began.

"Tamzin Pook," said the girl. Max thought at first it was another curse. "Grab what you need, but only what you need, and follow me," she ordered. "We've got the guards shut in a cupboard up top and I don't reckon it'll be too long before they find a way out."

"We?" asked Max. But she did not seem in the mood for further chitchat. He ran back into the bedroom to shed his pajamas and pull his clothes and shoes on. By the time that was done, Tamzin was already prowling back out through the open door into the darkness outside. Max went after her. "Are you sure there's nothing out here?" he asked nervously. "I've heard it some nights, I think."

Tamzin Pook stopped and looked back at him, a strange, watchful expression on her face.

"Maybe I imagined it," he admitted.

"Down!" she shouted, throwing herself against him, pushing him out of the way of something that dropped from the landing above. A falling blur of armor plate and razor-edged spines missed the pair of them by inches. Steel claws struck sparks from the stairs below them as it landed and turned to spring again.

The Daunt had been built in the likeness of a massive, armored wolf, with sharp spines jutting from its neck and vicious metal fangs. Dead green eyes watched Max and Tamzin unblinkingly as it started prowling slowly back up the stairs toward them. Tamzin scrambled away from it, dragging Max with her and then pushing him behind her as they reached the first landing. She recognized this Revenant. She remembered how the crowd had cheered when it came bounding out into the lights of the Arcade one half-forgotten night last season. She remembered it savaging two of her teammates before Ultra-Violent Violet finished it off with an electric spear. Its head had exploded, as she recalled.

But Mortmain must have built it a new head. He had given it

bigger fangs, and longer spines, and sharper claws as well, as if the version Tamzin had faced in the Arcade was just a prototype, and the life-and-death battle her team had fought against it had been nothing but a test. Perhaps gentlemen from Paris had been sitting with him in his private box that night, drinking his wine, eating baklava, watching the show. Perhaps at the end, as the bodies of the fighters it had killed were dragged away, they had turned to Mortmain and said, "It's just the thing we need — the perfect night watchman for the Oubliette . . ."

The thought that she had been doing nothing all her life but destruction-testing machines for Mortmain to sell made Tamzin so angry that she shouted at the Daunt to come and get her if it dared, and thumbed the button that switched her knife on. But instead of the reassuring buzz and judder she expected to feel there was a small, sharp crack, a spray of sparks, and a cloud of acrid smoke that almost blinded her. The shoddy electro-blade was just a blade now, and about half as long as the ones that jutted from the Daunt's jaws.

It kept prowling slowly up the stairs toward her, silent except for the metallic chink each time it set its feet down. Tamzin backed away from it, shoving Max behind her.

"Run," she growled at him, but he was just gawping at the thing, taking a step or two backward only when she shoved him.

The green light in the Daunt's eyes flared, the way the eyes of Revenants always flared when they knew a kill was near. Tamzin tried to think, tried to work out what it was planning to do (leap on her and tear her throat out, that was pretty obvious) and when it was planning to do it (in about ten seconds' time, at a guess). How to fight it without a weapon, without teammates to distract it? Think, Tamzin. She wondered why the Parisians had chosen this Revenant. Why not one of Mortmain's other monsters? Why not have a dragon or a dinosaur as their guard dog? But that was what this was: an actual dog. "Le Chien Diabolique," that jailer had called it. Tamzin knew enough of his lingo to work out that meant something like "Devil Dog." Inside its nasty armored skull some dead dog's brain was wired up to weird machines. It probably didn't even know it was dead. Poor dog. Poor dog . . .

She stopped backing up the stairs and stood as tall she could. The Daunt stopped too, suspicious, letting the light of its eyes lap her face.

It's just a dog, she thought. LeClerc had said the jailers sent it back to its kennels every morning, so it must obey their orders. And if it obeyed their orders, why not hers?

"Sit!" she said in the most commanding voice she could manage.

The Daunt stared at her, jaws agape, fangs glinting.

"Bad dog!" she shouted, not moving a muscle, staring straight into the green lamps of its eyes.

The Daunt drew back a little. Its head went down. It was hard to tell in the dim light and the shadows, but she thought it put its bladed tail between its legs.

"Sit!" said Tamzin again, thinking that, even if this didn't work, it might buy her time enough to get Max and herself back up the stairs to the exit.

But the Daunt sat. It went down slowly and reluctantly, but it sat, and stayed sitting, the eye light dimming slightly.

"Down," commanded Tamzin.

If Mortmain had thought to give the Daunt a voice box, it would have whimpered. It lay down sphinxlike on the stairs, then lowered its head between its paws.

"Good dog," said Tamzin. "Stay." She took a step toward it, and another. She did not trust it, but it did not move. She reached out and patted its head, between the vicious spines. "Stay," she told it again, and backed off, trembling.

Max was staring at her as if she had performed a magic trick. "Move away slow," she said. "Don't run, don't shout. Running and shouting will only anger it." She wished she could step back through time and share that tip with her old teammates. They had run shouting at the Daunt, and it had killed them. She looked at Max Angmering and wondered how long he would last in the Arcade. About two minutes, she reckoned. He was taller than her, half handsome with that haughty nose and flop of dark blond curls, but there was something soft about him. Miss Torpenhow was wrong about him, she thought. He had never had to fight for anything in his life. He would not know how.

"But . . ." he whispered, looking past her at the Daunt.

"It's just a dog," Tamzin told him. "It just wants somebody telling it what to do."

Max moved slowly backward along the landing to the next stair, and Tamzin went after him. As they started up, the Daunt made a small movement behind them, but Tamzin held up her hand and called out, "Stay!" and the movement ceased. Across the palm of the hand she had raised, Max saw a thick, pale scar. It made him feel safer, for he sensed this girl had been in scrapes like this before, but also more feeble, because he had never been in any situation at all that could have resulted in a scar like that.

They climbed again, and reached the exit. The door hung open. The hatch above stood open too, till Tamzin heaved it shut. In the office, a lady stood pointing a gun at the door of a broom cupboard from which angry French mutterings emerged.

"Max!" she said brightly, glancing around as he entered. "I am so pleased to see you."

Then Max considered seriously for the first time that he might be dreaming. The last time he had spoken to Lavinia Torpenhow, she had been dismantling his essay on the Zagwan Empire and telling him he must pull his socks up if he wanted to pass his examinations. He did, he had, and he'd not seen her since. But how could his old tutor possibly be here in the Oubliette with an angry girl who was able to tame Revenants?

"Miss Torpenhow . . ." he said.

"Please call me Hilly," said Miss Torpenhow. "Tamzin, was there any trouble with the Revenant? Is it . . . ?"

"I sorted it out," said Tamzin, trying not to look pleased with herself, but failing. "Now what? Your boy's out of the prison, but how do we get him out of the city?"

"There is an air terminal for fuel freighters not far from here," said Miss Torpenhow. "I'm hoping the customs men there are not as nosy as the ones on the mooring tower. Should we let these poor fellows out of the cupboard, do you think?"

"No," said Tamzin, shocked at the idea. "Leave them in there. Someone will let them out in the morning. We need to get off this city, quick and quiet."

"I am sure you are right," said Miss Torpenhow. But as she put away her gun and walked toward the door the office filled suddenly with light. Outside in the street, large lamps had been turned on, directing their beams through the Oubliette's grimy windows. Men could be seen running around out there, silhouetted against the glare as they took up their positions.

"Mademoiselle Torpenhow!" said a voice, amplified by a tin speaking trumpet, buzzing and echoey. "Mademoiselle Pook! Monsieur Angmering! Put down your weapons and come out with your hands up!"

13

PUTTING OUT THE TRASH

How do they know our names?" asked Tamzin. "How do they know we're here at all?"

"That voice sounded rather like — " Miss Torpenhow started to say, but, before she could say who it had sounded like, the men outside seemed to grow tired of waiting. There was a crash of shattering glass, a rolling roar of rifle fire and cheerful toy-xylophone noises as bullets plucked at the thin metal slats of the blinds and pinged off the walls. Tamzin, Miss Torpenhow, and Max fell flat, trying to hide themselves behind the table and the chairs, and feeling terribly conscious that none of those items was particularly likely to be bulletproof.

In the silence that came after, the same voice that had told them to come out could be heard saying in French, "Hold your positions, men. I shall check and make sure none of the miscreants survived. No, no, Melville, I insist. In the Bureau de Navigation, we believe in leading from the front."

"That definitely sounds like Patrice LeClerc," said Miss Torpenhow indignantly, from behind a chair. And there was Monsieur LeClerc himself, booting the bullet-riddled door open and stepping inside with a revolver in his hand. He swung his gaze across the office, and then down at the floor.

"So, mes amis," he said, seeing the three of them cowering there. "You got the young man out? I was not expecting that. Mademoiselle Pook, you are good — you defeated the Revenant even with a defective knife. I had assumed it would kill you and Max while you were trying to escape. But, alas, it seems I must do that disagreeable job myself." He raised his revolver.

"Monsieur LeClerc!" snapped Miss Torpenhow. "What is the meaning of this?"

LeClerc shrugged and beamed, and for a moment Tamzin glimpsed again the cheerful, friendly character who had bought them lunch at the Baguette Pneumatique. "I am truly sorry, my old friend. Très désolé. I have not been altogether honest with you. When I spoke earlier of certain members of the council who are in the pay of Gabriel Strega, I failed to make clear that I was referring to myself. I am not proud of it. But what can one do? To live well aboard Paris is expensive, and Strega will reward me most generously for your young friend's death."

A voice outside, shouting, anxious.

"Ah," said LeClerc. "Inspector Melville grows impatient." He swung the pistol to point at Max.

There was a loud bang. It came not from the revolver but from the inner room, where the hatch had been slammed violently open. Max, thinking it was a gunshot, flinched and put his hands in front of his face as if that might ward off LeClerc's bullet. So he did not quite see what happened next. He had only an impression of something fast and huge that came crashing through the door at the rear of the office and bowled LeClerc off his feet. The pistol went off, but the bullet went into the ceiling, and the sound of the shot was lost in the scream and ugly crunch as the Daunt landed on its prey. The men outside, hearing the noise, came running and found the Revenant standing over LeClerc with blood dripping from its fangs. Then there were more screams, shouts, orders, gunshots. Bullets ricocheted from the creature's armor and set off on excitable tours of the office like overcaffeinated bees. The men fell back along the short passageway that led to the front door, and the Daunt followed them.

Spread-eagled on the linoleum, Tamzin turned her head to see if her companions were all right. They were, and weren't. Miss Torpenhow and young Angmering seemed unharmed, but both had a look she had seen before on her teammates in the Arcade when things turned bad. They were frozen with fear. They needed someone to take charge, and Tamzin was the only one who could.

"We have to go back down," she said, snaking her way to Miss Torpenhow, and taking her hand. "There's no way out the front door with that lot shooting off their pop guns and the Daunt on the prowl."

Outside, so many orders were being yelled and so many guns were going off that it sounded as if every policeman in Paris had shown up. Fewer stray bullets were finding their way into the office now, which suggested that the Daunt had left the building and was now menacing people in the street. Tamzin stood up, keeping low, and ran to the back of the office, through into the vestibule with the hatchway. The hatch hung open, wrenched half off its hinges by the Daunt. She turned and shouted to the others, "Come on!"

They did as they were told, although Miss Torpenhow darted

back to fetch her carpetbag. Then they followed Tamzin down through the hatch, through the open inner door, which she should probably have locked, back onto the upper landing of the empty prison. Tamzin could see that Max wanted to go home to his cell. She seized him by his arm and pulled him away from the stairs. "You can't stay on this city. LeClerc might not be the only one here who wants you dead."

"I still cannot believe it," fluttered Miss Torpenhow. "Poor Patrice — he has behaved very shabbily, I'm afraid . . ."

"There has to be another way out of here," said Tamzin.

"I don't see why," Max objected. "It's a prison — that's kind of the point."

Tamzin had already gone hurrying off along the landing, and was hidden from him and Miss Torpenhow by the curving wall of the cell block. Her voice came back to them. "Something here . . ."

Max hesitated, still thinking wistfully of his cell, which seemed the safest place in Paris, whatever this fierce girl said. But Miss Torpenhow pushed him gently along the landing, saying, "We should put ourselves in Miss Pook's hands, Max. She is a most resourceful young woman."

The "something" of which Tamzin had spoken turned out to be a door, a heavy iron affair like the doors of the three cells, but set in the Oubliette's outer wall. A few seconds of frantic fumbling with the set of keys Miss Torpenhow had taken from the jailer produced the one that opened it. It let them into a dank corridor that led a few yards in darkness and ended at a hatch. The hatch was not locked. Swung open, it revealed a short walkway jutting out, rather like a diving board, into a large, shadowy silo.

"It stinks," said Tamzin, covering her nose with her sleeve.

"What is it?" asked Max. "Another prison?"

"A refuse silo," said Miss Torpenhow. "Waste from every tier of the city must collect down here. I imagine this walkway exists so that the staff at the Oubliette can dispose of their rubbish, and perhaps, in crueler times, the bodies of prisoners. Come, there must be other hatches that open into it. Perhaps we can find our way up into the city."

They went out along the walkway, Miss Torpenhow taking the lead now. When they reached the end, they jumped down a few feet onto a layer of old vegetable peelings, broken furniture, rags, bones, clock parts, crack-faced dolls, and other squidgier things too shapeless to identify in the half-light, which Max thought was probably a blessing. He guessed he was inside the vast steel blister he'd been able to see from the Oubliette's exercise balcony, jutting from the city's underside. It had never occurred to him what it was used for. Now, as he snagged his trousers on the spokes of a broken bicycle wheel, its purpose was clear. All over the roof above him were the mouths of garbage chutes, and sometimes streams of stuff came spewing out of them, spattering and clattering down into the morass where he stood.

"This is too dangerous," he shouted. "If we're passing under one of those holes at the wrong time, we'll be crushed by falling junk."

"I'm shocked at how much these Parisians throw away," said Miss Torpenhow. "I'm sure that much of this could be reused. I suppose in a city as big and prosperous as Paris, no one feels the need —"

"Look," said Tamzin, pointing to the far side of the silo where dim work lamps showed a row of metal rungs stitched up the rusty wall like a suture.

They started to scramble their way toward it across acres of the city's waste, while more came down in sudden avalanches from the chutes all around them.

"Who is throwing so much stuff away, in the middle of the night?" Max wondered.

"Refuse workers on the higher tiers," said Miss Torpenhow. "They must empty the bins in their districts each day, sort through for anything they deem worth recycling, and then send the rest here, ready to be jettisoned."

"Ready to be what?" asked Tamzin.

"Oh dear," said Miss Torpenhow, stopping suddenly.

New lights had suddenly come on, flashing, spinning orange lights, which flickered hellishly across the sea of trash. Somewhere high above, a siren began to sound.

"I think perhaps we should return to the walkway," said Miss Torpenhow. But, before any of them could move, the huge trap-door at the base of the silo opened. A mound of refuse the size of a small town went tumbling down into the mud between the city's tracks. And with it, their screams lost in the rush and slither of the garbage, went Max Angmering, Lavinia Torpenhow, and Tamzin Pook.

14

OUT-COUNTRY

On the Deuxieme Étage of Paris, in a pleasant apartment with a balcony and two cats, there lived a lady named Ermintrude LeBrun. Madame LeBrun had been complaining to her husband for at least six months about the state of their mattress, which she said had grown so lumpy, so soft in some places and so hard in others, that she could barely get a wink of sleep. Monsieur LeBrun had put off buying a new one for as long as possible. Mattresses were expensive items, he said, and should not be bought on a whim. Anyway, he slept perfectly well himself. But the previous morning at breakfast his Ermintrude had been so disagreeable that he had finally admitted defeat, and stopped in at a furniture shop on his way to work. The new mattress had been delivered that very afternoon, and Madame LeBrun enjoyed a peaceful night's sleep for the first time in months.

She was entirely unaware, until she read about it in the *Flaneur* over her croissants the next morning, that a Revenant had been let loose down in the engine district while she was sleeping. And she never did learn that her old mattress, which had been carted away by the refuse team that afternoon and found its way by various chutes down into the waste silo, had saved the life of Tamzin Pook.

It really was a horribly lumpy old mattress, and Madame LeBrun had been quite right to complain about it. But it was not so horribly lumpy as the rocks of the Out-Country, which were what Tamzin would have landed on if the mattress had not come down ahead of her and broken her fall. Indeed, if it had been a better mattress, she might have bounced off it and hit the rocks anyway. As it was, she lay there in the depression left by Madame LeBrun's un-sleeping body, and watched the towering wheels of Paris go rolling by on either side of her, and saw the stars appear as the city passed above her and moved away.

Then she sat up and looked about for her companions.

Max had landed not far off, in a gargantuan heap of vegetable peelings from the city's restaurants. They smelled worse than the mattress, but they had cushioned his landing just as effectively, and he stood up, shaking but unharmed, when Tamzin found him. Together, in the moonlight that was slowly brightening as the smoke of Paris blew away, they went searching for Miss Torpenhow.

"Over here!" they heard her call, out of the garbage mountain. They had to dig a little, throwing aside old boots, tangles of frayed rope, and anonymous bits of broken board, but she was not buried too deeply and they found her easily enough. She was still clutching her carpetbag. She started to rise to her feet, then gasped and sat back down. "I'm afraid I have sprained my ankle."

"Sit and rest awhile," said Max. "We can't do much till morning, anyway."

"We could get off this crap heap," said Tamzin. "And get upwind a bit," she added, holding her nose: not far off there was a literal crap heap, where a second silo had vented gallons of sewage.

"How quiet it is," said Miss Torpenhow.

It was. All three of them had spent so much of their lives aboard mobile cities that it was a shock to find themselves on the ground. As Paris trundled away from them and the sound of its engines faded, they were becoming aware that the bare earth had sounds of its own — the sigh of the wind blowing over the garbage pile, the drip and giggle of water falling into the deep, fresh trenches the city's tracks had clawed on either side of them, and a lot of other, less identifiable noises — patterings and rustlings and the fall of small stones. They all recalled suddenly the dreadful stories of the ghosts and nightwights that lurked in the wild places of the Out-Country — stories that seemed thrilling if a little silly when you were safe on the decks of your city, but that out here seemed entirely believable.

The silence did not last. They had barely managed to get Miss Torpenhow upright, and begun helping her down the scree slopes of the rubbish mountain, when there was a sudden skirl of engine noise and light blazed over them. Up out of the nearest track mark, scrabbling a path for itself with huge, clawed wheels, came a tiny town. It was little more than a single large house, many-turreted, fully articulated, and built mostly from wood. The ducts of a ramshackle engine seemed to have grown around it and through it like a strangler vine. Across its jaws, in large but uncertain letters, someone had scrawled its name in whitewash: WEECH.

"Scavengers!" said Miss Torpenhow. "They have come to feast on Paris's leavings, I expect. If they find us here, they will feast on us as well."

"What?" gasped Max.

"Not literally, but I imagine we would be sold as slaves, and then we'd never find our way back to Thorbury and that beastly Strega would have his own way. We must hide."

But how could they? For what Weech lacked in size and grace it made up for in searchlights. Dozens of them were arranged above its jaws and along its flanks, and they played their beams constantly across the rubbish mound. The jaws opened — not really jaws, more like barn doors — and out of them ragged figures came scrambling: men and women and children with dust masks over their faces and big wicker baskets on their backs, running up the slithering sides of the mound with eager shouts.

"Look here! New boots!"

"Look! Look! A bog seat!"

"Look! What a lovely mattress!"

Everything seemed to delight the scavengers. Even the vegetable peelings were being scooped into their wicker baskets. But they were not delighted to find three strangers stumbling down the side of their heap. The burlier ones came running to surround Tamzin, Max, and Miss Torpenhow.

"This claim's ours!" they growled, voices muffled by their leather masks, eyes hard behind their goggles. Some carried cutlasses and one held a sort of gun. Others wielded hooks on long poles, which were probably built for raking through the rubbish, but that looked as though they would serve as weapons too. "It's ours, it is!" they shouted. "This heap! Our heap! All ours! Get gone!"

"We are just fugitives who fell out of the city," protested Miss Torpenhow. "We make no claim upon your salvage . . ."

The scavengers didn't hear, or didn't care. One jabbed his pole at Miss Torpenhow. Max caught it and pulled, dragging the man off his feet. Things were turning ugly.

Tamzin said, "Stop! Stop!"

"'Ere," said one of the scavengers in a new tone. "'Ere," he shouted, "get a lamp on this one!"

One of the searchlights swung to pin Tamzin in its beam, blinding her.

"'Ere!" said the man again. "I know this one! I know who this is! What a find, mateys! What manna from the scrap gods! She's only Tamzin bloomin' Pook!"

❀

The summer before — or the summer before that, it wasn't clear — Weech had gone west, feeding on the droppings of a city called Grandeville, tracking it all the way to the sea. There, flush with scavenged wealth, some of the Weechites had gone aboard a raft resort that was anchored just offshore. The Mayor of Weech, a man named Absalom Croke, had watched a show in the Amusement Arcade, and it had made a big impression on him.

"Tamzin bloomin' Pook," he said, for about the thirtieth time, when they were seated in the big communal dining hall at the top of Weech. "I can't believe it's really you! An actual celebrity, aboard my town! What did you say you're doing here again?"

"She came with me to rescue Max here from a Parisian jail," said Miss Torpenhow. But Miss Torpenhow was of no interest to Croke. Nor was Max. Croke had not stopped them from following as he'd led Tamzin up the ramps into his town's jaws, but they were worthless as far as he was concerned.

"Tamzin bloomin' Pook!" he whispered, shaking his head.

A boy came hurrying in with a tattered pamphlet Croke had sent him to fetch. It was a souvenir program from the Amusement Arcade, with an engraving on the front of Tamzin standing triumphantly over a fallen Revenant Engine. Croke put it on the table in front of her and placed a stub of pencil beside it.

"Can I get your autograph, Miss Pook? Maybe you could put, 'To Absalom Croke, with best wishes.' Or — no — how about

'To my good friend Absalom Croke.' Or — well, you can put whatever you like really, 'cause I can't read. But I'm a big fan, Miss Pook."

A clanging noise began. Up in the rickety watchtower, which rose higher than Weech's tallest exhaust stacks, someone was beating a dangling hunk of scrap metal with a lump hammer.

"Cripes," said Croke. "Predator coming. They don't give us long these days."

He strode to the nearest window, and his guests followed, except for Miss Torpenhow, whose damaged ankle would not let her stand. Outside, the pale fingertips of the searchlight beams felt this way and that across the mountain of garbage. The scavengers who had been at work up there were all hurrying back toward Weech, casting frantic shadows up the drifting smoke. The alarm gong kept on sounding. A blaze of lights flared on the skyline like a low-budget sunrise. Another town, larger than Weech, was clawing its heavy way across the track marks.

"Come on, lads," growled Croke, watching as the last of his scavengers came blundering down the heap. Weech's engines were revving by then. The little town shivered, eager to be gone before the predator reached it. Farther along the raised ridge of earth between the track marks, another townlet was busy sucking up the dollop of Parisian sewage into the bulbous storage tanks on its top deck, where it would be rendered into fertilizer and sold to farming towns. Its people showed no signs of concern as they plodded around in their stained rubber muck suits, unclogging the suction hoses. But no predator town would go to the trouble of eating a dung harvester. A town like Weech, with its hold stuffed full of salvage, was a different proposition entirely.

"All aboard!" voices yelled, down in Weech's depths. The alarm gong stopped. The engines roared. The town went backward at speed, throwing Tamzin off her feet, almost throwing Max. Plastic cups and dishes slid from the tables in the eatery and bounced across the decks. The view outside the window slewed and swerved: Tamzin saw sky, earth, a dizzy glimpse into the maw of the oncoming predator. Then, its maneuver complete, Weech took off at a run, jouncing and barreling across the torn-up earth in Paris's wake, then onto flatter ground.

Croke went to another window, and again Max and Tamzin followed. Astern, between the soot-belching exhaust stacks, the predator's running lights showed now and then as it struggled across the track marks and gave chase. But Weech was going so fast it felt as though it were flying. It probably was sometimes, as it breasted a ridge and all eight wheels lost contact briefly with the ground. The predator kept up with it for a while, and even seemed to gain a little, but then decided that Weech wasn't worth expending any more fuel on. It turned aside, circling back toward Paris's track marks in the hope that other scavengers would soon be drawn to the great city's spoor.

Weech ran on into the night.

15

In Thunder City

To Helen Angmering it seemed impossible that less than two months had passed since Strega returned to Thorbury. When she remembered the events of that dreadful afternoon, or the golden times before, they felt like things that had happened in another age of the world, or to another person altogether. What a silly, happy, thoughtless girl she had been in those days! How much she had changed!

But everything had changed. In Bellevue Park, at which she looked out every morning from the window of the Werners' box room, the trees were being cut down and the lawns grubbed up. In place of the lawns, new vegetable plots and chicken sheds were being laid out. In place of the trees, bits of broken buildings were piled up in teetering mounds. The grand facade of the town hall lay there, along with pillars and statues from the Temple of Peripatetia and the ornate cupola of the Planning Office. One by one, all the glorious old buildings on the Command Deck were being torn to pieces, and the pieces lowered by cranes to the Upper Residential Tier, where they were stacked until there was room on the freight elevators to take them down to Base Tier. There, the rumors said, they would be used to enlarge Thorbury's jaws and Dismantling Yards. There was even talk of new auxiliary engines. Night and day, the city rang to the sounds of the ongoing work: the demolition gangs above, the renovations below.

No one objected. At least, no one objected anymore. In the early days, when people still thought Gabriel Strega had a better nature to which they might appeal, a few had tried. A delegation of councillors had presented a petition asking that the parks be spared. Strega had them shot, then sent his nomads to round up everyone who had signed the document and transferred them all to labor units on Base Tier. The High Priestess of Peripatetia protested about the demolition of her temple, and Strega demolished it anyway, but left one T-shaped section of girders standing, from which he had her hanged.

Strega never gloated over these cruelties, but nor did he show the slightest trace of mercy or remorse. Indeed, he never expressed any feelings at all. He stayed out of sight mostly, closeted in what remained of the town hall, drawing up his plans, and consulting with the men who were to put them into action. Some of these were nomads who had boarded the city with him, but others were Thorbury men, junior councillors and planning officials who had worshipped him in the old days. They called him the Architect, and they had become his loyal lieutenants.

It was left to these turncoats to explain the reasoning behind their master's actions. Strega never bothered giving speeches, but his allies gave speeches on his behalf. "We have no more need of Peripatetia," they said. "Once, before our city grew old and sleepy, it was called Thorburg: the City of Thunder. Thor the Thunderer is its proper god. We do not need gaudy temples in which to worship him. Our engine rooms shall be his shrine. The roar of our land engines shall be our hymn to him. And, besides, the city will be more streamlined without all those old-fashioned buildings catching the wind. The Architect has calculated that without the extra weight and drag of the temple and the Planning Office, Thorbury is two point five percent more fuel efficient."

"If only Miss Torpenhow would hurry up and bring my brother back," said Helen, listening to Mr. Werner read out this pronouncement on the morning it appeared in the city's newspaper. "Max would set things right."

Miss Torpenhow, before she left, had popped a note through the Werners' letter box, explaining where she was going and what her plan was. But that had been weeks ago, surely long enough for Miss T to have reached Paris, and for Max to have raised an army. From the window of the box room, where she stayed hidden through most of each day, Helen watched the sky, hoping to see the fleet of airships bringing her brother home.

The airships never appeared. Instead, when she returned to the box room on that particular day, she saw her own face. A rather unflattering portrait of her was being pasted up on a billboard outside one of the new chicken sheds. She was too far away to read all the things the poster said about her, but two words were printed large enough to make its purpose clear. WANTED said one, and the other: REWARD.

"I cannot stay here," she told the Werners. "It is too dangerous for you. If they find you have been hiding me, you might be killed. I shall go and surrender myself. I will throw myself on Strega's mercy."

"Except we know he doesn't have any," said Mrs. Werner. "He'll string you up next to our poor High Priestess."

"But Helen is right," said her husband. "She can't possibly stay here. It's clear that Strega suspects she is still aboard Thorbury, or he would not have gone to the trouble of having those posters made. He will keep looking until he finds her, and now there's no resistance left, he can spare more of his nomad thugs to conduct house-to-house searches and suchlike. No, it is high time we sent Helen down below, as I promised Miss Torpenhow we would if things got bad. Judith, my dear, we must drop a line to your brother and let him know there's a package on its way."

Helen wasn't sure at first what he meant, until she realized that she was to be the package. Every day, hoppers of salvaged building material from the heaps out in the park were being rolled along Circular Street to the freight elevators. Mr. Werner had a quiet word with an old friend in the Salvage Department, and it was arranged that one of the hoppers would pause outside his front door the next morning, just long enough for an extra crate to be added to its load.

"My brother will be waiting for you at the bottom," Mrs. Werner said as they helped Helen into the crate. "He's a good man. Him and his wife have a lad about your own age, Raoul. They'll keep you safe."

The crate looked too small to hold a whole person. Helen did not believe she could possibly fit inside. But she crouched down and somehow squeezed herself into the little space, and the Werners stuffed a lot of straw in around her and then closed the lid and nailed it down.

She waited in darkness, hardly daring to breathe in case the little air holes they'd bored for her were not sufficient. She heard the hopper rumble up outside and the Werners talking with the salvage men. Then the crate was lifted up, carried, dumped down, and her long, bruising journey began.

How have I come to this? she thought, cooped there in the stuffy dark, listening to men outside bellow instructions. *Where is Max? Why doesn't he come? Why doesn't he do something?*

She grew tearful for a while, imagining that poor Max was dead, and then very angry, because it seemed just as likely that her brother was still living it up aboard Paris and didn't care two hoots about beating Strega. Yes, knowing Max, he would be having a wonderful time, while his poor sister, stuffed inside a box, rode a rickety elevator into Thorbury's lower depths.

She was still angry when she reached the bottom. There her crate was thrown onto what felt like a truck, or possibly a conveyor belt. There was another long period of shaking and jostling, and a painful thump when the crate was manhandled some distance and landed upside down. The noise outside was so enormous and incessant that Helen could not hear if anyone was there until she was suddenly lifted the right way up again and the crate's lid was wrenched off.

She was in some dim hangar with a roof of rust. Two men in gray overalls backed away as she rose stiffly from the crate. One of the men was old, short, and fat: Mrs. Werner's brother, she supposed. The other was young, tall, and thin. His son, she guessed.

The older one held out his hand to her and said, "Come along, my dear, you'll be safe with us." As if she was just a child. Which, Helen supposed, was how everyone must see her. And she *had* been just a child really, until Strega came. But she had done a lot of growing up since then. So she ignored the outstretched hand, stood up, spat out some straw, and bowed with all the dignity she could manage, thanking these good men for the great risk she knew they were taking by helping her.

"My brother isn't coming back," she said. "And everything is going from bad to worse. If we want to save Thorbury, we shall have to do it ourselves."

16

THE SCAVENGER TOWN

Their were around fifty people aboard Weech, and most of them were Croke's wives, or children, or grandchildren. He was a dangerous man, Tamzin reckoned, looking at him the next morning as he sat at breakfast, surrounded by his tribe. A big old brute, decked out in tattered finery he'd found in rubbish dumps from one end of the Hunting Ground to the other: rings on his fingers, a fur coat on his back, a necklace of Ancient seedies slung around his neck. She wasn't sure what he would have done with the three fugitives if he had not been an Arcade fan. She was glad she wouldn't have to find out. As it was, he cracked a delighted smile as soon as she walked into the eatery, elbowed a wife off the throne beside him, and bellowed for Tamzin bloomin' Pook to join him.

As she picked her way between the salvaged tables where the others of his band were eating, Tamzin had a sudden, nasty feeling he might ask her to marry him, but it turned out all he wanted was her stories of the Arcade, and the secondhand fame he felt she could bestow upon him. "I had that Tamzin Pook aboard my town once," he would be telling other scavengers at trading meets and fuel stops, for the rest of his life, probably.

Max and Miss Torpenhow, sitting on mismatched chairs at the far end of the big room, could only look on in wonder. They had tumbled into an upside-down world where Max's breeding and Miss Torpenhow's education counted for nothing, but an Arcade fighter was treated like royalty.

"I have always known there was a subclass of small towns that live on the scraps our cities drop," said Miss Torpenhow, "but I had never bothered to imagine what such places must be like . . ."

What they were like, thought Max, looking around the eatery, was a junk shop in hell. Everything from the chairs and tables to the knives and forks had been salvaged from some city's spoil heaps. Nothing matched; nothing looked new; most things were bent, or had been broken and repaired at least once. Lights made from old bin lids swung from the ceiling, pictures of other people's dead relatives hung upon the walls, and everyone was dressed in rags and castoffs. Yet they seemed happy enough, these Crokes. The talk at the salvage-wood tables was of all the finds they had made in last night's midden, and the prices their loot would fetch at the trading cluster in the Gaunt Hills, where Weech was apparently headed.

"The Gaunt Hills," said Miss Torpenhow thoughtfully. She consulted some inner atlas, and looked unhappy at what she found there. "Oh dear me, no! The Gaunt Hills lie in entirely the wrong direction. No great cities hunt there. We must find our way to London, or Brussels, or Murnau, and tell the authorities there of what has happened in Thorbury."

"Why would they care?" asked Max.

"Because what Strega has done goes against all the rules and customs of Municipal Darwinism!" said Miss Torpenhow indignantly.

"The great cities may be rivals, but when Municipal Darwinism itself is threatened, they help one another."

"Paris didn't want to help," said Max. "Even the councillors who didn't want me dead were happy enough with Strega taking over. Why would the councillors of London or Brussels feel any differently?"

Miss Torpenhow fixed him with a look he remembered from his school days. "Max Angmering," she said, "that brave young woman and I went to a great deal of trouble to get you out of the Oubliette, and we did not do it for our own amusement. You are the rightful mayor of Thorbury. Your people are looking to you to free them from Gabriel Strega. Your sister, Helen, is waiting for you to save her."

Max looked at the green sludge in the bowl that a Croke child had just set down in front of him, and wondered what it was, and whether it had been made from the same peelings he had landed in when he fell out of Paris. He did not feel like breakfast, somehow.

"Poor Helen," he said.

His sister, in his memory, was just a pale and slightly annoying girl with blonde braids. How could she survive as a fugitive, in a city ruled by nomads and Stalkers? Hot tears filled his eyes, and he blinked hard to stop them spilling out. He remembered how he had planned to go and challenge Strega to a duel. His time in prison had knocked that confidence out of him.

"I don't know what to do," he said. "I am not a mayor! I am not a soldier!"

"But you did so much military training . . ."

"That was just parade ground stuff mostly — marching about

and saluting. I don't know anything about actual fighting. Last night, when we were under fire, and the Daunt, and . . . I was so afraid."

Miss Torpenhow looked stunned. She had been depending on him. She had risked so much to get him out of Paris. And he was no use to her after all.

Max felt himself blushing. He was not used to telling the truth about himself, not even to himself. "I am just a student," he said. "I am just a student, and not even a very good one. I am lazy, and not very clever, and the men who rule the great cities will see that. If I ask them for help against Strega, they'll laugh in my face. And they'll be right to! I don't know how to fight nomad warriors. And as for these Stalkers, the Scrap Metal Seven . . ."

Miss Torpenhow took a spoonful of the green broth, lifted it to her lips, then decided that she did not feel like breakfast either and returned it to the bowl. "You will rise to the challenge, Max," she said. "The hour produces the man, so they say."

"So who say?"

"It is a phrase from Ancient times."

"Well, this is not Ancient times," said Max sulkily. "And it isn't the age of the Nomad Empires, or the age of the Zagwan Deluge, when heroes walked the earth. This is just now, and I am just me. I could no more stand up to Strega and his army of thugs than you could."

"I see," said Miss Torpenhow. "I see. But to whom else can we turn for help?"

Max shrugged. "General Kleinhammer, I suppose. He's the head of the Defense Corps. It's his job to keep our city safe."

"He was away when Strega struck," said Miss Torpenhow. "He was taking a spa cure in Bad Luftgarten. A great many military gentlemen take their holidays in Bad Luftgarten."

"So where is he now?" asked Max.

"Still there, I expect. An exile, like ourselves."

"Then let's go to Bad Luftgarten," said Max. "Let's go there and find old Kleinhammer and set the problem before him. He'll be able to look at things objectively. Ask *me* how to retake Thorbury and I haven't the foggiest. Ask Kleinhammer and he'll say, 'Easy — a flanking movement up the lateral stairwells.' Or whatever. He's probably got a plan already. Probably just waiting to be asked. Kleinhammer's the man to lead the people in an uprising!"

"He does have a very impressive mustache," mused Miss Torpenhow.

"Exactly! They'd follow him anywhere, a man with a mustache like that."

Miss Torpenhow pondered this. She wondered why she had not thought of Kleinhammer herself. "Bad Luftgarten will probably be over the Middle Sea at this time of year," she said.

"Perhaps when we get to this trading cluster we can find an airship that will take us there," said Max.

The meal was ending. The other diners hurried off to work in the engine rooms or in the hold, where baskets full of junk were waiting to be sorted. Tamzin came to find her companions, wearing an expression neither Max nor Miss Torpenhow could read. She had spent the past twenty minutes explaining to Absalom Croke in detail how she had defeated Mortmain's Wheelie Shark, and then he had asked her about the thing with Eve Vespertine. She did not like talking about the thing with Eve Vespertine.

Croke swaggered up behind her just as she reached the table where Max and Miss Torpenhow were sitting.

"She's a diamond, this kid," he said. "A bloomin' diamond. You don't know how lucky you are to have her as a friend."

"We aren't exactly —" Tamzin started to say.

"We are well aware that we would both be dead without Miss Pook's skill and courage," said Miss Torpenhow. "And now, thanks to her, we may continue on our journey. Mr. Croke, may we stay aboard your charming town until it reaches the Gaunt Hills? We need to find an aviator with a ship that can carry us to —"

"You don't need to go all the way to the bloomin' Gaunt Hills to find an airy-ship," boomed Croke. "Not if Tamzin Pook is flying with you. We have our own bloomin' airy-ship right here on Weech, and Tamzin bloomin' Pook is welcome to use it any bloomin' day!"

17

SUCH A PRETTY CITY

Inspector Melville of the Paris Sûreté rode the elevator back to the Premier Étage as the day was breaking, and walked wearily home through the parks to his house on the Avenue Montparnasse. He was feeling somewhat shaken after the night's events. There had been rumors that the council had brought in a Revenant to guard the Oubliette, but he had never believed them until he saw the thing for himself, prowling out of the prison with poor LeClerc's blood all over it. It was mostly luck that had stopped it killing any of his men, for the bullets from their rifles just bounced off it. In the end, he'd managed to lower some of the heavy bulkhead doors that sealed off the different sections of the engine district in case of fire. Trapped behind them, the creature had clawed and thrown itself against the metal until Melville was able to bring in a heavy-weapons team to destroy it with armor-piercing shells.

All in all, it had been a long night, and now there would be reports to write, and scandals to deal with — the scandal of young Angmering's disappearance, and the scandal of the Revenant itself. Inspector Melville shook his head. He did not see how the council could survive this . . .

At his house, the servants were already up and about. The maid Delphine came twittering at him as soon as he was through the door. "Monsieur, monsieur! There are two gentlemen to see you!"

"At this hour?" grumbled the inspector, hanging his kepi on the hall stand and going after her to the drawing room.

"I told them you were not at home, but they insisted they would wait," the girl said. She hung back shyly as he pushed open the door, as if she were frightened of the gentlemen in there.

She was right to be, thought Melville when he got a look at them. They were not gentlemen — that was clear at a glance. The big one was sitting in Melville's best armchair, with his boots on the coffee table. The other — a scrawny little runt who nevertheless gave off an air of immense and imminent violence — stood by the stove, impertinently picking up and examining the knick-knacks and trophies arranged on the mantelpiece.

"Ah, Monsieur l'Inspecteur!" cried the big one jovially, not bothering to rise from Melville's chair. "A rough night, I gather? Mr. Lint and I arrived a few hours ago, and the mooring tower was simply *thrumming* with rumors. Was it not, Mr. Lint?"

"'Thrumming' is the very word I would have used, Mr. Coldharbour," said the little one. He turned and gave Melville a look that chilled him from the tips of his en brosse hair to the soles of his regulation boots.

"I gather there has been an escape from the prison down below," Coldharbour went on. "I believe a young man Paris wanted to keep *in* has been got *out*. But that does not concern Mr. Lint or myself. What concerns us is how he was got out. A Revenant Engine was on guard, I gather, and yet someone was able to nobble it. Is 'nobble' the correct term, Mr. Lint?"

"Once again, Mr. Coldharbour, you have picked the perfect word. The mot juste, so to speak."

"What is all this?" asked Melville. "What do you mean by coming to my home? If you know something about the escape, you should go to the police station and submit yourselves for questioning — "

"Ah," said Mr. Lint, "but we do not wish to be questioned, you see. We are the ones who wish to do the questioning. Don't we, Mr. Coldharbour?"

"We do, Mr. Lint!" laughed Coldharbour, as if it were all the most enormous fun. "And what we want to know is this. The person or persons who helped young Angmering escape — the person or persons who outwitted the Oubliette's guard dog — what became of them? Do you have them in custody, perhaps, Monsieur l'Inspecteur?"

"I will tell you nothing!" said Melville angrily. "You barge in here, frightening my servants, demanding to know official business — "

Coldharbour held up his hands. "I know, I know! You are a busy man, Monsieur l'Inspecteur. You want us gone. And as soon as you tell us what we need to know, we shall be! We shall hop back in our little airship and take flight, and you need never think of us again."

"But if you don't," said Mr. Lint, licking his lips, "we shall stay, and we might frighten your servants some more."

"Oh dear, Mr. Lint, do you think so?" asked Mr. Coldharbour.

"Such a pretty girl, your maid," said Mr. Lint. "And the inspector's wife — this is her portrait, I presume — a very pretty woman. And these children in the other picture, they are yours

101

too, I suppose. Such pretty, pretty children. Such a blessing, to be surrounded by pretty things."

"Mr. Lint has a passion for pretty things," said Coldharbour. "Don't you, Mr. Lint?"

"Oh, I do, Mr. Coldharbour. But somehow I always seem to break them."

"That is your tragedy, Mr. Lint," said Mr. Coldharbour. "But Inspector Melville does not have time to listen to our chitchat. I can see he is growing impatient. So just tell us what we wish to know, Inspector, and we shall be out of your house in a jiffy."

"Such a pretty house," said Mr. Lint with a meaningful look.

Inspector Melville swallowed, and then said gruffly, "We believe two women helped Angmering to escape. A young one and an older one. Poor LeClerc — the man who raised the alarm — gave their names as Lavinia Torpenhow and Tamzin Pook. We believe that after unleashing the Revenant to distract us they found their way into the aft waste silo, and were jettisoned when it released its load. Whether they survived, we cannot say . . ."

"Then let us worry about that!" said Mr. Coldharbour, jumping up and clapping Melville on the shoulder. "That is all we needed to know, and now that we know it we shall leave your lovely city, as we promised. But, ah, if I may offer some advice? It might occur to you to try to stop us leaving — to contact your colleagues on the mooring tower and have them try to detain us, for example."

"That would be foolish, wouldn't it, Mr. Coldharbour?" said Mr. Lint.

"It would, Mr. Lint," said Coldharbour, and, smiling down at the inspector, added, "Mr. Lint, though a mild-mannered fellow in ordinary circumstances, has a surprising temper on him. When vexed, he has been known to do some unfortunate things, things which I am sure he regrets deeply once the dust has settled, and the blood congealed."

"It pains me to think of them, Mr. Coldharbour," said Mr. Lint.

"So you can see it would be a great deal more pleasant for everyone if you simply let us go about our business, Monsieur l'Inspecteur, and we shall let you get back to guarding your city."

"Such a pretty city," agreed Mr. Lint as he followed his companion to the door.

18

THE HERCULES

Croke's airy-ship was tethered to a platform on the upper deck of Weech. Tamzin realized she had seen it when she first came aboard, but in the darkness she'd taken it for some sort of ugly shed. Like everything else in the scavenger town, it was made out of junk: a patchwork envelope stitched together from scraps of a dozen others, with a rickety gondola like a clinker-built shack. From its underside there dangled a lot of spidery extendable arms, ending in grabbers, scoops, prongs, and a couple of big, horseshoe-shaped magnets. The ship's job was to fly low over the Out-Country and pick up any useful-looking bits of debris the spotters in the gondola saw. It was called the Hercules, after the legendary steed that pulled the chariot of the scrap god and his son.

It did not look safe to Tamzin, Max, or Miss Torpenhow. But Croke was so proud of it, and so pleased to be able to offer it to the famous Tamzin Pook, that they were afraid he would be offended if they refused. He had the look of a man who might turn nasty if offended and his family and hangers-on had the look of people who were well aware of that, and who were already eyeing up their visitors' shoes and clothes and wondering if they would fit.

So they thanked him politely, and climbed into the gondola. Its walls were covered from deck to ceiling with a higgledy-piggledy collection of wheels that controlled the rudders, engine pods, and scrap-grabbers. A nervous young aviator, hired by Croke to fly the contraption, was peering worriedly at the gauges that showed gas pressure and fuel levels.

Croke made his goodbyes, kissing Tamzin's hand and telling the aviator to be sure to get Miss Pook safe to Bad bloomin' Luftgarten. Tethers were cast off. The engines sputtered and coughed and juddered. Gawky teenage Crokes were sent up stepladders to spin the big wooden propellors.

"Contact!" they shouted as the engines caught, and then "Aaaargh!" as the *Hercules* lurched laboriously skyward, knocking the ladders over. Looking back, Tamzin saw the horrible little town dwindle until it seemed only a model of itself, with a model Absalom Croke standing proudly on the deck to see her off. She watched until the low clouds hid it from sight.

The aviator seemed to speak no Anglish. "Bad Luftgarten" was all he would say, when Max tried making conversation. By gestures he managed to indicate that Bad Luftgarten was a long way off, and that they should relax. They climbed a ladder into the stuffy hold, which ran down the center of the envelope between two rows of alarmingly patched gas cells. Light came into it through small gaps in the fabric of the envelope. A pigeon was flying around up there, defying all Max's attempts to catch it. Miss Torpenhow, her ankle paining her, sat down on a heap of burlap sacks to rest. Tamzin sat down too, far enough away so that Miss Torpenhow would not try to talk to her. She had talked enough last night and this morning. Absalom Croke had asked so many questions about her time in the Arcade, and she had answered him for fear that not answering would endanger her and her companions. So she had talked and talked, telling him about things she had never spoken of before, victories and defeats and narrow escapes that she had done her best to forget. Now all the work of forgetting would have to be done again.

She leaned against a metal strut, which trembled softly with the beat of the airship's engines, and closed her eyes. She had not slept much aboard Weech, and she was still full of the deep weariness that always came on her after a fight.

A bit of a sleep will sort me out, she thought.

But sleep, when it fell on her, was full of dreams, and in all the dreams she was trying and failing again and again to save Eve Vespertine.

19

BAD LUFTGARTEN

The *Hercules* was tougher than she looked. Battering her way through headwinds that would have driven another vessel leagues off course, she crossed the snowy lower summits of the Shatterland Mountains the day after leaving Weech, and started down the spine of Italy.

The aviator's name was Stefan and, although he spoke barely a word of Anglish, he and Max were able to understand each other well enough that they became friends. At nights, when Stefan retired to his bunk at the stern of the gondola, Max sometimes watched the controls for him. He had flown his family's sky-yacht a few times and, although the oily clutter of the *Hercules's* instrument panel was quite unlike the sleek walnut console of the yacht, he was able to identify pressure gauges, altimeter, compass, rudder controls. Sometimes, taking the wheel to make a small adjustment to the airship's course while Stefan dozed behind him, he actually felt useful, which was a novelty. And on the last morning of the flight it was Max who looked through the airship's telescope and saw a speck on the sky ahead resolve itself into a bouquet of gigantic gasbags.

"Town-ho!" he shouted, the way the spotters on Thorbury's watchtowers did. "It is Bad Luftgarten!" he added proudly when Tamzin and Miss Torpenhow came clattering down the ladder from above. He supposed that some of the credit for bringing the *Hercules* so neatly to her destination must be his, and he felt surprisingly proud of it.

Tamzin took her turn with the telescope. The *Hercules* was crossing a rugged coastline with a line of white surf, heading out over the blue immensity of the Middle Sea. There was a darker patch upon the waves that looked like the shadow of a cloud, but when she raised the telescope up and up to where the cloud hung she saw that it was made of immense white gasbags, with buildings showing among them, and the glint of many windows, and a crowd of other airships coming and going.

"Why is it called 'Bad' Luftgarten?" she asked. "It looks all right to me."

Miss Torpenhow, who had been waiting for someone to ask that, explained that in the Tyrolean Mountains, where the town had started out, "bad" meant "bath."

Bad Luftgarten, she went on, had begun as a static settlement, built by a cult of physician-priests around some sacred springs in a high valley. When the Traction Era dawned and their neighbors started putting wheels on their towns, the folk of Bad Luftgarten were reluctant to follow suit. Their prosperity came from their location, and from the invalids who struggled up from the lowlands to breathe clean mountain air and soak in the pure waters. But Graz and Salzburg and the other hungry new all-terrain towns of the Tyrol were starting to look at plump little Bad Luftgarten like passersby eyeing up a delicious slice of Sacher torte in a café window. So the burgermeister of the time thought hard and decided that the air above the mountains must be cleaner still, and that water was obviously at its purest when it was falling as rain, before it ever touched the ground.

The town hired in aviators and airshipwrights from the East, and invested in gasbags instead of wheels and tracks. Ever since, it had been making its stately cruises around the sky, gathering water straight from the clouds, and selling it by the bottle or the bathfull to rich visitors from the lands below.

Other towns that had taken to the air, like Airhaven or Hawkshead, were trading hubs built on a single hoop of deckplate. Bad Luftgarten was altogether more stylish. Its buildings were arranged on seven different levels, tucked into gaps between its mighty gasbags like clusters of chalets clinging to a mountainside. The main air harbor was at the top, a coronet of mooring struts where delicate pilot ships nudged sky-yachts and pleasure cruisers to their berths. But the Hercules was directed to the tradesman's entrance: a lower docking ring serving the warehouses and waste refineries at the bottom of the town. There Stefan said goodbye to his three passengers, and set about finding fuel for his journey home, while they made their way by many stairs up to the higher tiers.

Bad Luftgarten in those days was a town of airy greenhouses and leaping fountains. It was a town of chill air and crystal-clear light, where artificial streams snaked through parks of alpine plants and whispering groves of silver birches, and fell from one deckplate to the next in waterfalls festooned with rainbows. It was a town where rich invalids in wicker bath chairs sat in ranks on sunny terraces, while handsome waiters brought them drinks of rainwater and pretty nurses rearranged the plaid rugs over their knees. It was a town where touring comedians told jokes so old they felt like long-lost friends, and reminded you that they were here all week, and to try the veal. It was a town where brass bands parped and boomed from airborne bandstands, and gilt statues of the gods of healing perched on the pediments of grand hotels like athletes poised to dive into the blue waters of the Middle Sea, five thousand feet below.

It was not Tamzin's sort of town at all. Even Max felt out of place there. But Miss Torpenhow, brushing off their concerns about her injured ankle, limped gamely up flight after flight of stairs, waving farewell to Stefan as the *Hercules* pulled out again, homeward bound for Weech.

There was an information kiosk on Level Four, where young men and women of extraordinary beauty, dressed in impeccable pastel uniforms, waited like kindly angels to greet arriving travelers and answer their questions. Miss Torpenhow asked directions to the Hotel Pegasus, where she believed General Kleinhammer would be staying. It was on Level Two, the angels told her, and she nodded as if a further climb was just what she needed and set off up the next flight of stairs, ignoring Max and Tamzin's offers of help.

The Pegasus was a confection of cupolas and domes and arches, white as a sculpted cloud. The lobby was filled with potted palms and bamboo furniture, and the receptionist looked like a young goddess of the sky. She called an attendant, who led the newcomers into a lounge where querulous colonels and gouty generals were discussing the benefits of rainwater baths and low-calorie diets.

Most of the great Traction Cities still had small armies, but now that Municipal Darwinism had more or less replaced war as a way for one city to capture another's wealth, the armies were mostly ornamental. The senior officers spent much of their time designing ever more magnificent uniforms for themselves and their men, or holidaying in places like Bad Luftgarten. The Pegasus was the place at which they all stayed, and its management had hung paintings of famous battles on the walls, and prints of manly looking fellows in the uniforms of famous regiments. There was a large table where some enthusiastic old gentlemen were re-fighting the Battle of Three Dry Ships as a war game, with a miniature London and armies of tiny Anti-Tractionist warriors, complete with war mammoths.

One of the players was General Kleinhammer. He looked irritated when the attendant interrupted him, then startled when he saw who his visitors were. Setting down his dice cup and measuring stick on a papier-mâché hill, he marched over to greet them.

"Maximilian Angmering, as I live and breathe! And Miss, ah . . . er . . ."

"Torpenhow," said Miss Torpenhow.

The general's mustache was as impressive as Max had remembered. Indeed, at first glance, he seemed to be mostly mustache, his white whiskers advancing before him like a smokescreen ahead of a dawn attack. When Tamzin dragged her eyes away from it and looked at the general himself, he was something of a disappointment: a small, plump man, his lavender dress tunic tailored to make him look slimmer than he was, his shoes built up to make him appear taller. Was this really the hero who could win Thorbury back from its captors? Tamzin doubted it. But the general returned Max's bow with military precision, clicking the heels of his built-up shoes as he did so, and bowed again to kiss Miss Torpenhow's hand, which made her blush. He did not acknowledge Tamzin. He probably thought she was their servant.

"And this is Tamzin Pook," said Miss Torpenhow, "without whose skill and courage Max would still be a prisoner aboard Paris."

"Oh, ah?" said the general, glancing briefly at Tamzin. "Charmed to meet you, m'dear. And delighted you are safe, Max, my boy. Delighted and relieved, for the news from home of late has all been bad. This Strega fellow — a very bad sort. Cunning, though. Dashed cunning, striking like that when I was not there to organize the defense. I was grieved to hear of your father's death, dear boy. A great man. A great loss. But thank the gods you were not there. No doubt Strega would have murdered you too."

"So what is to be done?" asked Miss Torpenhow when Max had thanked the general for his condolences. "I presume you have some plan to retake the city? It would be insufferable to let this Strega win."

"Indeed, indeed," agreed General Kleinhammer. "It sets a very poor example. Goes against all the customs of Municipal Darwinism. But as for plans, as for actual *plans*, well, my dear lady, you must understand, the situation presents many difficulties. It would take a sizable force to dislodge Strega. Those mercenaries he's employed, the Boethius Brigade, are legendary fighters, legendary. They have seven Stalkers with 'em, and they've had plenty of time to fortify the stairways and elevator shafts. It would need an army to take our city back, and we have no army."

"Then do you mean to just sit here?" demanded Miss Torpenhow. "Just sit here and play with your toy soldiers, while Gabriel Strega makes himself ever more secure in our city?"

"What else can I do, my dear lady?" asked the general. He turned to Max, as if ladies could not possibly be expected to understand such matters. "Ninety percent of soldiering is about knowing when not to fight. Without an army to send against Strega, we can only wait, and listen, and hope the situation alters in our favor."

"Could we not hire an army?" asked Max. "If Strega's mercenaries are so effective, perhaps we need some of our own."

The general snorted. "That would be most dishonorable. An Angmering, leading a band of sell-swords? Besides, mercenaries would want gold up front, and plenty of it."

"But if I promised to pay them once Thorbury was free again it would make them fight even harder, wouldn't it?"

General Kleinhammer's mustache quivered with amusement. "You could try that, I suppose? There is an establishment on the bottom tier called the Soldier of Fortune. You will find a few mercenaries propping up its bar, no doubt. But they will want gold and, pardon me for saying so, you don't look as if you have much of it."

Max reddened. Talking with the general had made him feel for a moment as if he were back in Thorbury; he had forgotten that he was a refugee, and penniless.

Miss Torpenhow stood up sharply. "Gentlemen," she said in a loud voice. The buzz of conversation in the hotel lounge died away, and a hundred curious faces turned toward her. "Gentlemen," she said again, "the city of Thorbury needs your help. General Kleinhammer feels unable to fight the brigands who have captured it. But a large army, well led, could surely oust them. The reward will be glory, and a place in the history books, and the undying friendship of Thorbury and of its rightful heir, Max Angmering."

Max stood up to let himself be seen. He wished he had a splendid uniform like the ones all the other men in the lounge seemed to be wearing, or at least that his civilian clothes had not gotten quite so stained and tattered during his escape from Paris.

"Come," said Miss Torpenhow. "There must be one of you who would like to try some real fighting? Or did you only join your cities' armed forces so you could wear fancy hats, and organize parades, and award yourselves medals?"

The assorted colonels, marshals, generals, subahdars, and duces bellorum who made up her audience mumbled excuses through their grand mustaches, or took a sudden interest in the carpet, or polished their monocles. One by one, they turned away, and went back to their own conversations.

"Very well," said Miss Torpenhow. Her face had become very pink. She had made a fool of herself, but it was not just that which made her blush. She was extremely angry. "Very well. I see that I made a mistake in coming here. I doubt any of these doddering old men has ever been in a real battle at all. Tamzin Pook here is a better soldier than the lot of them put together. We shall try the other place you mentioned, General: the Soldier of Fortune, I believe you said it was called? Perhaps we shall find someone there with a little more fight in them."

The hotel manager appeared, looking like an apologetic pencil, and murmured that there had been complaints and that Miss Torpenhow and her friends should leave. But Miss Torpenhow was already leaving, with Tamzin close behind her. Max, with a last despairing glance at General Kleinhammer, hurried after them.

20

THE SOLDIER OF FORTUNE

A town like Bad Luftgarten did not have slums, but if it had, they would have been on its bottommost deckplate. That was where the *Hercules* had dropped its passengers off earlier, and Miss Torpenhow heartily wished they had stayed there rather than wasting their time on the fancy upper tiers. Her ankle was hurting badly by the time she'd gone back down all those stairs.

The tavern called the Soldier of Fortune crouched at the end of a street of budget hotels and airship chandleries. It was a low building, its roof an arc of wriggly tin with skylights let into it, which cast dim sunbeams into the smoky interior. The sign outside portrayed a group of mercenaries in gaudy uniforms and feathered leather hats, and the walls and pillars within were decorated with blunt boarding axes and obsolete guns. But as for actual mercenaries there were none: just a grumpy-looking barmaid mopping tables, and a lone old man nursing a tankard of beer in a dark corner.

He nodded when he saw Max, Tamzin, and Miss Torpenhow looking at him. "I reckon you're in the wrong place, mates."

Miss Torpenhow drew herself up stiffly and said that she was not his mate and she had understood this was where one hired fighting men. That surprised the man enough that he leaned forward to look more closely at her. The light from one of the windows fell on his craggy, grizzled ruin of a face, seamed with old scars, one eye hidden by a patch, his scruffy week-old beard the shade and texture of iron filings. He wore a uniform like those of the mercenaries on the sign outside, and maybe it had been as colorful once upon a time, but it had faded from scarlet to a nasty pinkish gray, and the few strands of gold braid that still clung to it were dark with grime. If this was what real mercenaries looked and smelled like, Tamzin thought, she was glad he was the only one around.

He looked Miss Torpenhow up and down and let out a grunt of laughter. "You're a funny sort of general, missus."

"Miss," she corrected him. "I am Miss Lavinia Torpenhow, and this young man is Maximilian Angmering, rightful mayor of Thorbury. We are recruiting soldiers to fight against the usurper who has seized our home city. But it seems there are no soldiers present . . ."

"All off in Hamburg," said the old man, waving a hand in the general direction of the Central Hunting Ground. "You must have heard? Mad Mayor Odo is raising a grand alliance of cities to go and nibble down the walls of Batmunkh Gompa. He's promised good pay and plenty of loot to any man who can tell one end of a gun from the other."

"Then why are you not with them?" asked Miss Torpenhow. "Too drunk, I suppose?"

"Too old, ma'am," said the mercenary, and looked for a moment rather tragic. "Too old, and seen too much, and I seem to recall the walls of Batmunkh Gompa being a mile high, and armored with the wrecks of cities that have tried to nibble 'em before." Rising clumsily to his feet, he said, "But I'll fight your war for you, Miss Lavinia Torpenhow. Oddington Doom at your service. There was a time when that name was known round half the world."

"Really?" said Miss Torpenhow. "I must have been in the other half. I thank you for your offer, Mr. Doom, but you really are not quite what we were looking for. Come, Max, Tamzin."

Tamzin hesitated for a moment, just to show that she was not a servant and did not have to follow like a dog whenever Miss Torpenhow snapped "come." But she saw no point in staying either, so she followed eventually, out into the sunlight and the shadows of Bad Luftgarten's looming gasbags.

"What now?" asked Max as they started up the stairs again.

"I do not know," Miss Torpenhow admitted. She paused, leaning against the handrail on the first landing. Her ankle was swollen and hurting badly, her plans were all in tatters, and almost all of the money she had stitched into her skirts before she left Thorbury was gone. She was an optimistic sort of person by nature, but she could not at that moment think of anything more she could do.

"We could try London," said Max doubtfully. "They are old rivals of Paris. They might help us just to spite the Parisians . . ."

Tamzin was not an optimistic person by nature. She had always assumed Miss Torpenhow's plans would end in failure. She did not believe London would care about saving Thorbury any more than Paris had. She did not think Max Angmering had the makings of a mayor. She liked Miss Torpenhow, but she told herself she had already done all that she could to help her. It was time to leave, before she grew more attached.

She left them talking and hurried on up the stairs. The next tier was mostly greenhouses. The one above that was not as shabby as the bottom one, nor as smart as the higher levels. In one of the cafés there, Tamzin thought, she might find an aviator prepared to let her work her passage to some new city. She would do what she should have done the moment she reached Paris — take off on her own.

There was an enormous bathhouse in the center of that tier, surrounded by a circuit of small gift shops and galleries, and plenty of cafés with stripy canvas awnings. The air was filled with the sound of rainwater collected in the high reservoirs the previous night, now gurgling down long networks of rubberized pipes to feed the baths. Tamzin started toward the nearest of the cafés, and then stopped. Her attention had been caught by something in the window of one of the shops.

The shop was a picture gallery. TRUBSHAWE FINE ARTS read the sign outside it, once you had puzzled out all the curlicues of the gilt lettering. The windows were full of pictures. There were views of Bad Luftgarten, pictures of pretty ladies not quite in the nude and several portraits of a handsome young man in a large hat. But what had caught Tamzin's eye — what drew her like a sleepwalker across the metal pavement in front of the gallery until her face was almost pressed against the glass — was a large painting in a gilded frame that sat in pride of place at the center of the window display.

It showed a grand, domed space in which rows and rows of onlookers gazed down upon a lamplit patch of sand. In the lamplight stood a Revenant Engine a little like one of Mortmain's,

118

except that its eyes glowed red instead of green. Before it stood a young woman with the shining red-gold hair and shining white armor of a warrior angel. She was turning her face up to the light with a look that was somehow both tragic and smug, and clasping one hand to the spear that had pierced her breast. Three delicate little drops of ruby blood were spilling from the wound. In the sand at her feet crouched a girl who, despite her cowering posture and grin of greedy triumph, was still a great deal prettier than Tamzin. But she was clearly meant to be Tamzin, for that was what the plaque on the bottom to the frame announced to anyone who cared to look.

The painting was called An Incident in the Amusement Arcade on Margate: Eve Vespertine Betrayed to Her Death by the Coward Tamzin Poke.

❋

After the old bird and the two youngsters left, Oddington Doom thought about ordering another beer, and decided against it. He had the feeling, which came to him quite often these days, that he had made a prize plonker of himself. He wished he could have helped Miss Torpenhow. Twenty years ago, he would have captured the old girl's city back just for the laughs and the joy of battle, and never mind if she could pay or not. But twenty years ago he had been young and fit and running with the baddest, bravest band of freebooters this beat-up world had ever seen. Now he was old, and his comrades were all dead, or scattered down the wild winds, and there was not much left for Oddington Doom.

More strangers arrived. He told himself to mind his manners if they were looking for mercs; it wasn't like he could afford to turn work away. But these two looked more like mercs themselves. Or maybe debt collectors. Or maybe something in between. There was a big one in a huge fur coat, and a small one in black. Doom's instincts told him that the small one was the more dangerous.

The newcomers ignored Doom and sauntered over to the bar, where the barmaid was cleaning glasses. The big one put a friendly smile on his face while the little one's eyes went all around the empty tables and found Doom. The big one said, "Perhaps you can help us, my dear? We are looking for a young woman, a girl, really. A short, dark-haired girl. Name of Tamzin Pook. She is traveling with an older lady. We believe they are aboard this charming town."

The barmaid glanced over at Doom. "Haven't seen them," she said.

She was no fool, Doom thought. She could sense there was something sketchy about these two. Trouble came off them like fog off a marsh.

"How about you, sir?" asked the little one, trying to be as friendly as his companion, but not so good at it. "You look like an observant man. Sitting at your window seat, watching the world go by. I wonder if you've seen the young lady?"

He came over to Doom's table and held out a square of card. It was a photograph of the girl Doom had just met. She was glowering at the camera in a way that made Doom think the photographer had told her to smile and she had done the opposite just to be awkward. He respected that.

He took a good long look at the picture and shook his head. "Never seen her."

"Oh dear. Well, it seems we have drawn a blank, Mr. Coldharbour," said the dangerous little man, putting the picture back inside his coat.

"Most vexing, Mr. Lint," his friend agreed. "Nevertheless, we shall continue our search. Perhaps the upper levels will prove a more fruitful hunting ground."

"Perhaps they will, Mr. Lint."

After they had gone, the barmaid came and refilled Doom's tankard for free. He nodded his thanks. Lying to the two strangers had made a sort of bond between them. In the old days, Doom might have tried to build on that and chat her up, but although she wasn't young she was still young enough to make him feel like the old wreck he was. He thanked her and started drinking the beer, but he kept thinking about the girl and the old woman, and the two men who had come looking for them. When the tankard was still only half-empty, he set it down, stood up, and went out.

21

THE THING WITH EVE VESPERTINE

Eve Vespertine had not arrived in the Arcade as a slave, the way most players did. She was a volunteer. On Margate's upper decks there were attractions where visitors could pit their wits and strength against nonlethal versions of Mortmain's machines. These were simple automatons mostly, but still powerful. There was reliable entertainment to be had watching hulking holidaymakers get knocked down by the boxing gloves of the mechanical kangaroo, or the rubber-tipped lance of the clockwork Zagwan paladin.

But Eve Vespertine, a girl from the lower levels of some scabby passing town, had KO'd the kangaroo, and, sidestepping the Zagwan's thrust, grabbed hold of his lance and pulled him clean off his war zebra. She had done these things not once, but many times, so the growing crowd that gathered to watch her had been able to see it was not just a fluke. Their applause warmed her. A girl with no prospects and no status aboard her hometown, Eve had found something she did well, and she pictured herself growing both rich and famous aboard Margate. She was invited to dine with Mortmain in his Bouncy Castle that very night. The contract she signed waived all claim to compensation if she was killed or maimed, but promised her a small fortune if she survived a season in the Arcade. For someone like Eve, it was a pretty good deal.

The newcomer started out in the Blue Team, which fought when Tamzin and the other star athletes were resting. Her fellow players were contemptuous at first. She won't last, they told each other. When Eve survived her first show, they said it was beginner's luck. When she made it through her second and her third, they claimed Mortmain was stacking the deck in her favor, telling his Revenants to go easy on her. But Tamzin Pook, watching as the new girl easily took out machine after machine, saw she had a natural talent for the Arcade. Like Tamzin, she seemed to sense what the Revenants were about to do before they did it. Unlike Tamzin, she had a good figure, a clear complexion, and a winning smile. Her self-confidence was boundless. The joy she took in her own skill and daring was infectious. She was lighthearted and likable; generous when it came to sharing the gifts her admirers sent her. By her fourth fight, even the other players were won over. It was difficult not to like Eve Vespertine.

But Tamzin managed it. Because she could not help noticing that, as the end of the season drew near, the posters outside the Arcade were starting to feature Eve's face as often as her own.

That summer, as the season reached its climax and Mortmain promised visitors his most spectacular and dangerous Revenant Engines yet, the teams were rearranged. Several fighters Tamzin had grown used to working with were reassigned to Blue Team, and Eve Vespertine was moved up to Red.

"Hey, kiddo," she said, breezing into her first training session with Tamzin. "I've been watching you fight. You ain't bad. Ain't bad at all. We'll be a hot team, you and me."

Too shy to respond, Tamzin felt herself growing smaller, as if she were shriveling under the radiance of Eve's smile. She had often imagined dying in the Arcade, but she had never thought she might be replaced while she was still alive. She turned away from Eve without replying, and that was how it got started: the rumor that they were rivals.

POOK & VESPERTINE VS. MORTMAIN'S DEADLIEST ENGINE YET! the posters on the boardwalks screamed in the run-up to Eve's first outing with the Red Team. When the players made their way to the stage door that day, there were more people crowding outside the wire fences of the paddock to get a glimpse of them than Tamzin had ever seen there.

"Eve!" they bellowed, waving betting slips and souvenir programs, desperate for her to look their way. No one shouted Tamzin's name. And when the team fanned out across the Arcade's sawdust floor a few minutes later, the chants of "Vespertine! Vespertine!" rolled around the packed seats and echoed from the domed roof like thunder.

Eve Vespertine acknowledged them with a grace and cheerfulness Tamzin could never have mustered, waving her electric tomahawk in the air and turning to bestow her heartbreaking smile on each section of the crowd in turn. The other players seemed pleased, feeling some of Eve's glamour attaching itself to them. Tamzin was too self-conscious to join them as they swaggered around the edges of the arena, waving and blowing kisses. She had never needed to do that stuff before to get the crowd to notice her. Her reputation as the best fighter the Arcade had ever seen had been enough. She would have to remind them of it, she thought, watching the door from which tonight's Revenant would emerge. She could not let Eve Vespertine win this fight. Whatever horror Mortmain had cooked up for the season finale, Tamzin must be the one to put it down.

The Revenant, when it appeared, seemed disappointing. A bulky, bulbous thing, like the offspring of a giant turtle and an Ancient ground-car, its eyes blazing dull green hatred from a tiny armored head. "The Fretful Porpentine," Mortmain called it. Slabs of his amplified commentary fell around the players as they scattered, taking up positions around the thing. Its hulking shell had three-foot-long spikes poking out in all directions, making it difficult to approach, and its tail ended in a heavy club, but it lacked the elegance and speed of other Revenants the team had faced that year. For a moment, Tamzin wondered if Mortmain was making things easy for his new star. But when she glanced up at him in his box, she saw he was watching the game develop with his usual expression of amused anticipation. There was more to this machine than there seemed. She motioned to the others to stay back while she scouted closer, trying to guess what vicious secrets it was hiding. What sort of brain was watching her through those green lenses? And those spikes — why so many and so long, to defend a body that was already thickly armored? What was a Porpentine anyway? A made-up animal? A real one? Some monster out of Ancient myth?

"It's just a hedgehog!" jeered Eve Vespertine, ignoring Tamzin's warning to stay back. The crowd laughed, tickled by the contrast between Tamzin's cautious crouch and Eve's swagger. She circled the Revenant, graceful as a model on a catwalk, swinging her hatchet on its flex like this year's must-have accessory. "We ain't afraid of a hedgehog, are we?"

Determined not to let her rival make the kill, Tamzin edged closer still, putting herself between Eve and the Revenant. When Eve moved left to try to get around her, Tamzin moved left. When Eve moved right, so did she. Meanwhile, she kept watching the creature, and the creature watched her in a calculating way, working up to something.

It isn't a hedgehog, Tamzin realized. *It's a porcupine.*

She could not recall if porcupines were real or not, but she had heard about them somewhere. And what was it they did to defend themselves, those porcupines? What did they do with those spiky quills of theirs when they grew fretful?

She dropped just in time. She could have shouted "Get down!" or "Duck!" but for some reason (and she would spend a long time afterward wondering what that reason was) she said nothing at all, just threw herself down in the sawdust so that when the porcupine's quills suddenly shot from its body like a volley of spears, they passed straight over her.

Most of the other players, used to taking Tamzin's lead, had dived when she did. Eve Vespertine was the only one left standing, looking down at Tamzin with a puzzled expression, which turned to stark surprise when a porcupine spike slammed through her chest. The crowd, which usually cheered such fatal blows excitedly, let out a horrified gasp. So did Eve Vespertine. Like them, she had thought she was indestructible.

The sound of her body crumpling to the deck amid that eerie silence was the loudest noise Tamzin had ever heard.

Then the Revenant came surging forward, swinging its sledge-hammer tail, a new crop of quills appearing in the sockets from which the first volley had sprung. Tamzin grew preoccupied with saving herself and then the rest of her team. It was all the survivors could do to keep the thing distracted until finally one of the chainsword handlers sliced its tail off and Tamzin buried her knife in its brainpan. There were a few shouts of "Pook!" then, but they were muted, because the onlookers were still mourning Eve Vespertine.

When Tamzin scrambled down from the wreckage of the Revenant and went to look for Eve, the Arcade staff had already dragged the body away, leaving a long, red smear across the trampled sawdust.

✸

Afterward, the rumors flew. How Tamzin Pook had been so jealous of her glamorous new teammate that she'd failed to warn her of the Revenant's quills, so jealous she'd coaxed her into going closer to it, so jealous she'd literally pushed Eve into the path of the missile. There were cartoons about the incident in the *Margate Mercury*. Newspapers in other cities took up the story. Rumors from Traktionstadt Murnau said the composer Odilon Rusk was making it the subject of his next opera. There was a popular song that claimed, quite untruthfully, that Eve and Tamzin had been sweet on the same boy and Tamzin had cunningly used the Porpentine to dispose of her love rival. In their quarters under the Arcade, Tamzin's fellow fighters joined the rest of the town in mourning Eve as a sort of martyr, betrayed on the brink of a glittering career.

Tamzin did not mind too much the suspicious stares they aimed at her, nor the things they muttered when her back was turned. They had never been her friends. Why should she care what they thought of her? But she was troubled by what she thought of herself. Because she knew she should have warned Eve Vespertine what was coming, and she had not. And, although she had not meant or ever consciously hoped for Eve to die, in that moment when it had happened she'd felt the same sense of triumph that came to her when she destroyed a Revenant.

And here, more than a year later, more than a hundred miles away, outside an art gallery window aboard Bad Luftgarten, she stood gazing at a picture of that dreadful night, and trembled with guilt and growing anger.

127

22

A Spot of Art

The bell above the door of Trubshawe Fine Arts clattered as Tamzin burst into the gallery. "That picture," she was shouting. "That picture in the window . . ."

"Ah yes," said the man who roused himself from behind the desk in the far corner. He was a plump young man with dark curly hair going thin on top. "*An Incident in the Amusement Arcade on Margate.* I think you will agree that . . ."

His voice trailed off as he saw Tamzin's furious expression. It did not look as if she would agree with him about anything. Nor, frankly, did she look like the sort of person who was likely to buy paintings.

"Er . . ." he said uncertainly. "Now, see here —"

"It's all wrong," said Tamzin, coming up to his desk and slamming the palms of both hands on it, hard enough to topple a pile of unpaid bills and tattered sketchbooks off its edge. "Have you ever seen the Arcade? It is not so big as that, nor so grand, and the Revenants don't look like that one either. And Eve Vespertine was not half so pretty as that, and my name is not 'Poke,' it is Pook, and I did not betray her, and anyone who calls me a coward is a damned liar."

The plump young man backed away from her in alarm until he was pressed against the wall between a painting of the Fall of Birmingham and an icon of the goddess Peripatetia. Now that the first flush of her own rage was receding, Tamzin recognized him. He was the same man whose face was in several of the paintings in the window, except he did not have his large hat on, and he was much less handsome in real life.

"You painted it!" she said accusingly. "You painted all these pictures!"

"Indeed I did," he said, and bowed. "Giotto Trubshawe, at your service. Can I interest in you a spot of art? A souvenir of your visit to Bad Luftgarten? All these works you see around you are the fruits of my genius, and I have rented this gallery for the season so I may share them with the public. The *buying* public," he added meaningfully. "And I can assure you that *An Incident in the Arcade* is based on the most reliable eyewitness accounts, told to me by people who were aboard Margate on that fateful night —"

"I was aboard Margate on that fateful night," shouted Tamzin. "I was there! You have painted me in your silly picture, and made me look nothing like myself, and all squinty and villainous."

"You mean to tell me *you* are Tamzin Poke — I mean Pook?" asked the artist.

"She is," agreed Miss Torpenhow, entering the gallery at that moment. Tamzin's heart sank. She had not expected Miss T to come looking for her. Now she would have to slip away all over again.

"Tamzin, I am so glad I have found you!" said Miss Torpenhow. "We lost you on the stairway somehow, and have been looking everywhere. Max has gone up to search the next level, but my ankle is paining me so I decided to wait on this one, and heard you shouting. You are quite correct about Mr. Trubshawe's painting. It is a poor likeness, Mr. Trubshawe, both of Tamzin and of the Arcade."

"Well, naturally a, a certain amount of artistic license was involved," Trubshawe spluttered. "My public do not want to see life as it is, but rather as it should be, refracted through the lens of my genius —"

"Lies, you mean," said Tamzin. "You are a liar, is what you are saying."

"Is it a lie to find beauty and grandeur in the story of your battle with the fretful Porpentine, Miss Poke? Pook!" asked Trubshawe.

"Frankly, yes," said Miss Torpenhow, coming forward to take Tamzin's hand. "But there is nothing we can do about it, Tamzin. No law prevents Mr. Trubshawe from making his foolish paintings, and there is nothing to be gained by haranguing him."

"Oh, but there may be!" said Trubshawe, recovering himself and stepping away from the wall. "I mean, not by haranguing me as such, but if you would allow me to make a portrait of you, Miss Pook — a portrait of the actual, genuine Tamzin Pook — why, it might go very well for both of us. I could certainly pay you a fee, a modest fee. Of course, I should have to make you look a little less . . . That is, I should have to make you look a little more . . ."

"We have not time, sir," said Miss Torpenhow. "We are on urgent business, and will be leaving Bad Luftgarten shortly."

"I won't be," Tamzin started to say, but she was drowned out by the clatter of the bell as the door swung open again.

"Well, well, well," said Mr. Coldharbour, stepping into the gallery. "What have we here?"

23

AN EARLY BATH

"What do you spy with your little eye, Mr. Lint?" said Mr. Coldharbour over his shoulder, while keeping his eyes fixed firmly on Tamzin.

Mr. Lint, slipping into the gallery behind him like a shadow, licked his thin lips and said, "I spy a runaway, Mr. Coldharbour. I spy a naughty and ungrateful young person. I spy a young person who needs to be *punished* for all the trouble and worry she has caused poor Dr. Mortmain."

"Mortmain?" said Trubshawe. He had brightened when the two men entered, but now his shoulders sagged again as he realized they were not likely to be buying any paintings either. "Isn't he . . . ?"

"He is Margate's Master of Amusements," said Miss Torpenhow, placing herself between Tamzin and the newcomers. "These gentlemen are his hirelings, no doubt. I regret to inform you, gentlemen, that Tamzin is under my protection now. She will not be returning to your nasty little town."

"Oh dear, Mr. Coldharbour!" said Mr. Lint. "The Pook girl is under this lady's protection. So I suppose that is that. We are foiled. We must return to Dr. Mortmain empty-handed."

"He will be upset, Mr. Lint," said Mr. Coldharbour. "He will be most upset."

"On the other hand, Mr. Coldharbour," mused Mr. Lint, "it might be that this lady's protection is not worth much."

"Do you think so, Mr. Lint?"

"I believe I do, Mr. Coldharbour."

"Do you know, Mr. Lint, I believe I agree with you . . ."

They came farther into the gallery as they spoke, and moved farther apart, and their eyes darted from Miss Torpenhow to Tamzin and back again.

"Tamzin," said Miss Torpenhow, quite calmly. "Run."

"She has run quite far enough, you foul old harpy," snapped Mr. Coldharbour. He lashed out with one big fist, knocking Miss Torpenhow to the floor. Tamzin went backward to avoid Mr. Lint as he made a grab for her. She collided with Trubshawe's desk, somersaulted over it, and made for the open door, but Coldharbour was there ahead of her, blocking her way with his burly body. She turned back and there was Mr. Lint again. A knife as thin and sharp as a surgeon's scalpel had appeared in his hand. His eyes gleamed with a cold light. She dodged around him as if he were one of Mortmain's Revenants. Trubshawe was helping Miss Torpenhow off the floor, dragging her into a corner. Tamzin snatched a bronze statuette of the Goddess of Art from a plinth and turned, swinging it, as Mr. Lint lunged at her with his bright little blade. He hissed and drew back. She vaulted the desk again and kicked open a door she had noticed in the wall behind it. It let her into a narrow staircase, stairs steep as a ladder. She scrambled up them and through another door into a room full of half-finished paintings and the smell of turpentine. She could hear Mr. Coldharbour climbing the stairs behind her, the whisper as his fur coat brushed the walls on either side. She slammed the door, found to her joy that there was a key in the lock and turned it.

She hoped Miss Torpenhow was all right.

The door handle rattled. Mr. Coldharbour's voice said, "Open it, girlie. There's no way out. We're not going back to Margate without you."

Tamzin did not answer. She looked around the cluttered studio. Mr. Coldharbour was wrong. There was a way out. The far wall was all big windows, and beyond the grubby glass she could see a low dome — the roof of the bathhouse, she presumed. She went quietly between the easels, past a big packing crate half covered by a moth-eaten velvet curtain. Trubshawe's models probably sat on that. Someone had probably posed there as her. There were swords and axes propped against the wall behind it, but they were only made of painted cardboard. On a messy table she found a knife that Trubshawe must use for sharpening his pencils, so she helped herself to that. Behind her, Mr. Coldharbour's big body hit the locked door like a battering ram.

Tamzin unlatched one of the windows and climbed out, shutting it behind her. Doves took off, rising into the sunlight all around her like low-budget angels. A band was playing somewhere. Tamzin scrabbled across the shallow slope of the roof, hoping to get the bathhouse dome between her and Mr. Coldharbour by the time he reached the window. If she could break into one of the buildings on the far side, she could find her way back down to street level and vanish into the crowds . . .

Behind her, Coldharbour punched the window out. She looked back. He had a big gun in his hand and he was using it to clear the last shards of glass from the window frame.

"Come back here, girlie," he said affably.

133

Tamzin was going crabwise across the dome on her hands and knees. The dome was not slate or metal, just lacquered paper over a wooden frame. A flying town had to watch its weight. Confident that Mr. Coldharbour could not follow her out onto this flimsy surface, she stopped and looked back at him again.

"You won't shoot me," she said. "Mortmain wants me back. He wants me alive."

Mr. Coldharbour's big red face stretched into a kindly grin. "Oh, Mortmain wants you back," he said, "but if he can't get you alive, he will have you dead. All we really need bring him is your head and your spine; that's what he told me and Mr. Lint. Isn't that right, Mr. Lint?"

Mr. Lint appeared in the window beside him. "That's right, Mr. Coldharbour. Dr. Mortmain has grown weary of using animal brains in his creations. He plans to use a human one next. He'll pop your tiny little brain into one of his engines, Miss Pook, and then you shall work for him for ever and ever, and spend your days slicing and dicing all your former teammates. What fun you'll have! What japes!"

"So what'll it be?" asked Mr. Coldharbour. "Will you come back over here like a good girl? Or shall I put a slug in you?"

Tamzin crouched there, starting to understand the full horror of what he had said, starting to wonder if it would not be better to go back to the Arcade alive rather than let Mortmain make her into one of his Revenants. Mr. Coldharbour watched her for a few seconds, then shrugged, cocked his pistol, and aimed it at her. But, before he could fire, the roof gave way under her.

In the bathhouse below, twenty or thirty fat old men bobbed in the rainwater pool beneath the dome like dumplings in a watery stew. "Great gods!" and "'Pon my word!" they cried as Tamzin and a largish portion of the roof splashed down among them. She surfaced, spluttering, and made for the side.

"Outrageous!" the bathers blustered. "Attendant! Get this young woman out of here! And bring us towels!"

"She has a knife!" someone bellowed.

"A terrorist! An Anti-Tractionist!"

It was like a stampede in a piggery, thought Tamzin, running for the door while plump pink and brown bodies went wobbling out of her way. She knew Coldharbour and Lint would not give up. They knew where she had gone. They would be on their way down to hunt her. They would be pushing their way into the bathhouse by now, and who would stop them?

She barged through a door and found herself in a steam room. A hot pool smoldered like a witch's cauldron. More old men, their bellies like barrels, sat along the poolside, heads turbanned in hot towels. Most were fast asleep. The few who noticed Tamzin only stared. She felt the sweat squeezing out of her pores as she went quickly around the edge of the pool, her boots slithering on wet tiles. There were signs on the wall that read NO RUNNING and SLIPPING HAZARD, but she ignored them. She had worse hazards to worry about than slippery tiles.

A bullet smacked into the wall beside her. Bathers sprang up in confusion and Mr. Coldharbour's voice, somewhere in the steam clouds, said cheerfully, "Do you think I hit her, Mr. Lint?"

Tamzin found a door and fell through it into a dark room where soft, chiming music played and bottles of lotion and shampoos gleamed like dim lamps on shelves around the walls.

"Would you like to try an exfoliating scrub?" asked a young woman in white, standing beside a tub of what looked like pea soup. Then she let out a shriek, catching sight of Tamzin's knife. She fled to a door at the far end of the room and shoved it open. Tamzin ran after her. The open doorway was a rectangle of bright, hopeful sunlight in the dark; she knew if she could get through it there would be dozens of places outside to hide in. But just as she reached it the woman running ahead slammed it in her face and Tamzin heard a bolt slide into place.

Sobbing with frustration, she shoved at the door anyway, but it did not budge. Behind her, the door she had come in by opened again. Mr. Coldharbour stood there, haloed by the light from the steam room behind him. He raised the gun, waiting for his eyes to adjust to the gloom. But Mr. Lint pushed past him and said, "Perhaps I should handle this, Mr. Coldharbour. A blade is so much neater than a bullet. We would not want to damage Dr. Mortmain's property too much, would we?"

"Oh, we certainly would not, Mr. Lint," agreed his friend. "But do be careful. The naughty girl has a little knife of her own."

"She will not use that, Mr. Coldharbour," said Mr. Lint, coming into the dark room. His own blade glinted as he walked cautiously toward Tamzin, who stood waiting with her back to the locked door. "Miss Pook is very skilled at killing Revenants, but she is far too soft to hurt a fellow human being."

"You sure about that?" said Tamzin through tears and gritted teeth, and flailed at him with her pencil-sharpening knife so that he went dancing backward.

"Oho, this is a fierce one, Mr. Coldharbour! This one has spirit! This one is a wildcat in a tight corner! But when the moment comes, she will not have the nerve. My pretty little blade will open her throat and let her life out as easy as turning a key in a lock."

"I look forward very much to seeing it, Mr. Lint," said Mr. Coldharbour, folding his arms and looking on approvingly. "I have always admired your artistry with a knife."

"You are too kind, Mr. Coldharbour," said Mr. Lint, but he spoke in an undertone, as if he were no longer really aware of what he was saying. His attention was all fixed on Tamzin, his bright little eyes watching her very keenly. She felt that he understood people as well as she understood Revenants, and that he had already anticipated every possible move she might make to try to escape him.

"Leave her alone!" said a loud voice.

Mr. Lint blinked and glanced behind him. Mr. Coldharbour looked around too. The clouds of steam in the open doorway swirled and parted to reveal a shabby figure. Mr. Coldharbour laughed. "Why, it is our friend from the tavern — the drunk in the window seat."

"I'm not so drunk that I can't sort you two out," said Oddington Doom, blinking as he came shambling into the dark room.

"He has a gun, Mr. Doom!" warned Tamzin.

"I suggest you shoot the old fool, Mr. Coldharbour," said Mr. Lint, keeping his eyes on Tamzin.

"I think that is an admirable suggestion, Mr. Lint," said Mr. Coldharbour, and pointed his gun at Oddington Doom. But before he could pull the trigger Doom sprang at him and grabbed hold of him by the wrist of his gun hand. The gun fired, but only into the wall, and then twice into the ceiling, as Doom drove three crunching punches into Mr. Coldharbour's face. Coldharbour staggered backward. Doom wrenched the gun from him and fired at Mr. Lint, who squealed with fright and scrambled away. The flash from the gun lit up the black, scuttling shape of him once, twice, three times, then it clicked empty.

"I hate guns," grumbled Oddington Doom, stuffing it into his belt. "It's this blind eye of mine. It messes up my depth perception . . ."

"Mr. Doom!" shouted Tamzin, for she had seen Mr.

Coldharbour rising from the floor where Doom had left him, lumbering at him from behind.

But Doom had heard him coming. He snatched the heavy dish of pea-soup stuff from its plinth and slammed it into Coldharbour's bloody face so hard it shattered. Green goop sprayed everywhere. Coldharbour toppled like a felled tree. "Consider yourself exfoliated," growled Doom.

"Mr. Coldharbour!" shouted Mr. Lint, alarmed, then disbelieving. "Mr. Coldharbour?"

Doom dropped to his knees, rifling through Coldharbour's pockets. He came up with a handful of bullets, but before he could fit them into the gun Lint was on him, hissing, slashing at him with the dreadful little knife. Doom scrambled backward, snatched a fluffy white towel from a rack behind him, and wrapped it around his forearm as a shield. Lint's knife tore white flakes from it. Doom groped on the shelves beside the towel rack and grabbed a loofah, which he flourished like a sword, driving Mr. Lint backward until Lint realized that — well, it was a loofah. Tamzin found a shelf with bottles of lotion on and started throwing them at Lint.

"Leave him to me, girl!" grunted Doom. "Run."

Tamzin made her way around them to the open door of the steam room. She did not want to leave Doom to face Mr. Lint alone, but nor did she have the courage to attack Lint with her blunt little knife. And as she stood hesitating in the doorway Lint made a lunge that caused Doom to dodge backward and collide with the towel rack. The rack fell, Doom went down under it, and Lint turned and saw Tamzin standing there.

Tamzin went backward away from him, through the doorway, and out into the steam room, her feet sliding on the wet tiles beside the pool. Lint came after her. His pallid face wore a strange, wide smile. She held her knife out in front of her to ward him off, but that only made him smile still more. He was so close that she could smell coffee on his breath, mingled with the prettier smells of the lotions she had flung at him. He was humming a little nursery song. Then, as Tamzin stepped away again, and he stepped after her, he must have slipped on the tiles. He seemed to lunge at her. His knife snagged in the shoulder of her tunic; his free hand grabbed her arm. She shrieked. His weight drove her backward a few more paces before she was able to shove him away. His eyes, pale blue and slightly bulging, looked wonderingly into hers, and then down at his own chest.

Tamzin looked down too, and saw the handle of her little knife sticking out of Mr. Lint's shirtfront, and a red stain spreading around it like spilled wine. The look on his face reminded Tamzin of Eve Vespertine in the Arcade: that same dreadful astonishment. She found herself saying, "I'm sorry . . ."

"Mr. Coldharbour?" said Mr. Lint in a gasping way. "It appears I was mistaken about the girl . . ." His knife dropped from his hand and tinkled on the tiles, and he fell backward into the steaming pool and floated there, with the water turning pink around him.

A terrible groan drew Tamzin's attention back to Oddington Doom. She ran into the dark room and found him struggling out from beneath the wreckage of a towel rack.

"Are you stabbed?" she asked him, lifting the rack out of the way to help. "Are you shot?"

"No, no," Doom grunted, flinging towels aside. "Nothing like that. It's just my back is killing me. I'm not as young as I was."

He stood up. Tamzin stepped back, and a hand grabbed her from behind, for Mr. Coldharbour had risen too. Dripping blood and exfoliating scrub, spitting out broken teeth, growling with animal rage, he flung Tamzin at the wall and himself at Oddington Doom. But at some point while Tamzin was busy with Mr. Lint, Doom must have found time to reload the pistol he had confiscated, and Mr. Coldharbour was close enough that his lack of depth perception was not an issue. He put two shots into Mr. Coldharbour's wide chest, then stood over him and shot him once more to make certain.

"Always the trouble with these big blokes," he said conversationally, as the echo of the last shot faded. "They won't stay down. But it was the little one we had to worry about. Something nasty looking out through his eyes; I noticed it soon as I saw him. That's why I came after you, mostly. You dealt with him?"

"He is dead," said Tamzin. "I killed him," she added. She was almost as shocked by it as Mr. Lint had been.

People were approaching through the steam. One of them was shouting Tamzin's name. Miss Torpenhow appeared, with the artist Trubshawe behind her, and numerous nervous-looking men in the sky-blue uniforms of Bad Luftgarten's police force.

"All's well," Doom said, putting his gun down, raising his hands. "Slave-catchers tried to snatch this young lady, but they chose the wrong quarry. She's as tough as they come."

But Tamzin did not feel the least bit tough. Mr. Lint had said she hadn't the strength of character to kill anyone, and perhaps he had been right. Perhaps that was why, now that her enemies were dead, she was shaking so. And why, when Miss Torpenhow fussed the policemen away and came to her, Tamzin collapsed into her arms, and buried her face in Miss Torpenhow's blouse, and cried, and cried, and cried.

24

THE AIR B&B

The Bad Luftgarten authorities were terribly apologetic. The burgermeister and the chief of police could not stop apologizing for the oversight that had allowed slave-catchers to operate aboard their town, and bring a gun through customs, contrary to both their civic values and their safety regulations. They apologized so much that Tamzin began to wonder if they had been in on the whole thing. Their apologies wearied her as much as their questions had.

She felt drained by what had happened, and ashamed that she had broken down and wept in front of Miss Torpenhow. What was happening to her? She had never cried after a show in the Arcade, not even after the thing with Eve Vespertine. Crying in front of the other players would have felt like an unthinkable display of weakness. They would have lost all respect for her. But Miss Torpenhow did not seem to think any less of her. She had held Tamzin tight and said, "There, there" and "You poor, brave child," which had made her cry even more.

At last the chief of police said they were free to go. The burgermeister, in a gesture of goodwill, announced that he had arranged luxury accommodation for Miss Torpenhow and her party. It was the least he could do, he said, after all they had endured. On the outer edge of Bad Luftgarten's cloud of gasbags was a cluster of individual floating chalets called "Air B&Bs." One of these would be home to Miss Torpenhow and her friends until they had recovered from their terrible ordeal.

On the landing stage outside the police station, Max Angmering was waiting for them. He felt slightly ashamed that he had not been there to help Tamzin, but also secretly relieved, for he was not at all sure he would have had the courage to tackle Mortmain's hunters. Still, he said how sorry he was to have missed the fun, and how he would have liked to have dealt with Mr. Coldharbour and Mr. Lint himself.

"That is quite all right, Max," said Miss Torpenhow, fingering the bruise on the side of her jaw where Coldharbour had hit her. "Tamzin and Mr. Doom were perfectly able to cope."

Oddington Doom, who had emerged from the police station with her, seemed strangely shy now that there was no more fighting to be done.

"Mr. Doom," she said, "I hope you will join us aboard this chalet? The least we can do is offer you an evening meal, and a bed for the night if you wish it."

"I won't say no, miss," Doom replied. "I'm bunking in a cheap boardinghouse by the sewage farm, and the bed's rock hard, which won't help my back any. I'm getting too old for this lark."

"Nonsense, Mr. Doom, you are no older than I am," said Miss Torpenhow. "You have strained yourself, that's all. I know some very effective exercises that will soon put you to rights; I shall demonstrate as soon as we reach our chalet."

It was already growing dark as the air taxi weaved its way through the labyrinth of envelopes and supporting hawsers to the town's outer edge, where the Air B&Bs hung. Each was a charming little wooden house, set on its own deckplate, and supported by its own gasbag, attached by heavy cables to the rest of Bad Luftgarten. The chalets' names were painted on their gasbags — FALLING WATER, SURPRISE VIEW. The one that had been reserved for Miss Torpenhow and her companions was called THE OVER-LOOK. It was the largest, and had a garden with a small private swimming pool on the deck outside. As they stepped out of the taxi, Tamzin thought how good it would be to strip off, dive into that pool, and let the rainwater wash away all the fears and weariness of the long day. But she had no swimsuit, not even a change of underwear, and she could not go in naked, otherwise the people in the neighboring chalet really would get a Surprise View, so she went indoors and made do with a brief soak in the bathtub instead.

By the time she emerged, Miss Torpenhow was busy cooking a simple dinner from the well-stocked larder, and Oddington Doom was lying on the living-room floor, doing complicated stretching exercises. Max had poured wine into five tall glasses, and he handed one to Tamzin without bothering to ask if she wanted any. She had never drunk wine before; it tasted so sour it made her wince.

"Why five glasses?" she asked. "There are only four of us."

"The fifth is mine," said Giotto Trubshawe, entering through open French windows from the garden. "Miss Torpenhow asked me to join you — I believe you were bathing when I arrived."

Tamzin returned his bow uncertainly.

"Mr. Trubshawe was most helpful when those thugs attacked us in his gallery," explained Miss Torpenhow. "It was he who helped me out of harm's way, and he who ran to fetch the police. And they did a great deal of damage to his property, so the least we can do is offer him our hospitality . . ."

"His picture is still stupid," said Tamzin warily.

Trubshawe just bowed again, sweeping off his wide hat. "Then pose for me, Miss Pook!" he said.

Ever since his talent for drawing became clear, when he was just a little boy aboard Trieste, Trubshawe had felt that he was destined to be famous. But although people admired his paintings they very seldom bought one; despite the airs he gave himself, he could barely pay the rent on his little studio and gallery. He had convinced himself that a painting of Tamzin Pook would turn his fortunes around, and he was not about to let her go. "Pose for me, and I shall paint an even better picture, and show you in a more heroic light."

"I don't want it to be heroic," said Tamzin. "I just want it to be not stupid."

"How is the back, Mr. Doom?" asked Miss Torpenhow.

"Worse than ever," groaned Doom, stretched out in a curious position on the hearthrug. But Tamzin noticed that he sprang up easily enough when Max called out from the kitchen that dinner was ready.

❈

They ate thin slices of lamb, pan-fried in rosemary and chili oil, with sautéed potatoes and asparagus. They drank more wine. The gardens faded into darkness, then reappeared as a moonlit ghost of themselves.

Trubshawe was an entertaining companion, and so good at

putting his fellow diners at ease that when he said, "So what is your story, Mr. Doom?", Doom actually told it.

"I was born on the far side of the world," Doom said. "Farther away and longer ago than I care to think of now. Aboard a little town called Boomerang that spent its days creeping around the dusty interior of Oztralia."

"The Great Southern Hunting Ground!" said Miss Torpenhow, most impressed. "I have never spoken with a native of the place before. I thought you had a peculiar accent, Mr. Doom."

"Oh, it is mostly rubbed off me now," said Doom. "I left as soon as I was able, for Oztralia is an awful place. There are snakes there whose bite will kill you dead in half a minute, and spiders the size of hands in hairy gloves. Crocodiles lurk in the shallow creeks, waiting to drag folk in and eat 'em, and bunyip suburbs skulk in the deeper ones, waiting to do the same to passing towns. There are predator platforms in the outback that can shoot their jaws hundreds of feet in the air to snatch down passing airships. I've seen it happen. There are flying towns called Drop Boroughs that fall out of the sky on top of passing villages and strip 'em bare. I've seen that too.

"Even when I was a nipper, it seemed to me there couldn't be any place much worse, so I jumped aboard a passing raft town as soon as I was old enough and went to seek my fortune elsewhere. There wasn't much I was good at, but I've never been afraid of a fight, and there's always fighting to be done somewhere in this world, so that was how I earned my living. It was a good one too, back in those days. I ended up running a band of my own. Doom's Stormcrows, we called ourselves, and wherever there was trouble you'd find us in the thick of it. We fought off a whole flock of sky pirates once that was attacking Puerto Angeles. And we held out for weeks against a pack of pirate towns looking to eat Los Muros Viellos . . ."

"But Los Muros Viellos is a static city!" said Max, shocked. "You mean you fought on the side of Anti-Tractionists?"

"We fought on the side of anyone who'd hire us, mate," said Doom. He smiled, recalling old campaigns as fondly as other old men thought of long-ago love affairs. "But war is a dangerous trade, and one by one my Stormcrows all went down."

"Are they all dead?" asked Trubshawe, who was sketching a deft little likeness of Doom in his notebook while he listened.

"Dead, or gone off to start up on their own, or retired for a quieter life," said Doom. "The fighting business ain't what it was. And I'm not the man I was. Even that little scuffle in the baths today has left me aching all over. If I had the sense, I'd have got out long ago. But there's no other trade I've ever been much cop at, so here I am."

A silence fell. Doom had grown sad, and the others all felt his sadness too. But Miss Torpenhow topped up his glass and said, "Well, we're glad to have you, Mr. Doom. If you'll help us gather some fighting men and come with us back to Thorbury, I think we can promise you a battle as fierce as any you fought back in the old days."

Doom raised the glass she'd filled. "Thorbury," he said thoughtfully. "Young Max was telling me earlier about your city, and what's happened there. The Boethius Brigade, eh? They're a tough crew. And if they have the Scrap Metal Seven with them . . ." He shook his head. "No wonder those chocolate soldiers at the Pegasus didn't fancy taking on that fight. They might mess up their pretty uniforms."

"But what about you?" asked Max. "Would you take it on?"

146

Doom sipped his wine in silence for a while, then slowly nodded. "Reckon I might," he said. "Maybe it'll be my last. It would be no bad thing if it was. To go out in a blaze of glory, like. That's how old soldiers dream of dying. And it would let you off paying me when you've got your city back, wouldn't it? But let's hope for the best: a fair fight and a fair fee."

"A fair fight and a fair fee," said the others, raising their glasses, but Tamzin only pretended to drink — she did not like the taste of wine, and even the little she had already drunk was making her feel muddy-headed. She had a suspicion that Trubshawe had finished his drawing of Oddington Doom and started one of her, so she sat stiffly, slightly afraid to move, listening to the talk and laughter of the others.

"How bright the moon is," said Miss Torpenhow.

"You would think it would have gone behind the gasbags of the town by now," Max agreed. He stood up, glass in hand, and went out into the garden. The others talked on for a moment, until they were interrupted by Max bursting back in, shouting, "It's gone! It's gone!"

They all looked up at him. "What's gone?" asked Tamzin.

"The town! Bad Luftgarten! It's vanished!"

A couple of chairs fell over as everyone jumped up and followed him out into the moonlight and the cool night air. It was very quiet out there. What had happened to the purr of Bad Luftgarten's big engines? What had happened to the song of the night wind through the rigging? What had happened to Bad Luftgarten itself? For the sky was empty. A wreath of high cloud framed the waning moon. The ocean stretched out below to all horizons.

Then, as the chalet turned with the wind, Bad Luftgarten came into view again. It was already several miles away.

25

FIRE IN THE SKY

We are adrift!" said Trubshawe. "The cables that tether us to Bad Luftgarten must have broken!"

"Cables that thick don't just break," said Oddington Doom darkly, but only Tamzin heard him.

Max ran to the edge of the little garden and stood at the handrail, waving his arms toward the lights of the flying town and shouting. Miss Torpenhow joined him and they both shouted together for a while, but Tamzin could see it was useless. The same wind that was carrying their chalet so quickly away from Bad Luftgarten would carry their voices away from it as well. She went back inside the chalet and ran from room to room, turning on all the lamps, hoping some lookout on the flying town would see their light.

By the time that was done, the others had come back inside.

"This is an outrage!" Miss Torpenhow was saying. "The burgermeister assured me this was a first-class chalet, but truly first-class accommodation does not slip its moorings in the night! I'm astonished they have not launched rescue ships!"

"Perhaps they haven't seen us yet," said Max.

"Perhaps someone does not want us rescued," said Tamzin.

"She's right," said Doom. "Someone cut us loose deliberately."

"Who?" cried Trubshawe. "Was it Mortmain's men? Perhaps there were more of them aboard?"

"They want to capture Tamzin, not lose her in the sky," said Miss Torpenhow. "My guess is this is Gabriel Strega's work. He must have agents aboard Bad Luftgarten. Perhaps Kleinhammer himself is in the enemy's pay, and that was why he was so conveniently away on his holidays when they seized the city. We are betrayed at every turn! It is too bad!"

"The first thing we must do is bring this chalet under control," said Doom.

"I must get back to Bad Luftgarten," said Trubshawe, as though he were thinking of flapping his arms and flying there. "My studio! My gallery! All my work!"

"The chalet must have an engine of some sort," suggested Tamzin. "For emergencies."

They ran through the rooms, opening all the cupboards, and at last, forcing open a narrow, padlocked door next to the linen closet, Oddington Doom found a control panel. But no engines, alas — just a lot of copper pipes and a set of wheels and switches that controlled the chalet's heating and electrics.

"What's that?" asked Max, pointing over Doom's shoulder while he stood glaring at the useless controls.

A contraption of colored wires and brown-paper-wrapped cylinders had been bolted to the pipes. The hands of the quietly ticking clock attached to it stood at a minute to midnight.

"That is a bomb," said Tamzin, and she was surprised by how calmly she said it, and how calm she felt as she ran with the others away from the cupboard, through the house, and out into the cool night air beside the swimming pool.

The explosion when it came was only a soft popping sound, as if someone inside the chalet had just eased the cork from a particularly fizzy bottle of champagne. For a moment afterward, they were still able to tell themselves that all would be well. Then the interior of the chalet began to glow, and with surprising speed the flames rose up through the flat roof and started to tickle the underside of the big envelope overhead.

"Those villains!" shouted Miss Torpenhow, over the roar and crackle of the blaze. "They let us drift far enough away that we can't set Bad Luftgarten on fire and then, *boom!*"

The base of the envelope had caught, and it was starting to glow from within like a huge paper lantern as the flames spread up between the gasbags inside it. Sparks and burning flakes of envelope fabric danced excitably on the updraft as if they were delighted to be on fire. One of the gasbags caught, a rush of bluish flame mingling with the orange of the blazing envelope. As the gas burned off, the chalet started to tilt steeply. Charred cables snapped and lashed dangerously across the garden. A procession of high-end patio furniture and potted shrubs slid down the sudden slope of the deck and collected against the handrail until it gave way under their weight. The slope steepened. The swimming pool emptied itself in a waterfall over the deck's edge. Tamzin and the others clung to whatever handholds they could find while whole chunks of the burning chalet tumbled past them and down into the ocean.

The debris did not have far to fall. With its gasbags emptying, the chalet was sinking rapidly toward the sea, which was close below now, speckled with the white splashes of falling debris. The descent was quite graceful at first, but then it became faster and faster, and with a rush they were in the water, and then under it.

Tamzin surfaced, gasping. She had been taught to swim three summers back for the Arcade's Aqua-Spectacular (a Revenant kraken, the fighters hobbled by sequined mermaid tails). She was glad of it now. She trod water on the cold swell, turning herself in circles as she looked for her friends.

They popped up one by one. Their shocked faces were lit by the glow of burning fragments that bobbed upon the waves. The chalet had sunk. The fiery remnant of the envelope lay down upon the sea and died. Slowly the burning fragments guttered and went out too, and darkness fell.

"Is everyone all right?" asked Miss Torpenhow. Then, recognizing that "all right" was not quite the correct term, she asked, "Is everyone present? Tamzin? Max? Mr. Trubshawe? Mr. Doom?"

"Yes," they each said, and Oddington Doom said, "Yes, ma'am," like a schoolboy hearing the roll called.

"Now what?" asked Trubshawe.

"There!" said Tamzin. "Look, a boat . . ."

A low, wedge-shaped profile showed against the night sky, riding the swell nearby. They swam toward it, and reached up with wet hands to clutch its slippery sides. Max heaved himself clumsily up and over its edge, and reached back to help Tamzin after him. Then, together, they dragged the others aboard.

It was not a boat. It was the swimming pool from their chalet. It had been molded from a single sheet of plastic, and apparently only gravity and the weight of the water inside it had held it in its hole in the chalet's deckplate. Empty now, it floated face up on the waves. There was some seawater sloshing in the deep end, and the diving board was charred, but otherwise it seemed shipshape.

The castaways collapsed in the shallow end, and lay there through the night, sleeping sometimes, waiting for rescuers to find them. "Even if the burgermeister is in league with Strega," Max reasoned, "everyone on Bad Luftgarten must have seen the fire. They'll send airships out to look for survivors."

"We were not far from the southern coast of Italy when we were set adrift," said Miss Torpenhow, consulting the schoolroom atlas in her head. "If the winds and currents are favorable, we may wash ashore on some beach."

But no airships came, and the winds and currents were not favorable. When the sun came up and Tamzin woke from bad dreams with a taste of burning in her mouth, she peered over the pool's side to see an empty ocean, and an empty sky.

26

THE SWIMMING POOL

How long do you think it will be before we find another town?" asked Trubshawe.

The five bedraggled castaways were sitting at the shallow end of the drifting pool, bedazzled by the low, new-risen sun. Their damp clothes were beginning to steam as the air warmed.

"There are towns out here, aren't there?"

"Oh yes!" said Miss Torpenhow. "The Middle Sea is the cruising ground of many raft cities. Brighton, Alexandria, Cannes . . . Banvard's Gazetteer of Traction Towns lists more than a hundred, I believe. I'm sure we'll run into one of them sooner or later."

But Max guessed she was only saying that to keep everybody's spirits up. The Middle Sea had always seemed like quite a small sea when he only knew it from maps. Now that he was adrift on it, it felt huge. Even a great raft city would be just a tiny speck upon its blue immensity. A floating swimming pool could vanish here completely.

"What will we eat?" asked Trubshawe. "What will we drink?"

No one had an answer.

"Let us hope we are rescued before that becomes a problem," said Miss Torpenhow.

They made crude awnings from coats and shirts to give some shelter from the midday sun. In the afternoon, Doom spotted the smoke of a passing raft town in the distance, but the town itself was out of sight below the horizon, and must have been heading away from them, for the smoke soon vanished. Toward evening, a swell came up, and the waves started to slop through a vent on the wall of the pool's deep end. The castaways took turns at bailing, scooping the water out with their cupped hands and Trubshawe's hat.

So the long day wore away, and the sun went down into an empty sea, and no rescue came.

❇

Next morning, they woke to find that a little condensation had formed on the plastic of the walls and floor. It helped to take the edge off their thirst.

Tamzin sat on the metal ladder at the pool's edge and watched the horizon until her eyes ached. The heat and light were appalling, and there was no escaping them; the sun beat down at her out of the sky, and up at her from the blue plastic of the pool and the bright, reflecting waves. On Margate, residents and visitors alike had always grumbled about the rain and fog that hung so often over the shores of the Anglish Sea, but Tamzin would have welcomed a good thick sea mist now. She could not quite believe this latest evil turn her luck had taken. To have been killed by Mortmain's slave-catchers would have been one thing: a fitting end for an Arcade fighter. But to die in an empty swimming pool, killed by heat and thirst and hunger, which she could not hope to fight, just seemed absurd. The merciless sun would roast her body black, she thought, and all the others too. They would lie here like five overcooked sausages and no one would ever know who they had been.

Oddington Doom was not ready to give up, though. "I've been in worse scrapes than this," he kept saying, although he did not go into detail about what they had been. The dew would be enough to drink, he promised. As for food, they would just have to catch some. He pulled the laces from his boots and knotted them to make a line, and made the others do the same. They pried the glass off Trubshawe's drowned pocket watch and detached the hands to fashion little fishhooks. Soon they were ready to go fishing.

Doom sat on one edge of the pool and Max took the other, dangling his feet in the cool sea and casting the makeshift fishhook out as far as it would go. There was nothing to bait it with, but perhaps the fish in this remote patch of sea would not know what hooks were, and would come and take a bite just out of curiosity. When he caught one, he thought, he could cut it up with Doom's pocketknife and serve it raw, à la Tokyo. Or perhaps the glass from Trubshawe's watch might be used to focus the sun's rays, so they could roast small pieces.

His mouth watered a little just imagining it. Lost in his daydreams, it took him a while to register the fact that a telltale triangular fin was circling the floating pool. He dropped the fishing line into the sea and fell backward, sliding down into the puddle at the pool's deep end.

"Shark! Shark! Shark!" he shouted.

Twice that night, the castaways inside the pool were woken by the sound of a big, powerful body rasping against the other side of its thin walls. By the following day, five sharks were following it.

155

The smallest was perhaps three feet long, the biggest a monster twice the length of a man. Tamzin climbed cautiously up onto the edge again and tried casting out a line, hoping to lure the small one nearer, but it showed no interest in the baitless hook. Even if she had caught it, it seemed unlikely that it could have been hauled aboard before its companions ate it.

"They look no different to the prehistoric sharks whose fossils I saw in the London Museum when I was a girl," said Miss Torpenhow, looking down at the creatures through the clear water. "They swam in these seas before there were people at all, before ships sailed or cities moved. They will swim here still when we are all gone."

"What a picture this will make!" mused Trubshawe. "The end-less sea, the brave mariners, the circling sharks. I shall have to make the swimming pool something more romantic, like a raft, and have the sharks behave more dramatically, but, even so, it will be my masterpiece. If I ever, ah . . ."

"If you ever get home to paint it," said Max gloomily, complet-ing his thought for him.

"You all talk too much," said Tamzin. She was trying to resign herself to death, and thought it would be easier without idiots talking about sharks and art the whole time.

Oddington Doom said nothing. Heat, thirst, and hunger were taking their toll on the old soldier. He lay on the sun-warmed plas-tic, too weak to move, too dizzy to even raise his head. The others wet his mouth sometimes with water from their dwindling reserves of dew.

❦

That night, or perhaps the next, something jolted Tamzin from her dreams. The others slept on, curled up on the plastic around her, impervious to the faint scratching sounds that had awoken her. Another shark, she thought, scraping its old barnacled hide against the outside of the pool. But it sounded more purposeful than that.

Over the edge of the pool, not far from where she lay, a glistening tentacle appeared. It felt around, and gripped, and another slithered into view beside it. Tamzin forced herself to stand up. She tried to call out to the others, but her mouth was too parched. She went to the pool's edge and peered over. The octopus's body was just beneath the water, a bulge of dark against the pallor of the pool's side. Another tentacle rose, not far from her, and this one gleamed with something more than water. The tip of it was sheathed in metal, as if a long, narrow thimble had been fitted over it. The thimble tapped against the plastic of the pool. The suckers of the tentacles made the faintest popping sounds as the octopus adjusted its grip. Its eyes glinted, looking up at Tamzin through slot-shaped pupils. There was metal on its body too, she saw: a sort of harness, and a hard little blue light shining like a sapphire there.

"Is this real?" she whispered.

And it wasn't. Of course it wasn't. She surfaced groggily from her dream. The sun was shining. Trubshawe was on his feet, shouting something she did not understand.

Tamzin sat up. Max, lying beside her, was still asleep. Doom lay like a dead man, and although Miss Torpenhow opened her eyes a little, she lacked the energy to move. So it felt like Tamzin's job to drag herself upright and go to stop the artist as he scrambled up the ladder at the side of the pool.

"Stop it, you fool!" she shouted, slithering her way across the shallow end to seize him by both legs. She thought he must have gone mad and decided to take a swim with the sharks.

"Let me go!" shouted Trubshawe. "There is a ship, an airship!"

He kicked free of her and clambered up to stand on the charred diving board. He waved his shirt over his head and shouted, "Help! Help!"

Was there really an airship? Tamzin could not tell. Maybe it had been a dream, like her octopus. A tiny speck showed, very low on the western horizon, but it might have been a cloud. She let Trubshawe keep shouting and waving until his voice gave out and his arms were too tired to wave anymore.

The airship — if there had ever been an airship — did not come. Trubshawe slumped to his knees on the diving board. Tamzin helped him back down the ladder. Max and Miss Torpenhow were awake. A shark bumped against the underside of the pool, gentle and ominous.

Oddington Doom could not be woken. His breathing was very shallow. Max and Trubshawe dragged him into the shade and collapsed beside him. Miss Torpenhow crawled over to join them. Tamzin forced herself to stay upright, stumbling restlessly to and fro along the pool's shallow end, pulling herself up a few rungs of the ladder now and then to scan the empty sky. The floaters drifting in her eyes all looked like airships flying to the rescue. A dark idea circled just outside her conscious thoughts — *When Mr. Doom dies, we could use him as bait and catch ourselves a shark.* Even further out, another lurked, still darker. *When Mr. Doom dies, we could eat him* . . .

As if to punish her for thinking such a thing, the sea began to boil. Huge white bubbles rushed up from the depths and burst, threatening to swamp the swimming pool. Up through the bubbles came a glistening black body. Tamzin had not realized sharks could grow so big. It dwarfed the swimming pool. Its massive dorsal fin jutted like a dark tower.

Her terrified shout woke Max, who scrambled up onto the poolside with her. They watched together as the monster surfaced, barely ten yards from them. But as the spray settled it became clear that the towering fin was much more tower than fin. Painted on it in white was the symbol of an octopus clutching a broken wheel, like a strange echo of Tamzin's dream.

Hatches began opening. Men and women clambered nimbly out onto the hull. They had brown faces and white uniforms, and some carried guns, which they pointed in the pool's direction. But others smiled, and one of the smiling ones called out, "Swimming pool ahoy! Are you in need of assistance?"

The castaways were in no mood for banter. "Of course we're in need of assistance, you subaquatic twit!" Max shouted angrily, but his voice was gone and the words were barely a whisper, which was fortunate, perhaps.

Tamzin, beside him, managed to croak, "Yes!"

"Stand by, then," said the submariner. "We'll throw you a rope."

27

SQUID SQUAD

She dreamed that it had all been a dream. Miss Torpenhow, Max, Bad Luftgarten, the swimming pool, all of it. She dreamed she was still on Margate, fighting a Revenant with the bulk and general demeanor of the nomad war mammoths Miss T had told her of. And when she woke, to the throb and shudder of big engines and a low ceiling covered by a tangle of pipework, she assumed it was Margate pipework, and Margate's engines rumbling. Had she been injured? Had they dragged her out of the Arcade unconscious? She sat up in a panic, checking to make sure all her limbs were still attached, feeling for her pendant with its smiling sun. It was still there, hanging around her neck.

"How are you feeling?" asked a young woman in a crisp white uniform, who had apparently been watching her. "You've been asleep for a day and a night. It is the best thing for you, of course."

She was not much more than Tamzin's age. She had very big, very dark eyes, and spectacles that made them look bigger still. On the breast of her white tunic was a brass badge in the shape of an octopus wrapping its tentacles around a broken wheel.

Memories fell into place in Tamzin's fuddled brain: the

swimming pool, the octopus in her dream, the submarine surfacing.

"You're aboard the Imperial Zagwan submersible *Haile Maryam*. I am Dr. Posie Naphtali. I've been keeping an eye on you."

"You're young, for a doctor," said Tamzin suspiciously.

"I am in training still," admitted Posie Naphtali. "And I am training to be a marine biologist, not the doctor sort of doctor, but the *Haile Maryam* is without a medical officer at present, so Captain Kardos asked me to look after you."

"And my friends?"

"They are all well."

Tamzin nodded. "What is a marine biologist?"

"I study things. Under the sea. Creatures. That's why I'm on this boat."

"But it's a warship?"

Posie Naphtali shrugged. "In the struggle against Tractionism, even marine biologists must do their bit."

That was what the broken wheel meant, Tamzin remembered. She had been rescued by a submarine of the Anti-Traction League. The Zagwan Empire, whose ship this was, had been one of the founders of the League, and had fought for centuries against the whole idea of moving cities. From what she had heard, they were as likely to enslave or murder her as any pirate suburb. She wondered what the octopus symbol meant.

"If you can walk," said Posie Naphtali, "I'll take you to the mess. Your friends are there."

Tamzin did not entirely trust this young doctor, but a tempting smell came through the door she opened, and there was nothing to be gained by lazing on the hard bunk, so she stood up and followed. She found that her ruined clothes had been replaced by a white shirt like Dr. Naphtali's, a pair of wide blue trousers, and

161

rope sandals. Looking down at the sandals, she almost failed to notice that the young doctor was leading her along a walkway beside an enormous glass tank, until a sudden swirl of movement in the corner of her eye triggered her Arcade-honed senses and sent her into a defensive crouch, reaching for a knife that was not there.

Inside the tank were weathered stones, gardens of coral, waving weed. It was difficult to make out the exact shape or size of the creatures who lived there. They seemed small at first, clinging to the stone and so close to it in color and texture that it was hard to believe they were not stone themselves. Then one seemed to swell, and flashed pale yellow and then mottled red. It billowed like a banner, unfurling marbled limbs. Rows of suckers fastened themselves carefully to the glass. A weird golden eye stared out at Tamzin from the fleshy bag that was its body, or perhaps its head.

"It is only Thomas," said Posie Naphtali, glancing back to see Tamzin crouching there, appalled. "You have met him before. If Thomas hadn't reported you, we would never have found your raft."

"An *octopus* told you where we were?" Tamzin remembered her dream: the tentacles gleaming in the moonlight, that weird metal thimble. Thomas was still wearing the thimble. He raised it now to tap against the glass, and Posie Naphtali tapped back. The second octopus, more shy than its companion, turned deep red and made movements with its tentacles that Posie repeated with her hands.

"So that part wasn't a dream?" Tamzin said.

"We are training them as scouts," said Posie Naphtali. "Thomas has a vocabulary of over a hundred and eighty words. And Abela knows almost three hundred. We are hoping that they can be taught to spy on raft towns, and perhaps help us to sink any that threaten our coastal settlements. It's meant to be a secret, but this

162

is a small boat so you're bound to find out. That is what my badge means — I saw you look at it before. We are part of the League's Cephalopod Corps. It is an experimental unit. We are also called the Squid Squad, but that is a very foolish name, because Thomas and Abela are octopuses, not squid, as anyone can see; squid have ten arms, and an entirely different bodily structure . . ."

She did like to talk about her octopuses, Tamzin thought. She got so excited that her words started tripping over each other as they tumbled out of her mouth, and she stopped and smiled a little shyly as if she suspected she'd been boring her guest.

"Come, please — your friends will be waiting."

She tapped out a little pattern on the glass of the tank before she led Tamzin on along the corridor.

Saying goodbye to her octopuses, Tamzin supposed, and she gave them a little wave herself.

Posie Naphtali showed her through a bulkhead doorway and up a companion ladder. The deck and walls were white, and so was the spaghetti of plumbing that mostly hid the low, curved roof. The engines throbbed like a headache, but their sound was fainter than before, so Tamzin guessed she was moving toward the sub's bow. She ducked after Posie through another low, oval doorway, and there was a cramped little mess with three wooden tables. Her friends were gathered around one of them, all dressed like her in odds and ends of Zagwan naval uniforms, all rising to greet her as she came in.

Tamzin was so glad to see them. Even Mr. Trubshawe, who had painted that stupid picture of her. A bond between the five of them, the sort of bond that had linked the other fighters in the Arcade, but that Tamzin had always been too wary to let herself feel before. She was still wary of it now, for it felt dangerous to her to care so much about other people. But something had happened to her aboard Bad Luftgarten or in the swimming pool, and there was no going back.

Posie Naphtali returned to her octopus tank, and the others made space for Tamzin at the table. There was coffee to drink, hot and sweet in small glass cups with metal handles. There were rounds of dry bread, which seemed to Tamzin more delicious than any food she had ever tasted.

"Not too much," warned Oddington Doom, who seemed completely recovered. "Dr. Naphtali said it can be bad for our stomachs to eat much after a fast like we had."

"She is a doctor of octopuses," said Max. "What does she know about our stomachs? You heard about the octopuses, Tamzin?"

Tamzin nodded, mouth too full to answer.

"Typical Anti-Tractionist cunning," said Trubshawe, "training those eight-legged brutes to spy on decent, law-abiding raft towns. Not that I'm not grateful to young Dr. N and her tentacular pals, of course. If they hadn't happened by when they did, we would all be dead."

"But I do wish they had not been Anti-Tractionist octopuses," said Miss Torpenhow. "For although the Haile Maryam's crew have been most kind to us, there is no getting around the fact that we are their prisoners. What will become of us when we arrive at their home port, I do not know . . ."

Oddington Doom patted her shoulder. (He meant to reassure her, but Miss Torpenhow just looked startled; she had never considered herself a pattable person.) "We can worry about that when we get there," he said. "For now, let's just be glad we're still alive, and in good company."

"Well, I am glad of that, of course . . ." said Miss Torpenhow, and Tamzin thought that she was blushing, although beneath the sunburn it was hard to tell.

✻

The sunburn faded. Lying in her bunk, Tamzin amused herself by peeling the scorched outer layer of skin from her arms and neck. It came off, if she was careful, in big patches, parchment-thin and raggedy-edged, like maps of unknown countries.

Meanwhile, the Haile Maryam moved west, traveling mostly on the surface, with the hatches open to let fresh air in. The crew treated the rescued castaways with distant friendliness. Most of them did not speak Anglish; most of them did not trust anyone who came from a mobile city, but the rules of the sea had been set long before cities moved: You saved shipwrecked mariners whoever they were, and treated them as well as you could, for who knew when you might be shipwrecked yourself?

Most afternoons, Dr. Naphtali and her two assistants brought their octopuses in leather buckets up through the forward hatch, and let them free. Thomas and Abela looked grotesque on deck: glistening alien bags of snot and muscle that groped their way toward the Haile Maryam's side with arms that seemed to grow or shrink at will. Their colors shifted with their moods, and their skin seemed sometimes spiny, sometimes smooth. But as soon as they were in the water they became oddly beautiful. They circled the sub with graceful, undulating movements, then vanished, darting away to locate whatever target Dr. Naphtali had set them. They wore steel thimbles and other, more complicated tools on several of their arms, and Thomas sometimes sported a leather harness with a contraption on it, the glowing sapphire light of which Tamzin had seen that night in the swimming pool. A camera?

"Best not ask where they're going or what they're doing,"

165

warned Oddington Doom. "The Anti-Traction League might not like outsiders knowing its secrets."

The Anti-Traction League might not like outsiders knowing its secrets, but Posie Naphtali was very bad at keeping them. She was so proud of her pupils that she could not resist boasting of their achievements to anyone who would listen. Since Captain Kardos and his crew were busy with the running of the submarine, that was often Tamzin and her friends.

One day, the submarine suddenly submerged, its hull creaking as the water pressure outside increased. The engines shut down. An order went around that no one was to talk. Sitting in silence, Tamzin and her friends looked up anxiously at the low roof, wondering what was above them that Captain Kardos was so keen to hide from. Faint clangs echoed through the corridors as hatches opened and closed.

After an hour or two, the emergency was over. The engines came back to life, the submariners began to talk again, and the Haile Maryam changed course.

"Thomas has gathered information on a corsair town," Posie Naphtali confided, joining the castaways at their table in the mess that evening. "We think it may be looking to raid our harbors in Sardinia. Captain Kardos is sending a message to warn them."

The Zagwan Empire had been technophobic in the past, and still had strange taboos against machinery. Submarines did not offend their god, it seemed, but they drew the line at radios. When the Haile Maryam surfaced, Tamzin went out on deck with Dr. Naphtali and the others to watch as one of the crewmen released a messenger pigeon from a basket. Trubshawe sketched the scene as it flew away northward.

"If the raft town is driven off, it will be our first victory," said Dr. Naphtali. "The first victory won by the Cephalopod Corps, I mean."

"You will have to give Thomas a medal," said Trubshawe. "I shall design one for him. Though I am not sure how you would pin it on . . ."

"Seeing how intelligent and helpful the creatures are," said Miss Torpenhow, "I am surprised the Ancients did not make more use of them. Yet I have seen no reference to octopuses in the Ancient texts, except as meals."

Dr. Naphtali, always happy to talk about her favorite subject, explained, "The cephalopods of Ancient times were not so intelligent, we think. Or perhaps they did not live as long as modern ones, and had less time to learn in. Something happened to them — either the Ancients bred special ones, which have replaced the old sort, or they were mutated by the poisons released during the Sixty Minute War, or perhaps God in His wisdom raised them up to replace human beings, in case we died out entirely in the Centuries of Winter. At any rate, some octopuses are almost as long-lived as people now, and almost as clever, I think. And Professor Yamaishi, the founder of our corps, believes something very strange is going on in the deep trenches of the Pacific. There are stories of lights underwater where no lights should be, and the oddest artifacts have been washed up on beaches there."

They sat on deck with her while it grew dark and the stars came out, listening to her spin tales of the cephalopod civilization, which she believed was thriving down in parts of the ocean that even sunlight could not reach. Miss Torpenhow thought it sounded unlikely, but to Tamzin it seemed no less impossible than Revenants or airborne towns or any of the other things she had seen. She liked the idea that squid and octopus were getting on with their own world down there in the deeps. She hoped it would be less filled with cruelty than the human one.

28

ROCK OF AGES

The next day, with much hooting of alarms and flashing of red lights, the *Haile Maryam* slammed shut all its hatches and submerged, staying deep beneath the waves for hours and moving west under full power. Whether something was hunting her, whether it was the corsair town Thomas and Abela had sighted, or another town, or merely a training exercise, the castaways never found out. When she surfaced again and they were allowed out onto the deck, it was evening, and in the hazy, golden air Tamzin saw land on the horizon, both north and south.

"The Pillars of Hercules," said Max, recalling old geography lessons. "It must be — isn't it, Miss T?"

"It is indeed," said Miss Torpenhow. "We are in the straits between Africa and Europe. Oh, look! You see that great ruinous structure on the African coast, like a squared-off mountain with the surf breaking at its feet? That must be one of the anchor points for the great pontoon bridge that the Zagwan Empire built in the height of its power. Three hundred years ago, the Zagwans and their allies from Trarza and the Tibesti Caliphate marched across that bridge on their way to try to stop our cities moving. It was a misguided effort, and doomed to failure, but so brave! What a sight it must have made: the banners waving, and the spearpoints shimmering, and the Zagwan paladins riding on their war zebras. It was they who gave the bridge its name, of course — the Zebra Crossing. Now all that is left is that crumbling pier, and another like it on the European shore . . ."

Captain Kardos, looking down from his conning tower, saw what his passengers were pointing at, and lent them his own telescope so they might see it in more detail. He felt it would do them good, these Tractionist barbarians from the north, to see what marvels his forefathers had built here. But by the time Tamzin got her turn with the glass the Haile Maryam was moving quickly northward, and she could see no more of the ruins than she had with the naked eye.

But it did mean she was the first to sight the submarine's destination. Ahead, with lights coming on upon its lower slopes as twilight advanced out of the east, something big crouched lionlike just off the shore of Europe.

"I can see a harbor," she said, trying to hold the telescope steady as the submarine adjusted course. "There are many ships in the sea, and many airships above it . . ."

"A city!" said Trubshawe. "But which?"

Max took the telescope from Tamzin. "It is not a city," he said, after a moment. "Just a dirty great rock."

"Not a rock, Max," said Miss Torpenhow. "It is the Rock. Djebel Tarik, Gibraltar of the Ancients. The last foothold of the Zagwan Empire in Europe, and an important Anti-Traction League stronghold nowadays. So that is where they are taking us."

"And will we be able to find airships there to carry us home?" asked Trubshawe. "I for one have wandered long enough. I need to get back to my studio, my gallery. The sketches I've done will make a marvelous suite of paintings, just the new direction I've been looking for . . ."

"It will depend on how the authorities on the Rock are feeling," said Oddington Doom. "And that will depend on how many of their static settlements have been eaten up by hungry cities lately. If they are in a good mood, they may let some of us go free. If not, your new direction will probably take you into one of the League's slave-labor camps."

※

The Rock had been among the first strongholds the Zagwan Empire had established when it began its war against Europe's Traction Cities, and when at last the Traction Cities banded together and drove the Zagwans back into the sea, the garrison there had held out stubbornly. It was still holding out today. Cities had turned their guns on it; hungry amphibious suburbs had raided its shores; it had defeated them all.

These details of the stronghold's past were explained by Miss Torpenhow as the castaways were rowed ashore. She might be bound for a slave camp, but she could not resist the opportunity to give her companions a history lesson. She had never expected to see Djebel Tarik with her own eyes, and now that she was, the sight awoke memories of all the great stories she had loved as a girl: the wild, romantic history of the early Traction Era.

"I doubt it was that romantic," grumbled Oddington Doom when she mentioned this. "War is war in any age: hard luck on the warriors, and harder still on the ordinary folk who get in the way of their rampages." He was in a bad mood, for he alone understood how much trouble they might be in. The Zagwan Empire was a fading power nowadays, but some of its regional governors dreamed fondly of its old glory days. They might not be above making a grisly example of any Tractionists who fell into their clutches.

Tamzin paid little heed to any of this talk. She looked back over the boat's stern to where the *Haile Maryam* lay at her moorings, her hull and conning tower silhouetted against the afterglow in the west. She was sorry that she had not had a chance to say good-bye and thank you to Dr. Naphtali and her octopuses. Now that it was over, she felt that the past few days aboard the submarine had been among the happiest of her life. It had been like a holiday, away from all her troubles. Now she was returning to dry land, where they would all be waiting for her.

They were waiting in the form of a detachment of Zagwan soldiers, much sterner and better equipped than the shabby submariners, who shouted orders as the boat bumped up against the harbor stairs.

"They say we are to be taken straight to the governor's palace," whispered Doom as the castaways climbed out of the boat and the soldiers took charge of them.

"Is that good?" asked Trubshawe nervously.

"I doubt it . . ."

It was dark by then. With guards going ahead and following behind, the newcomers were marched up slopes and stairways, through fortified gates in one ring after another of thick walls, until they came to a terrace high on the rock's western face. There fountains played outside a pillared portico, beneath which was the entrance to the governor's warren-like residence. He was waiting for them in a reception room, the walls of which were decorated with sections cut from the deckplating of shattered traction towns.

The governor was a big man, and growing rather portly, but there was still a tigerish grace about him as he came down the steps from the dais where his throne stood. His bald head shone like something carved from dark, well-polished wood. Gold braid decorated his smart white uniform, and at his side hung a huge sword. His eyes moved quickly from one face to the next, as if weighing up whose head he should lop off first. From Max, to Miss Torpenhow, to Tamzin, to Trubshawe, who said, "It is an honor to meet you, Your Excellency . . ."

The governor ignored him. His eyes lit on Oddington Doom and narrowed, as if he had sighted his prey. Then his face broke into a delighted smile.

"Doom! Oddington Doom! I saw your name in the message the bird brought from the *Haile Maryam*, and I thought it must be you, for there cannot be two men with such a ridiculous name. My God, but you've grown old!"

Doom laughed. "And so have you, Kush Tundurbai. Old and fat. I would not have known you."

Max and Tamzin glanced uneasily at each other. It seemed unwise to use words like "old" and "fat" about this powerful man who held all their fates in his hand. But Tundurbai just laughed even more loudly than Doom, and strode forward to enfold the old mercenary in a bearish hug.

"We fought together at Los Muros Viellos," Doom explained, when he surfaced again. "Kush Tundurbai here was the Anti-Tractionist commander who hired us to reinforce his garrison."

"And Doom fought like a devil!" said Tundurbai. "Three big suburbs attacked together at the end, and we were hard pressed to deal with them. All through a black day and a red night we

172

battled. But when morning came again, two of the slug towns were in flames and the third took flight . . ."

"It did not get far," said Doom. "We had damaged it so badly it could only limp along at half speed. When it reached the plains below, it was eaten by the city of Badajoz."

Kush Tundurbai seemed to remember that his old friend was not alone. He looked inquiringly at Miss Torpenhow and the others, and Doom introduced them.

"Barbarians from the moving cities?" asked Tundurbai.

"I'm afraid so," admitted Doom. "But Miss T and young Max Angmering here are from Thorbury, which is a peaceable enough kind of place, and Trubshawe is only an artist, so it doesn't matter much where he comes from. And as for Tamzin there . . ."

"I came from Mayda," Tamzin said, "though I do not remember it."

"Then you at least are civilized, my child," said Tundurbai, taking her hands and looking down at her with a fatherly smile. "Mayda was a great city once, and I weep that the League grew too weak to save it. So will you vouch for these Tractionistas you are traveling with?"

"Yes," said Tamzin.

"Me too," agreed Doom.

Tundurbai nodded. "Then that is good enough for me. You will stay here tonight, and we shall eat together, and you shall tell me how you came to be adrift together in — what was it Captain Kardos said in his message? A swimming pool?"

29

KUSH TUNDURBAI

By ancient Zagwan law, no alcohol could be served anywhere within the bounds of the Empire. But the crews of merchant airships liked a drink or two, and Governor Tundurbai liked the money that could be made by selling them those drinks, so he had come up with an elegant compromise. The pubs and bars of his town remained decently shuttered during the hours of daylight. But when night fell they would fold open their roofs, inflate the gasbags they stored in their attics, and rise into the air. Anything above fifteen feet was considered far enough outside city bounds for the sale of wines, beers, and spirits to be permitted, but most pubs nowadays went higher, offering their customers spectacular views across the straits. "Pub-rise on the Rock" had become a popular subject for painters. There was even a famous air shanty called "The Voyage of the Dog and Duck" about a pub that had slipped its moorings in a brisk northeasterly. (The people inside it had been having such a good time that they had not noticed, until they emerged, blinking, the next morning in Madeira, seven hundred miles away.)

The pubs were rising now, their envelopes gleaming in the light of the moon. Tamzin watched them from the windows of the governor's elegant dining room while servants brought in plates of mezze and skewers of spiced lamb. Kush Tundurbai, his senior officers, and his fat, beautiful wife all listened closely while Miss Torpenhow told the tale of their adventures.

"Well," said Tundurbai, when she was finished, "that is quite a story. This Strega fellow sounds a very bad egg. You may be a barbarian, Mister Angmering, but your father did not deserve such treatment, and nor did his citizens. I despise and curse all motorized cities, of course, but I am damned if it does not almost make me wish I could do something to help . . ."

"You can," said Max boldly. He was a little flushed. The governor had provided wine for those not bound by Zagwan customs, and Tamzin suspected Max had drunk a little too much of it. "You can help us, Your Excellency. We have seen all the ships and troops you have stationed here. If you could lend us two or three airships, a hundred men or so . . ."

Tundurbai laughed, then realized Max was in earnest, and scowled. "You are impertinent, my young Tractionist friend," he said. "The Anti-Traction League does not send its warriors to settle disputes among squabbling barbarians. Your plight moved me, but it makes no difference to the League whether your city is ruled by you or Strega."

"Does it not?" asked Miss Torpenhow.

Tundurbai looked sharply at her. He was obviously unused to being interrupted, and Tamzin feared for a moment he might send them to the slave camps after all. But he raised one eyebrow questioningly, and waited for Miss Torpenhow to explain.

"I think who rules Thorbury might make a great difference to the League," she said. "Consider. For many years, under the

Angmerings, our city has been minding its own business. It survives by trading, and by eating those smaller towns that submit to being eaten. It does no harm to anyone."

A rumble of disapproval emerged from the governor, like a volcano preparing to erupt. "All Traction Cities do harm. They do harm to God's good green earth."

"But Strega is a man of an entirely different sort," said Miss Torpenhow, ignoring him. "He has a fierce and predatory nature, and he wishes to remake Thorbury in his own image. He intends to turn our city into one of the great terrors of the Hunting Ground. And do not think it is only mobile towns it will devour. There are still many static settlements among the mountainous and marshy parts of Europe. Bigger cities are too cumbersome to reach them; smaller ones can be driven off by their defenders, as you and Mr. Doom proved so memorably at Los Muros Viellos. But Thorbury is of medium size, and nimble enough to be a threat to them."

"You seem to know a great deal about this Strega."

"I remember the proposals he submitted to the Planning Department, before he was sent into exile," said Miss Torpenhow. "And I am quite sure it would be better for the League if he were disposed of, and replaced by a mayor who would look upon you and your fellow Anti-Tractionists as his friends."

Tundurbai stared at her in silence. Then the rumbling started in his chest again, and turned into a huge laugh, which echoed around the pillared room.

"Oddington Doom," he roared, "I like this new woman of yours! She has spirit!"

He fell silent again, apparently too deep in thought to hear Doom explain that Miss Torpenhow was not his woman, and Miss

176

Torpenhow declare indignantly that she was not anybody's woman, except her own. Then he shook his head.

"I am sorry," he said. "You speak sense, but the Empire and the League would not permit it. This long war may have grown quiet in recent years, but it is a war, for all that. My own people would call me a traitor if I let you have men, or ships, or weapons."

"I understand, sir," said Max. "I am sorry . . ."

Tundurbai held up a hand to silence him, and turned to his wife and the officers who sat with him. They all talked together for a little while in a language that Tamzin did not recognize, and that even Doom seemed unable to follow, judging by the way he shrugged when the others looked at him.

"There is a ship in my air harbor," said Tundurbai at last, turning back to them. "A worm smuggler's ship our patrols captured. It is only a Goshawk 20 from the shipyards of London, but its former owners fitted it with keener rudder controls and more powerful engines. I will let you have this ship, if you will use it to defeat Strega."

"An airship?" said Max, too loudly. "That's wonderful! We can fly on to Cittamotore or Lisbon or London, demand they help us —"

"What's the catch?" asked Oddington Doom.

"Why would there be a catch?" asked his friend innocently.

"I know you too well, Kush Tundurbai. You don't just go giving airships away."

"I do if it is in the interests of the Anti-Traction League," said Tundurbai, but his wife tugged at his sleeve and murmured something at him, which made him say, "Very well, very well, yes. It is a bad-luck ship, which is why none of my aviators will touch it. Its name is Fire's Astonishment, and fire is bad luck in an airship, for obvious reasons."

"And then there is the fact it is cursed," Madame Tundurbai reminded him.

"Yes, of course, my love, there is also that," agreed her husband, as if it were a very minor detail, and scarcely worth mentioning.

"It was found drifting on the high-level winds," said Madame Tundurbai. "Drifting with full fuel tanks and its cargo intact, but not a single living soul aboard. So obviously it is cursed, and anyone who flies it will be cursed too."

"But," said Tundurbai, and dazzled them all with his smile again, "you are all city dwellers, so you are cursed already, and it will not matter."

"I do not believe in curses," announced Max. "It is a most general offer, generous. I mean, a most generous offer, General . . ."

He fell silent, looking uncertain of himself. The others looked uncertain too. Oddington Doom had seen too many strange things in his time to dismiss the idea of the curse so lightly. Trubshawe was recalling ghost stories he had heard, and hoping he was not about to feature in one. Tamzin was reflecting on how bad luck had followed her like a dog ever since the thing with Eve Vespertine.

Miss Torpenhow did not believe in curses either, but she did not see how much help a single ship could be. "However fast this ship is," she said, "it cannot help us defeat Strega. We will need an army for that, and I still have no notion of how to find one."

Kush Tundurbai yawned. "If you have Oddington Doom on your side, you hardly need an army. But it grows late. Let my people show you to your sleeping quarters. In the morning, we shall go together to the air dock, and you can see the cursed ship for yourselves."

30

Worm Runner

At first light, the airborne pubs were winched back down to earth like wayward dreams. Aviators stumbled out of them, or were carried out by their friends, still singing drinking songs and exchanging news. Their voices echoed in the steep, cobbled streets as they made their way back to their ships and bunkhouses.

"Tamzin Pook is here."

"The Arcade star? *That* Tamzin Pook? The girl who ran?"

"*Now a pub's a fine place to get right off your face on wine and rum and beer-o . . .*"

"Yes, that Tamzin Pook! She's the governor's guest. My girl's brother's mate's a servant at the palace — he saw her there."

"Tamzin Pook, eh? We saw them posters about her when we docked in Margate, remember? It said there was a reward."

"*So let's drink to the luck of the old Dog and Duck for she carried us safe to Madeir-o!*"

"Shut up singing, you doughnut! This is important, this is! There was a big reward for this Pook girl, that's what them posters said."

"She's the governor's guest, though . . ."

179

"'A reward to whomsoever finds and brings back Tamzin Pook.' That's what them posters said. 'Whomsoever' — that's grammar, that is, which proves it was official."

"Ain't you listening? She's Tundurbai's guest, I said. Under his protection, like. Untouchable."

"It was a big reward, though."

"You're sure your mate said it was Tamzin Pook?"

"I could use a big reward . . ."

Far, far to the east, where the old Earth's wrinkled skin reared up to form immense mountains, lay the kingdom of Shan Guo, which had taken over the leadership of the Anti-Traction League as the Zagwan Empire fell into decline. In one of the high temples there, monks had preserved a breed of silkworm that the Ancients must have modified in the years before their world was swept away. The silk these worms produced was as soft as thistledown, but, when woven, produced a fabric with the tensile strength of steel. Carefully, the lords of the Mountain Kingdoms had cultivated these useful worms, for when the silicon-silk was turned into gasbags and envelopes it gave their airships a powerful advantage. But, gradually, the people of the cities came to know of it, and to realize that there was money to made by anyone who could spirit some of the worms out of Shan Guo.

The worm smugglers who had flown the *Fire's Astonishment* must have had a whole crate of silkworm larvae aboard, judging by the size of the secret compartment they had built behind the paneling of their control cabin. They had come a long way with it too, before something happened that left their ship empty and drifting, to be salvaged by Kush Tundurbai's patrols.

What had become of the crew, Tamzin and her friends did not

care to wonder. Madness? Murder? Suicide? Some hungry demon of the upper air? It was better not to think about it. But the ship herself looked quite unharmed by whatever horrors she had seen. She was moored at a rusty old gantry on the outer edge of the air dock, at a safe distance from luckier ships. She was no bigger than the Hercules, but much sleeker and more streamlined, and her powerful engine pods seemed to have come from a bigger and more expensive vessel altogether. She stirred at her moorings like a living thing, and the wind boomed softly against her tailfins. The silken panels of her envelope were all different shades of orange, the colors of a bonfire.

"She has no armaments, of course," said Tundurbai. "But you have Oddington Doom with you, so what do you care? If air pirates threaten you, all you need do is get the Fire's Astonishment above their ship and drop him on them; he will do the rest."

He strode away laughing, his aides and officers hurrying along behind him like small boats following a great liner. Max went aboard the airship and sat down in the pilot's chair. The labels on the control panel were in an alphabet he could not read or even name, but the dials and levers looked much like the dials and levers of his family's sky-yacht.

"You can fly her?" asked Miss Torpenhow.

Max nodded, and wished he had not drunk so much of the governor's wine. He had woken with a foul taste in his mouth and a pounding headache.

Doom made his own inspection of the controls, and pried access hatches open to check on the rudder controls and electrics. Miss Torpenhow and Trubshawe climbed up inside the envelope. Their voices could be heard echoing about up there among the gas-bags, commenting on how neat it all was, how well made.

Which had not been any help to the previous crew, thought Tamzin, standing alone on the mooring gantry at the foot of the gangplank. The airship's reputation still made her uneasy. Arcade fighters took luck seriously. Tamzin's seemed to have taken a turn for the better lately — first the submarine, then the kindness of Kush Tundurbai. But she sensed that the gods, who were as fickle and bloodthirsty as any Arcade audience, were toying with her. What if her run of good luck was just a way of making her lower her guard before they unleashed more of the bad? It would be hardly fair to make her friends take such an ill-starred girl with them aboard this already unlucky airship. They would be safer without her. But to leave them now would hurt her more than she could bear . . .

"Miss Pook?" a woman called.

A group of aviators was standing at the gantry's end, where stairs went up and down to busy terraces of shops. Tamzin went toward them, thinking they might be some of the governor's people.

"Miss Pook?" the woman said again, smiling. She was a northerner, wearing the shabby flying suit of a merchant aviator. "We heard you was in town! I saw you in the Arcade once! Could you sign your autograph? It is not for me — it's for my nephew."

She held out a scrap of pink paper and a pencil. As Tamzin stared at it, the wind came gusting up the face of the rock and ripped the paper from the woman's hand and carried it tumbling over and over high into the sky. At the same moment, someone who had gotten around behind Tamzin struck her on the back of the head, a blow so hard that she felt bewilderment and then the beginnings of anger, but no pain at all. And as they pulled a bag over her head and she fell backward into darkness, she was thinking only of that pink square of paper, whirling upward for ever and ever, through the sunlight and the tall, white castles of the clouds.

31

DOWN ON BASE TIER

Helen Angmering walked briskly along one of the main streets of Thorbury's engine district while Thorbury rolled and bucked beneath her, chasing its prey through the maze of track marks some bigger city had made.

She had been several weeks on Base Tier, and this was the farthest she had yet ventured from her friends' home, in a block of flats on the rear edge of the city. She felt alarmingly vulnerable out in these busy thoroughfares, but excited too, and free. She had been hidden too long. She had been itching to do something. She had been pleading for days with Raoul and his father for something useful to do in the struggle against Strega, and they had finally relented.

She turned left on Conduit Street as they had told her to, and there ahead was the elevator station. No one recognized her as she walked toward it, and she felt fairly confident that no one *could* recognize her. She had cut her hair short, which Raoul said suited her, although anyone could see it really didn't, and she wore a set of Raoul's gray work overalls, which his mum had altered for her, taking up the cuffs and trouser hems. She also wore a smog mask, as most people did down here to keep out the smuts and fumes that filled the streets when the engines were working. And, since Strega had taken over, the engines had been working day and night.

"A Traction City is like a shark," the Architect was reported to have said, "it must keep moving or it dies." Helen wasn't sure that was true of sharks or cities, but Thorbury had not stopped for ten days now, and each town it gobbled up was dismantled on the move while it went chasing after the next.

The elevator station was a welcoming blaze of light in the sub-terranean gloom of these deep streets. How strange to think that directly above her was the Upper Terminus, and the park where it had all begun, with Strega shooting her father, while the starlings blew like smoke across the evening sky. Ten weeks ago, but it already felt to Helen like ten years, or ten thousand . . .

She walked past the station, keeping on the far side of the street, not stopping, not risking more than a quick glance. Then onward with her head down along narrow ways between the sal-vage holds, carefully memorizing what she had seen. Six nomads on guard outside the station, bored-looking, two of them with heavy weapons. Three Stalkers, standing inside like spiky statues, near the elevator gate. She turned right and took a walkway that led her to the open air, out on the city's skirts, above the tracks. She would go home and tell Raoul and the rest what she had seen, and they would add it to the picture they were assembling of Strega's forces. Before anything could happen, they had to know how many nomad warriors they were facing, and where they were, and what their routines were.

It did not feel like much. But it was a start. Walking aft through the spray and screeching din of the huge tracks below her, she remembered how she had once watched the sky and waited for her big brother to come and save her.

Some hope, she thought scornfully. Old habit made her glance up anyway, but smoke and fumes were spewing so thickly from the Dismantling Yards that she could not see the sky at all.

Back at the apartment, Helen found a man with a gun in the kitchen. She knew the gun: a carbine that had been stolen from one of Strega's drunken nomads and brought to Raoul's father for safekeeping. The man was a stranger, but obviously a friend, since Raoul's mother was cheerfully cooking dinner while he sat there at the kitchen table with the gun in his hands. Raoul and his father, standing on either side of him, looked up guiltily as Helen entered.

"Are you all right?" asked Raoul. "Did it go as planned?"

"I was only scouting out the station," Helen reminded him. Raoul and his family still thought she was a Command Deck girl, fragile as a porcelain figurine, and that annoyed her sometimes. "I counted six men and three Stalkers, same as the night shift. Who's this?"

The man with the gun remembered his manners and stood up.

Raoul said, "This is Carl. He used to be in the Defense Corps. He's teaching us how the gun works. How to reload it and stuff like that."

Helen hung her smog mask on the back of a chair. She held out her hands for the gun.

"Show me," she said.

32

Missing Tamzin

For the rest of that day, and all through the long night that followed it, Tamzin lay bound and gagged in the hold of an air freighter called the *Mutley Plain*. The people who had kidnapped her were not bounty hunters, just hookey air-traders who had seen an opportunity to claim the price Mortmain had put on her head. At first Tamzin thought that might play to her advantage. When one of these amateurs untied her to let her drink or eat or go to the toilet, she might be able to overpower him and force his mates to set her down upon some passing city.

But her luck was running bad, just as she'd feared. For it turned out her captors were such amateurs they never thought to let her eat, or drink, or use the toilet. She lay in her own filth, hungry, thirsty, weeping sometimes with rage and despair. The sorrow she felt at being torn away from Miss Torpenhow and the others was like a wound. *I didn't even have a chance to say goodbye*, she thought, over and over. *They must think I just ran off. They must think I never cared about them at all . . .*

❈

In fact, it had taken some hours for Tamzin's friends to notice she was gone. While they were exploring the Fire's Astonishment, a sky-train tug docked on the neighboring quay. Its captain had towed his string of grubby cargo balloons across half the Hunting Ground, and along the way he had stopped at Thorbury.

"The place is under new management," he said when Miss Torpenhow asked him about it. "A man named Strega has taken over. A strong man. Quite a change from all those spineless, chinless Angmerings."

Max started to let the fellow know he was talking to an Angmering, and that this Angmering was neither spineless nor chinless, but Oddington Doom elbowed him sharply in the ribs from one side and Miss Torpenhow kicked his shin from the other, so he kept quiet.

"Could you tell us all you saw in Thorbury?" asked Doom. "Come, we'll buy you some dinner in the harbor canteen."

"Where's Tamzin?" Max said as they walked along the bustling docks to the canteen. But it seemed no one had seen her for half an hour or more. "Gone back to Tundurbai's palace, I reckon," said Doom. "Or down into the town."

Max felt a momentary chill of worry, as if a cloud had crossed the sun. But it did not last long. It had been rude of Tamzin not to let them know where she was going, he thought, but Tamzin often seemed rude, and he was learning that she did not really mean to be. She was a shy, solitary, prickly sort of person, and she probably wanted some time to herself after being cooped up with them all for so long in the swimming pool and then the submarine. She must have gone off to explore the markets or the waterfront. He decided he would leave her to it. He would look for her later, once he had learned what was happening at home.

The sky-train captain was not a friendly man, but the prospect of a free lunch made him talkative. "Strega's got Thorbury all sorted out different," he said between mouthfuls of songbird pie. "He's driving it northeast, chomping up any town they meet along the way. They say he keeps the Dismantling Yards running day and night. Half my cargo is stuff Strega didn't think worth keeping — books and furniture and carvings and suchlike, taken off the towns he's eaten. And the stuff he does keep, the deckplates and super-structure, is all being recycled into new engines and buildings for Thorbury. He's planning to build a whole new tier."

"A new tier? Above the Command Deck?" Miss Torpenhow was aghast. "But that will throw the town hall and all those fine old buildings into shadow! And what about the parks?"

"All being grubbed up," said the train captain. There was a pause while he bolted the rest of his meal and eyed up the dessert menu. "Strega reckons lawns and trees are a waste of space. They say he's planning to get rid of the farming terraces too — he reck-ons his new engines will make Thorbury so fast that whenever it needs fresh produce it can just catch a farming town. It was eating one when I was there — a place called Poltavia."

"But we had treaties with the Poltavians!" said Max. "We meet them on their travels every year, and buy up their asparagus crop! Poltavia is Thorbury's friend!"

"Well, it's Thorbury's lunch now," said the train captain. "Speaking of which, I'll have the sticky cinnamon pudding, please, with plenty of cream, and another bottle of this rice wine — very kind of you to offer."

On the way back to Tundurbai's palace, Max said angrily, "It is an outrage! It is a disgrace! It is pure greed!"

"It was a very large lunch," Miss Torpenhow agreed. "I would not have thought anyone could manage *three* helpings of sticky cinnamon pudding. And so quickly . . ."

"I don't mean the sky-train lout. I mean Strega, and what he is doing to our city. It's against all the customs and conventions of Municipal Darwinism! Thorbury should set an example to the smaller towns, not barge about behaving like a pirate suburb!"

"You are beginning to sound like a mayor, Max."

"Am I?" Max looked pleased, then angry again. "But I am a mayor without a city. The sooner we get back and kick this Strega out, the better."

They reached the palace and he ran up the steps to their quarters, eager to tell Tamzin what they had learned. But Tamzin was not there, and nor had any of Tundurbai's people seen her since she'd left with the others that morning.

"Perhaps she just decided to leave us," said Miss Torpenhow, a little sadly. "I told her from the start she should feel free to go her own way."

"She would not leave us without saying goodbye," said Max. He was not sure how he knew that, but he did. "You don't think — I mean, those slave-catcher fellows who came after her in Bad Luftgarten — you don't think Mortmain might have set others on her trail?"

✺

They went back to the docks, but dozens of airships had left the Rock since Tamzin disappeared, and she might have been on any of them.

"So we don't know who took her away," said Oddington Doom. "But we know where they are taking her. Back to Margate, and that foul Amusement Arcade."

"We must get her back!" said Trubshawe. "I mean," he added as the others turned to look at him, "*you* must get her back. You are the warriors, the planners. I am merely the humble servant of my muse. But I shall help in any way I can, of course. That poor girl . . ."

"I don't see how we can get her back," said Miss Torpenhow. "I freed her from the Arcade once before. Mortmain is sure to have tightened up his security since then."

"You are planning to seize Thorbury from Strega, aren't you?" said Oddington Doom. "How can you hope to do that if you can't seize one girl from this mountebank Mortmain?"

"It is not just one girl," said Max. An idea had come to him. That did not often happen, and, when it did, he tended to keep quiet about it, because his ideas usually turned out to be foolish ones. But he did not care if this idea was foolish or not, for he knew it was the right thing to do.

"We have to free all the Arcade fighters," he said. "Firstly, because they deserve to be freed, but secondly because they're fighters. Perhaps some of them will join with us against Strega. That's the army we need, Miss T! It's been waiting for us in Margate all along."

Miss Torpenhow looked doubtful. "Tamzin told me I should free the others, the night I got her out. But I did not see how it could be done . . ."

"Ah, but you didn't have Oddington Doom with you then, did you?" said Doom. "Trubshawe, there must be a copy of Cade's *Traction Towns* or Banvard's *Gazetteer* somewhere in this place. Get hold of it, and make me a drawing of Margate, as detailed as ever you can."

"Yes, Mr. Doom," said the artist, and saluted like a soldier in a play.

190

"Max," Doom said, "young Dr. Naphtali took a shine to you, didn't she?"

"I don't think so," said Max.

"Of course she did! I could see it a mile off, and I've only got one eye. So get down to the harbor and find her if you can. Tell her Oddington Doom would like a word."

"I, um, right," said Max, and went to do as he was told.

"And what may I do, Mr. Doom?" asked Miss Torpenhow.

Doom grinned at her. "You," he said, "will come with me to find that old villain Kush Tundurbai, and persuade him to have his ground crews fuel and overhaul the Fire's Astonishment as fast as they can, and get his armorers to spare us swords and guns."

"Can you not ask him yourself? He likes you, though I cannot think why."

"That's just it," said Doom, leading her through the crowded streets toward Tundurbai's palace. "We're old mates, and he might not take me seriously. But point that beaky nose of yours at him and give him that schoolmarm look you do. That's enough to put the fear of the gods into any man."

"Why, Mr. Doom, you say the nicest things . . ."

"I mean it as a compliment, Lavinia. You're the toughest old bird I ever came across."

Miss Torpenhow was about to tell him that she was not a bird, but someone carrying an enormous basket of fresh crabs came the other way, forcing her to step into a doorway, and by the time she caught up with Doom again the moment had passed. Besides, she felt rather pleased that he thought she was tough. "I have always disliked the name 'Lavinia,'" she told him. "My friends call me Hilly."

"Why?"

191

"It is a sort of joke. Torpenhow means 'hill' in three different Ancient languages — 'Tor,' 'Pen,' and 'Howe.' So I am Hilly Torpenhow, you see."

Doom stopped to think about it, on a high stone landing at the rock's edge. Far below, the Middle Sea swarmed with busy specks of sunlight.

"All right," he said. "Hilly it is."

He held out his arm, and after a moment she took it, and they went on together down the steep streets.

33

THE PRODIGAL STAR

Summer had come to the shores of the Anglish Sea, which meant that a watery sun peeped out occasionally through gaps between the fog and rain. It lit up all the little winding watercourses of the broad salt marsh that lay at the sea's eastern end. Beyond the marshes, where the North Sea had once rolled, lay the old Fuel Country. Oil could still be gotten out of the deeper wells there, by drilling towns whose snouts were long enough, while other towns scratched at the salt pans, or raked up relics from the Nomad Wars. Margate had steamed east to entertain them. When the *Mutley Plain* found it, the raft resort was anchored in the mouth of one of the wider channels that led into the marshes. A dozen scruffy towns were drawn up on the shore nearby.

"Miss Pook!" said Mortmain, when they brought her (cleaned and dressed in an Arcade fighter's jumpsuit) to his Bouncy Castle. "So our prodigal star has returned to us!" He sat behind his big bronze desk and beamed at her. Tamzin stared out of the window at the gently bobbing battlements and the billowing veils of the rain. She felt as if her travels and adventures had all been a dream, and now she had awoken to real life again, which consisted of this town and this man.

"Miss Pook, Miss Pook, Miss Pook," said Mortmain. "We are so happy to have you home. The Arcade has not been the same without you. I'll be posting announcements to let the public know you have been found. And we shall get you back in training immediately, of course. A new season starts on Friday. You will be the perfect opening act."

No, Tamzin decided, this was not real life. Real life was Miss Torpenhow, and Max, and Doom. They must have worked out by now what had befallen her. They would not abandon her.

"My friends will come for me," she said.

Mortmain cupped a hand to his ear and made a show of not having heard her. "Your what? Your *friends*? Oh, Tamzin Pook, do you think you have friends? An Arcade star cannot afford friends. I'm sure that if the chips were down you would betray them as easily as you betrayed poor Eve Vespertine. And in your place they'd do the same to you. No, no; forget them, Tamzin. If anyone was coming to save you, they would be here by now, don't you think? Concentrate on your performance. We shall draw a big crowd on Friday afternoon. Bigger, once people hear you are back. That's what you need to be thinking about, Tamzin my dear. I have something very special waiting for you on Friday."

✻

Tamzin's fellow Arcade fighters were not exactly delighted to have her back. In her absence, Skip Recap had taken her place as the fans' favorite. He was good-looking in spite of the scar where one of the Porpentine's quills had gashed his face the night Eve Vespertine died, and he was far more of a team player than Tamzin had ever been. The others thought he brought them luck, even though quite a few had been killed and maimed since Tamzin left.

They thought Tamzin would bring them luck too, but not the sort they wanted. When her name replaced Skip's on the boards outside the Arcade entrance in the run-up to Friday's big show, they were offended on his behalf, and they did their best to let Tamzin know it. In the training sessions, they refused to talk to her, but they talked about her none too quietly when her back was turned. Tamzin found herself jostled and tripped by players who claimed it was only an accident. Perhaps it was also an accident that the padding kept slipping off the wooden swords and axes they trained with. By the session's end she was bruised all over.

Her quarters had been given to Aya Munoz, the Bad-luck girl whom Tamzin remembered crying with terror the night they fought Mortmain's dragon. The papers said Aya was Skip Recap's girlfriend, which Tamzin reckoned was a lie, since Skip liked boys, but the publicity had done neither of them any harm, so now Aya was a big star too, which was how she'd gotten Tamzin's old rooms.

Tamzin slept in a narrow cell too near the engine room, with a shackle on her ankle chained to a ringbolt on the wall beside the bunk. The others kept her awake at night by tapping on the pipes that ran through all their rooms.

"Rev's gonna get you, Tamzin Pook," their voices whispered in the long hours of the night, drifting through the air ducts like the voices of ghosts. "It's gonna slice you into fish food. Mortmain will take you on deck in a bucket. He'll throw you overboard to feed the eels."

She still had her sun pendant at least: They had not taken that from her. Curled up on her bunk, she clutched it for comfort as she had used to when she was younger and newly come to the Arcade. In those days, the pendant had been the only evidence she'd had that someone had ever cared for her. Now it made her think of Miss Torpenhow saying, "It is a token of the sun god Apollo . . . Rather unusual in our part of the world." And remembering that reminded her of Max, and Oddington Doom, and Trubshawe, and her memories of them kept her company, and saved her from despair. She could almost see their faces in her mind's eye, and the memory of their voices drowned out the mean-spirited whispering of her teammates. She was not alone anymore. Her friends would find some way to help her.

❊

"Mortmain won't feed me to the eels," Tamzin said in the dining room the next morning, her eyes dark-rimmed from lack of sleep. "He's got other plans for me. For all of us. He means to start using human brains inside those Revenants of his. And whose brains do you think they'll be? Dead Arcade slaves, that's who."

Some of the others looked uneasy, as well they should, thought Tamzin.

But Skip Recap laughed loudly and said, "That ain't true. Nobody's allowed to make human Revenants. All the cities agreed on it."

"Who'll stop Mortmain, if he wants to?" Tamzin demanded. "He sells his Revs to the government of Paris, and probably half the other great cities too. He's rich and powerful. He can do as he likes. Pretty soon getting killed in the Arcade won't mean the end. It'll just mean you get stuck inside a Rev. The only way out now is to get off Margate. I've got friends coming to help me. They could help you too."

"Oooh!" jeered the others, flicking gobs of porridge at her. "Tamzin Pook's got *friends!*"

Skip Recap silenced them just by standing up. "Why would anyone take the trouble to try and rescue you, Pook? You're a snake. Nobody trusts you. Nobody likes you. Everybody remembers what you did to Eve. When we get into the ring on Friday, you'd better watch yourself, because we'll be too busy looking after one another to care what the Rev does to you."

The others murmured their agreement, and fell to wondering what sort of monster Mortmain had cooked up for Friday. Tamzin finished her porridge and went under the watchful eyes of Mortmain's guards down to the fighters' gym, where she spent the rest of the morning trading blows with a mindless clockwork thing called the Quintain. Its feet were bolted to the deck and only its upper half moved, its three long arms waving three padded clubs she had to duck beneath to reach the kill switch on its torso. She had got so good at avoiding the clubs she had barely bothered with the Quintain in the year before Miss Torpenhow took her away. But somewhere on her travels she had lost the knack, and it knocked her down again and again.

At last, she gave up and lay on the deck, watching the clubs whirl by above her, wondering where Max and the others were. Skip was probably right. There was no reason why her friends would risk themselves to help her. She had done the thing they needed her to do. They might not even guess where she had gone. Even if they did, they could not afford a detour to Margate and a pointless fight with Mortmain's guards. Doom would say it was a bad strategy. Miss Torpenhow would say it was sad but unavoidable. Max would protest, but even he would have to admit that the plight of Thorbury was more important than Tamzin. And

Trubshawe would just be glad she was no longer around to tell everyone how bad his painting was.

But, however often she told herself this, she never quite believed it. She kept waiting for something to happen, for Oddington Doom to burst into the training hall and fetch her out, or Miss Torpenhow to arrive and give the overseers what for with her carpet bag.

It was a constant distraction, and Tamzin, distracted, found it impossible to return to the icy detachment that had made her such a menace to Mortmain's Revenants in the past. The Quintain knocked her down; her surly fellow fighters knocked her down; the trainers watched her fall and shook their heads and muttered that she'd lost her mojo.

The day before the show, the women's trainer, whose name was Wispa Naasti, visited the Bouncy Castle to tell Mortmain her concerns.

"The girl's not ready, boss. She needs another month."

"A kick up the backside is all she needs, Miss Naasti."

"Oh, she's had plenty of those, boss. And kicks and blows on every other part of her as well. Something's gone out of her. Or something new's got in. She won't be ready for the match tomorrow. She'll throw the others off their game too."

Mortmain shrugged, and ground out the cigar he had been smoking in an upturned seashell painted with the words A PRESENT FROM MARGATE. "Her name is on the signs," he said. "Her face is on the posters. Flyers have gone out to half the towns of the Fuel Country announcing that Tamzin Pook is returning to the Arcade tomorrow. So return she shall. We'll send her in alone, before the others, as an amuse-bouche for my new Revenant."

"A what, boss?'

198

"An appetizer, Miss Naasti. A tidbit to toy with, so the new machine can get a taste for blood before it has to fight in earnest."

"Oh, one of them," said Wispa Naasti, and limped away, shaking her head. She had fought in the Arcade herself until a Revenant's buzz-blade took her leg off. She'd been training fighters ever since. She was a hard woman, and she'd seen some ghastly things, but Mortmain's latest creation scared the wits out of her, she didn't mind admitting. She felt almost sorry for that poor Pook girl. But she consoled herself with the thought that at least it would be over quickly.

Evening was falling by that time. The illuminations were being lit on Margate's upper decks, and an airship the color of bonfires was circling the docks at the raft town's stern, awaiting permission to land.

34

MAXIMUM CONFUSION

I still think your plan is too complicated," said Max, peering through the raindrops on the gondola windows, and wishing the ill-fated worm smugglers had thought to fit the *Fire's Astonishment* with windshield wipers.

"That's your nerves talking," growled Oddington Doom, standing just behind him. "It's normal to feel nervous on an op like this, but you have to learn not to listen to your nerves. Step outside yourself. Make yourself calm."

"That's easy for you to say," grumbled Max, frowning as he eased the airship in toward a rusty mooring gantry. Ground crew in oilskin ponchos were waiting there to seize the ropes he lowered.

"Now here is why we need a complicated plan," said Doom as a group of armed men appeared out of the rain on the dock outside. "That's a lot of security for a raft resort. I'm guessing Dr. Mortmain hired those blokes after Hilly's last daring escapade."

"It was not so very daring," Miss Torpenhow said modestly from the bench seat at the stern of the gondola where she sat waiting with Trubshawe. "It was quite easy, really."

"Well, Mortmain's making sure it ain't going to be easy for anyone else to pull the same trick," said Doom. "And that is why we have to pull a different one."

Max extended the gangplank and he and Doom went down it into the rain, followed by Trubshawe. Miss Torpenhow waited in the gondola, keeping to the shadows, but still terribly afraid one of those men outside would look up and recognize her. They crowded around Doom as he stepped off the gangplank, demanding to know his name, his business, and whether he was bringing weapons aboard their town.

"Weapons?" asked Doom, all innocence, holding out his arms to let the men pat him down. "Do I look like I'd be carrying weapons? My name is Nutley Cluster, and this is my son Clem and our passenger, Mr. Trubshawe. We've come to see the big show at the Arcade tomorrow."

"You and half the rest of the Hunting Ground," grumbled one of the men. He wore an official-looking hat, and rain was dripping off the peak, so that he seemed to be peering at the newcomers through a veil of glass beads. "You got papers?"

They had papers, all proper and official. Mr. Trubshawe, when they came to him, said, "I am Giotto Trubshawe, artist at large, and I mean to capture your Amusement Arcade in pastel, as preparation for a great painting —"

"Whatever," said the customs men, searching his bag for concealed weapons and finding only pencils and sketchbooks. "And what about that ship of yours? There is a mooring fee, you know."

"Oh, the ship's just dropping us off," said Doom, and, sure enough, an aviatrix could be seen in the gondola, signaling to the ground crew to cast off. The *Fire's Astonishment* revved her idling engines, rose a little uncertainly, and took off toward the shore, where the lights of a few traction towns could be seen gleaming through the murk.

"Good girl, Hilly," murmured Doom, watching the airship fly away. "She learns fast, your governess."

Max said nothing. He was wishing he was still aboard the airship, not down here on this tacky town, where the decks rose and fell beneath his feet in a most disconcerting way. "I still don't see why we have to wait till tomorrow. Why not just blast our way into the players' barracks, rescue Tamzin, and blast our way out again?"

"Because there'd be a couple of dozen blokes blasting back at us, that's why," said Doom patiently. "And more locked doors than we could deal with too. The time to get Tamzin out is on her way to the Arcade tomorrow. Fewer guards. Maximum confusion. Trust me."

"Look," said Trubshawe, pointing to a tavern called the Short-Sighted Mermaid, with a sign outside announcing rooms to rent. "We can stop the night there. And perhaps we might share a bottle of wine to help us get the chill of this wretched rain out of our bones."

"Not me!" said Max hastily, remembering how ill he had felt in Djebel Tarik.

"Nor me," said Doom. "I need my wits about me for tomorrow."

"Oh, come on, old boy!" said Trubshawe, leading them toward the inn. He was even more full of himself than usual, after how easily the papers he had forged had fooled the Margate customs men. "Just one little glass of wine. Or maybe two. What harm could that possibly do?"

❉

The *Fire's Astonishment* flew westward through the rain. Miss Torpenhow kept the ship low, letting the line of white surf along the ragged shoreline guide her, and frequently checking the helpful labels that Max and Oddington Doom had pasted below the more important controls. Strange to think that a few months ago she had never set foot aboard a flying machine, and now here she was, piloting her own! She would have felt very proud of herself had she not been so nervous of doing something wrong, and so worried about her friends.

She wished she could have gone ashore on Margate with them. She knew she could not, for fear of being recognized, but she still felt as if she had been left out, the way her cousins used to leave her out of games when they were children, because she was a girl. What if something went wrong on the raft resort? What if it had *already* gone wrong? She had half a mind to pull that lever labeled RUDDER CONTROL, turn the airship around, and go back to help.

But she had promised to fly west, and she was the sort of person who kept her promises, however disagreeable. So the *Fire's Astonishment* flew onward through the rain while, on the dark land beneath her, clusters of lights turned into small towns, mostly heading east, probably hoping to catch tomorrow's show in the Arcade.

In times gone by, thought Miss Torpenhow, this coastline would have glittered with the electric lamps of Ancient settlements, and the million lighted windows of people who never bothered moving their towns at all. And in that way that sometimes happens to people who study history, she suddenly found herself looking at her own era as if from a great distance, and wondering what those Ancients would have made of her. She supposed it might seem very strange to them, this world where cities rolled about and ate up smaller ones.

"But no one gets a choice about which age they are born in," she told herself, thinking out loud to keep her spirits up. "We are all castaways, carried along for a while on the river of history. All we can do is enjoy the passing view, and do our best to help our fellow castaways, if we can."

The rain was slackening. Moonlight lay upon the sea below, and on the marshy pools and flooded track marks of the land. The Fire's Astonishment passed over the desolate island of Wight, and flew on into the west.

❋

Max knew he was dreaming, because in real life he could not swim. There had never seemed much point learning, living as he always had on the upper tiers of land-crawling cities. But here in his dream he was swimming like a fish, following Posie Naphtali down through swaying tresses of kelp into one of those Pacific deeps she'd told him of. And there, on a pale abyssal plain where the skeletons of whales and cities moldered, an immense octopus was waiting for him, with its long limbs strewn about it in the ooze like spilled intestines.

"Don't worry," said Posie Naphtali. She could breathe and speak underwater, it turned out. She wore the same pink polka-dot bathing suit as the mermaid on the sign outside the tavern where Max lay dreaming of her on a lumpy mattress. "He is a friend," she explained, and the octopus raised one of its disgusting tentacles and patted Max's face, then wrapped it around him and began to shake him till he came awake with a shout, and realized it was not an octopus who had him in its grasp, but an artist.

"Wake up, Angmering!" Trubshawe was saying. "It's a disaster!"

Max rolled off the hard little bed, rubbing his eyes to rid himself of the memories of his dream. The details were fading fast, but the unsettling atmosphere remained. "What's wrong?" he asked, glancing at the door, the window. "Is Mortmain onto us? Are we discovered?"

"No, no, nothing like that!" said Trubshawe. "It's that blighter Doom! He's as drunk as a skunk!"

"What's a skunk?"

"I don't know — some extinct animal that was partial to a drink, I suppose."

"But he was all right when — " said Max, pulling on his coat and boots and following Trubshawe down the winding stairs to the larger room that he and Doom had shared. Doom had been all right when Max said good night to them both; they had been sitting in a quiet corner of the bar, enjoying what Trubshawe promised was just one glass before they retired to bed.

"But one glass turned into two," said Trubshawe, "and then we thought it was a shame not to finish the bottle, and then Doom ordered whiskey, and then I went to bed. But I suppose Doom thought it would be a shame not to finish that bottle too, and now look . . ."

Doom lay sprawled across the rumpled bed, snoring thunderously. Trubshawe splashed water on his face. Max drew back the curtains and opened the window to let in the raucous dawn chorus of Margate's gulls, but the old soldier did not stir. Only when Max slapped him hard across the face did he half open his one eye and mumble something about a cauliflower, before going back to sleep.

"Even if he does wake up," groaned Trubshawe, "he'll be no

use for anything today. I've got a bit of a morning head myself, but poor old Doom's going to feel as if he's been hit by a Slow Bomb. What are we going to do? What about the plan? Should we call it off?"

"The plan!" said Max, who had forgotten it. "What time was the rendezvous?"

"Seven thirty. But Doom's in no state to —"

Max snatched up Doom's battered old pocket watch from the bedside cabinet. Seven fifteen. Outside the window, through a gap between the neighboring buildings, Tamzin's face stared sullenly at him from a poster advertising that afternoon's show in the Arcade.

"I'll go," he said. "Get some coffee or something into him, and give me the map you drew."

Two minutes later, he was making his way aft along the raft town's greasy decks, clutching the plan that Trubshawe had copied from the books in the governor's library in Djebel Tarik, and praying that it was accurate. Margate, being a party city, was mostly asleep until midmorning, so the only people he passed were street sweepers clearing up the litter of the previous night's revelries, and a few revelers stumbling back, bleary-eyed, to their hotels. Neither group paid any attention to him as he went down to the midlevel and then down again, by rusty metal stairways, to the engine deck.

The engines were sleeping too, and the narrow streets between them were empty as Max followed the map toward the town's edge. There, in the shadow of the massive paddle wheel, a ramp of wet timbers led down into the water. It was used for the launching of maintenance boats, which waited in a chained-off enclosure nearby. Another chain was stretched across the top of the ramp, with a notice hung from it to say NO ENTRY. No one was watching but the gulls, so Max climbed over the chain and went carefully down the slope to where the oily wavelets lapped.

It was 7:26. He waited, crouched there, horribly aware of all the windows in the rusty buildings that rose behind him, and all the eyes that might look down and see him there. Seven twenty-seven. Seven twenty-eight.

They are not coming, he thought. *Something has gone wrong. It hasn't worked.* And maybe it didn't matter. Maybe Tamzin Pook didn't need rescuing, and wouldn't want him here. Maybe she would be glad to be a star again, with her face blown up big as a building, staring in at people's windows. Maybe . . .

But at 7:30, just as they had arranged back in Djebel Tarik, the water at the ramp's foot swirled and seethed as if a tangle of fat worms was writhing there, and the worms became an octopus — Thomas, he thought. The creature had taken on the color and texture of the ramp's slimy timbers, and raised up sections of his skin into sharp-looking peaks, like whipped meringue, which had turned the orange and russet of rusty metal. He looked up at Max with his gilded eyes, and the bundle he was towing bumped gently against the timbers of the ramp.

Max dragged the bundle out of the water. It was an oilcloth bag, with cork floats tied around it to stop it sinking to the bottom, but not so many that it floated on the surface. Something inside it clanked weightily. The octopus watched him. Max wished he'd paid more attention to the sign language Dr. Naphtali used to communicate with the creatures. As it was, all he could do was wave.

"Tell Posie we'll see her soon," he said, as if Thomas could understand him. Could he even hear him? Did octopuses have ears? He would have to ask Posie, he thought. But he could not do that until the Haile Maryam surfaced to take the rescue party off. There was a whole complicated plan to put into action before that. With Doom out of the picture, Max was not sure any of it would work.

Thomas — Max was pretty sure it was Thomas — slid off the launching ramp like phlegm, and the sea swallowed him. Gulls wheeled and shrieked. With luck, Posie's other octopus would be delivering a second package on the far side of the town about now, the distraction that would enable Max and his friends to get away once the operation was complete. If it didn't . . .

But there was no point worrying about that until the time came. Max shouldered the bundle and started back up through the town. He felt that everyone he passed must know at a glance what was inside the oilcloth. But no one stopped him, and when he got back to the Short-Sighted Mermaid with his prize he found Doom sitting up in bed, while Trubshawe made him drink black coffee.

"The octopus came through," said Max. "Bang on time, just like Posie promised." He threw the wet bundle down on the floor and opened it. There were three layers of oilcloth, with a plastic bag inside. Within that, wrapped in more plastic, were knives, guns, bullets, percussion caps, and a pair of heavy-duty wire cutters.

"So far, so good," said Trubshawe hopefully, and Max grinned at him, feeling suddenly lighthearted, suddenly sure again their plan would work.

"Uuuuuuurgh," said Oddington Doom. Which they took to mean that he agreed.

35

SURVIVING CONTACT WITH REALITY

There was a plan. It had been worked out over strong coffee and sweet pastries in Kush Tundurbai's palace. In the sunlight of the Middle Sea, it had seemed pretty watertight.

Margate and its Master of Amusements had long been of interest to the Anti-Traction League's intelligence agents, since captured League personnel sometimes ended up in the Arcade. There were detailed reports about the place, which Tundurbai had been happy to share. According to the League's informants, the Arcade was heavily guarded. So were the barracks farther aft where the slaves lived and trained. But half an hour before each show began, when the fighters were escorted through a covered walkway to the Arcade's backstage area, they crossed an open section called "the paddock" where fans could gather to get a look at them.

Oddington Doom reckoned the paddock was the weak point. "The fighters are only escorted by four men. That's where we'll get Tamzin out."

Watching him circle the paddock in red pencil on Trubshawe's map, Max had felt as if the rescue was already accomplished. They would ambush the party, Tamzin and her friends would help to overpower the four guards, and they would all fight their way together down to the same slipway where he had met the octopus that morning. There the *Haile Maryam* would surface to pick them up. It felt as neat and right as a good story, and since Mortmain and his thugs were so obviously the story's villains, and he and Doom and Trubshawe so plainly its heroes, it did not occur to Max that they might fail, or that he himself might be captured, or wounded, or even killed.

At least, those things had not occurred to him when the plan was being laid, while he ate pistachio-nut pastries and looked down from the heights of the Rock at sun speckles swarming on the Middle Sea. They had not even occurred to him that morning, while he and Trubshawe did their best to sober up Oddington Doom with pots of black coffee and a massive fried breakfast.

Now, as he pushed his way through the crowds on Margate's cluttered upper deck, he realized with a kind of sick horror that he might not be this story's hero after all. What if he was just the brave fool who tried to defeat the villain, and died a horrid death? For all he knew, the real hero was somebody he had not even met, someone stronger, wiser, and better looking, who was still waiting in the wings and would be along to avenge him later. But small comfort that would be to Max, who would be a ghost in the Sunless Country by then. Following Doom and Trubshawe through the stench of the fried fish stalls and doughnut stands outside the Arcade, it was all he could do to stop himself from throwing up.

The Arcade looked like a condemned wedding cake: a white building that rose in many overdecorated tiers, all drizzled with gull droppings and scoured by the salt sea winds. The echoing ticket hall inside the entrance seethed with spectators, queuing for tickets, queuing for snacks, queuing for the toilets, queuing to lay bets on which of today's fighters would survive.

"There is the place!" said Trubshawe, pointing to a doorway labeled PADDOCK. Max paid for their tickets, and they followed the sign down ten stairs and along a corridor lined with posters for old fights. They emerged on an open windswept section of deck behind the Arcade. There was a fenced-off section about thirty feet long, walled and roofed with rusty wire mesh. At one end of it was the entrance to a covered walkway; at the other loomed the door of the Arcade's backstage area.

The place was already crowded. Fans of Skip Recap and Aya Munoz were waiting by the fence to throw flowers to them and wish them good luck. Gambling men in gaudy suits were waiting to see if any of the fighters looked off-color or particularly confident.

Trubshawe pushed his way through them all to a place at the fence, saying in his loudest and most self-important voice, "Let me through! I am an artist. I am here to capture this event in all its tragic grandeur . . ."

Surprisingly, nobody punched him on the nose. Max and Doom went after him before the crowd closed in again, and stood close behind him while he fussily set up his little folding stool and sat down on it. Opening a sketchbook, he began to draw the view of the paddock. "I am planning a grand painting of the fighters on their way to battle," he said as he worked, to any of the crowd who might be listening. "Some brave and noble, some half fainting with fear; the grim faces of the guards; a beautiful girl who glances up at us, hoping perhaps to catch a glimpse of her lover, who has come to rescue her . . ."

"Fighters don't get rescued from the Arcade," said a woman scornfully. "It ain't possible. The Master of Amusements has guards all over. If they caught somebody trying to do any rescuing, he'd be chucked in the arena himself, as a mouse for Mortmain's cats to play with."

"Really?" said Trubshawe, looking pale. "Well — ah — never mind; it is artistic license. A work of art must have some hope in it, or it is scarcely art at all."

"There's not much hope for Tamzin Pook today," said one of the gamblers to another. "I heard Mortmain's sending her in first, as an amuse-bouche for his new Revenant."

"What's an *amuse-bouche*?"

"It's a kind of snack. Don't you know nothin'?"

"I heard this new Revenant's his fiercest yet."

"Quiet! Here they come!"

A silence fell on the crowd. The tramp of footsteps echoed from the covered walkway. Max glanced at Doom, who was standing beside him. The plan was for Doom to cut a way through the wire, so that the three of them could burst into the paddock and free the fighters. But Doom was asleep again, his face gray, his eye closed. He was being held upright only by the press of the crowd around him.

"Doom!" hissed Max. Realizing he would have to do something himself, he reached inside Doom's coat and groped around until he found the wire cutters. The crowd was pushing forward, all eyes on the walkway, everyone waiting for a glimpse of the fighters. Max crouched down with the cutters and began snipping the strands of mesh, starting at the bottom. He worked fast, the rusty wire parting easily under the blades: one strand, then another, and a third, and —

"'Ere! 'Ere! 'E's cutting the fence!" screeched the woman who had spoken to Trubshawe.

A fourth strand parted, then a fifth. Three more, Max reckoned, and there would be a gap just large enough to squeeze through. But mutterings of disapproval were spreading through the crowd. Shouting Tamzin's name, Max threw himself against the mesh, but he had not cut enough of the wires and he simply rebounded. Doom, awake now but still decidedly groggy, fished in another pocket and brought out a pistol, but one of the gamblers grabbed his wrist before he could raise it.

"This one's got a gun!"

"Assassins!"

"Anti-Tractionists!"

Contrary currents surged through the crowd. Some people were trying to get as far as possible from Doom, some were struggling forward to help capture him, and some had not noticed what was happening at all and were still shoving for a view of the paddock. Pressed up against the mesh, Max saw the players emerge from the tunnel: a group of young men and women, looking very much as Trubshawe had described, led by two guards with guns and more behind. He glimpsed Tamzin, near the back of the group, glancing around with an irritated frown at the commotion.

"Tamzin! Tamzin Pook!" he yelled.

Someone thrust him aside, eager to get a look themselves. Doom was struggling in the grip of half a dozen guards. More guards had seized Trubshawe.

"There was another one!" a man yelled. "Where's the young one gone?"

Max dropped to his knees and crawled through a forest of legs. Someone kicked him. Someone had dropped a cheap felt hat with

KISS ME QUICK printed on the band. Max snatched the hat and crammed it on his head. He wrestled his jacket off and let it fall behind him. No one seemed to recognize him when he surfaced in a new part of the crowd. Guards were blowing whistles over by the wires he'd cut, clearing people aside so they could search for him. Doom and Trubshawe were both prisoners. There was nothing Max could do but watch as they were bundled back along the corridor and up the stairs to the ticket hall.

Max went after them. Not through choice, or out of some delusional belief that he could help them, but simply because the guards behind him were clearing the paddock and the whole crowd was funneling back down the corridor, carrying him with it. By the time he reached the ticket hall, there was no sign of his friends, but guards were hurrying around everywhere, so he did not look too hard, just pulled his new hat down to hide his face and kept moving, shuffling along with the rest of the crowd toward the arched opening that led into the arena. In his trouser pocket, he still had the strip of pink paper tickets. He tore one off and handed it to the woman at the door, who ripped it in two and gave him one half back without looking at him.

And then he was in the heart of the Arcade. He found a seat, and sat there trembling while the seats around him filled with loud, excited spectators who did not notice him. Below him, men were raking the sawdust on the oval fighting floor where Tamzin Pook would soon be fighting for her life.

Reason told him he should leave now and save himself, because Thorbury needed him. Once the show started and everyone was watching the action, he reckoned it would be easy to slip out unnoticed. And in another few minutes they would be even more distracted, for there was one last part of the plan that might still work, even though the rest had gone to pieces. If it did, he could get off Margate in the confusion and no one would blame him for leaving Tamzin, Doom, and Trubshawe to their fates.

But what would that make him? What Thorbury needed was a hero, not someone who left his friends to die. He had to stay. He had to help Tamzin. Even though he was alone, and he did not know how, and was not sure whether he had the courage.

36

IN THE DEAD CORNER

Tamzin thought she heard someone shout her name as she came out of the tunnel into the sudden sunlight of the paddock. But some sort of scuffle broke out among the watchers up above, so she could not see who had shouted it, and so many other voices were yelling the names of other fighters that she could not be sure she had heard it at all.

Then the guards in front opened the stage door, the guards behind urged the fighters through it, and Tamzin was back in the cluttered backstage space where she had waited so often before.

But never like this. Never so nervously as this. She tried and tried to find that old, cold numbness in herself that had allowed her to face Mortmain's creations without fear, but it was gone. The things that had happened to her out there in the world had made her a different person. A better person, maybe — a happier one, perhaps — but one far less capable of surviving the Arcade.

A burly stagehand loomed over her. It was Nobby Murk, a brutish-looking man, but not a bad one — he always did his best to look after the players, and Tamzin had seen him weep over their deaths in the past.

"Good luck," he said, pressing her favorite electric blade into her hands, then going round to fit the battery pack onto her belt. "You're on first today."

"Just me?"

"Mortmain's orders."

That was not good. Arcade fighters did not fight alone. The only ones who went out solo were condemned criminals, who served to test the Revenants' mettle and get the crowd's bloodlust up before the main event. Fighters who went out solo never came back again.

Nobby knew it too. His big hand gripped Tamzin's shoulder for a moment, saying goodbye. "You're a good kid, Pook," he said.

The other fighters were in a huddle, talking tactics, making plans. Few of them even glanced at Tamzin as she took her place inside the arena door. She remembered how she had told them her friends would come for her, and how they had laughed, and how they had been right. What a fool she had been to hope. No one was coming for her. No one had her back. She did feel numb now, but it was the wrong sort of numbness, as if she were already dead.

The door slid up. Nobby did not push her forward as he should, so a guard stepped up and gave her a hard shove in the back, which sent her stumbling out into the sawdust and the roar. The Arena was in darkness as usual, but a follow-spot on the high roof swung around to pin her in its cone of light. Another fingered Dr. Mortmain in his gaudy robes and massive silver turban, who stood a few yards off, in the center of the arena.

That was new, thought Tamzin. He was usually safe up in his box. She gripped the handle of her knife and wondered. But the door behind her was still open, and the armed guards waited,

217

watchful, there. She guessed she would make it no more than half-way to Mortmain before they cut her down.

Out of the shadowy dome above them a silver microphone came dropping on a long cable like a spider on a thread. Mortmain caught it, and his voice boomed out around the arena, quieting the cheers and jeers and laughter of the crowd.

"Ladies and gentlemen . . ." he said, and waited for total silence before going on.

"Ladies and gentlemen, we will begin this afternoon's presentation with single combat. A display of skill and savagery such as few of us have ever witnessed . . ."

There were cheers again. Again, Mortmain waited.

"In the red corner," he said at last, flinging out one hand toward Tamzin, "is a fighter who needs no introduction. Tamzin Pook has been sadly absent for several weeks, but she is now restored to us. She has survived forty-nine shows here in the Arcade. Will she survive her fiftieth?"

"YES!" roared the crowd, and "NO!", and "TAM-ZIN POOK! TAM-ZIN POOK!"

Mortmain smiled, turning in a circle, eyes on the wall of faces above him. "And in the *dead* corner," he said, "another fighter some of you know well. Perhaps you were here when she was mortally wounded on this very spot. She was taken from the Arcade straight to my workshop. There we installed in her dead brain a device from before the Sixty Minute War: a device that had the power to call her back. Just like Miss Pook, she learned that no one leaves the Arcade. And so here she is, returning from the Sunless Country to take her revenge. Ladies and gentlemen, please give a very warm Margate welcome to the late, the great *Eve Vespertine*."

He took a firm grip on the microphone cable and it lifted him up out of the ring as the door on the far side opened. Through it stepped his newest Revenant. The crowd forgot to cheer. Max Angmering, busy steeling himself for what he had to do, forgot for a moment even to breathe. A shocked murmur ran around the Arcade as everyone leaned forward to see what Mortmain's art and science had made from the corpse of Eve Vespertine.

She was taller and broader than the living Eve had been: armored all over in shiny blue metal like the bodywork of an Ancient ground-car, with gleaming chromium trim. Bizarrely, though, she still had her long red hair, and her own face, although it was gray and expressionless and her eyes were hidden behind goggles whose lenses glowed with a green light.

That is the weak point, Tamzin thought, stowing away her shock and trying to size up her opponent as the new Revenant walked slowly toward her. The armor looked too tough to pierce, but Mortmain had been forced to leave the face bare to show the crowd this thing really had been Eve. The face was the place into which Tamzin would have to drive her knife.

But, even as she thought that, she knew she could not do it. She remembered something the dreadful Mr. Lint had said: It was one thing to kill a Revenant, but quite another to stick a blade into a human being. And, although she knew Eve Vespertine *was* only a Revenant now, she still *looked* like Eve. And wasn't it Tamzin's fault she had died in the first place? That was what the gods had been punishing her for, dragging her on a switchback ride of good luck and bad like cats toying with a mouse. She could not kill Eve *again.*

"Let the grudge match begin!" boomed Mortmain, swinging

overhead on the microphone cable. "For years we have been told by wise men in the great cities that we must not build Revenants in human form. But why should the great cities tell us what to do? This is Margate, where Amusement is everything!"

The cable deposited him safely in his box above the arena, where various important visitors and Margate bigwigs were waiting to congratulate him as he took his seat between this year's Miss Margate and the mayor.

The crowd, finding its voice again, began to cheer. Max twisted around in his seat to check the time by the clock above the exit, and prayed it was correct.

The new Revenant, with a sort of shrug, unsheathed a cruel-looking blade that was housed inside its forearm. It held the blade up and looked at it, as if it were surprised to find it there. It turned it this way and that, admiring the way reflections of the arena lights trickled along the sharp edges.

Tamzin glanced behind her, with some vague idea of running, but the door into the backstage area had shut. She could see faces at the small viewing windows there. Skip Recap and the other fighters and the guards and stagehands were all jostling one another for a view of the fight.

The Revenant had finished admiring its weaponry. It circled Tamzin, confident but cautious, drawing slowly closer. Tamzin turned with it, watching. Its name, VESPERTINE, was written on the breastplate of its armor in raised silver script. Its bottle-glass goggles were bolted to its face. Behind them, unpleasantly, Tamzin could see Eve Vespertine's dead eyes. They did not appear to be looking at her, but something in there was.

"You are Tamzin Pook," said the Revenant. Its voice was a whisper and a creak, like wind in dead branches. Some contraption

220

clicked and hissed as it worked the dead jaw. The microphone on its spider cable came swinging overhead again, for Mortmain wanted everyone to hear. None of his creations had ever spoken before.

"I am here to kill you," said the Revenant Vespertine. She spoke flatly, without feeling. Tamzin guessed she was parroting lines the stagehands had fed her. "I have come for my revenge."

"Better get on with it, then," said Tamzin. She kept thinking of Max and Miss Torpenhow, and how she would never see them again, and the pity of that made tears come into her eyes so that the hulking Revenant in front of her was just a blur. She reached behind her and unhitched the battery pack from her belt. She threw her knife aside, and the pack with it. She stood unarmed, and waited for the Revenant to kill her.

Up in the cheap seats, Max saw that he could wait no longer. He stood up. He climbed over the back of the seat in front of him, then over the next, shoving his way between the people who sat there.

"Sit down!" someone yelled.

"Get out the way — we can't see!"

"What are you playing at?"

"Get off, you loon!"

Angry voices drifted down into the arena. The Revenant looked up, seeking the source of the disturbance. Tamzin risked a sideways glance too, and was just in time to see someone half jump, half tumble over the railing above the arena and drop down into the sawdust. He wore a white shirt and a stupid hat. Tamzin knew him instantly.

"Max!" she shouted, astonished that he had really followed her to Margate, and then pleased that he had, more pleased and happy than she had ever been, and then appalled, because now Max was in the same peril she was.

The Revenant swung around, reacting to this new threat. It hissed, a dangerous sound, half cobra, half gas leak, mostly drowned out by the boos and jeers of the crowd as Max stumbled to his feet and came crabwise across the sawdust toward Tamzin. KISS ME QUICK said his stupid hat. His mouth was saying something else, but Tamzin couldn't hear it over the mass of voices chanting, "Kill them! Kill them!"

"Don't hurt him!" Tamzin begged, raising her empty hands, speaking loudly enough to draw the Revenant's attention back to her. The numbness of a moment earlier had vanished. She was her old self again, determined to keep her teammate safe. Max snatched up the knife she had thrown away, but she turned fast and tripped him, grabbing the knife back as he fell, hurling it farther still, well out of reach.

"You can't fight it," she told him. "Don't let it see you as a threat. Run to the door there. Get backstage and you'll be safe."

"And what about you?" asked Max. "I came to help you. We all did — Doom and Trubshawe are here too, but it's all gone wrong. They're prisoners . . ."

Tamzin wished she hadn't thrown the knife so far out of reach. She had been thinking only of keeping Max alive, but now she wanted to live too.

Max was staring past her at the Revenant. "If you can just hold it off for a minute, Doom's plan might still work. Well, part of it."

"Hold it off?" said Tamzin, watching the Revenant, waiting for it to strike.

"Talk to it, like you did that dog-thing back in Paris."

222

"This is no dog," said Tamzin. "Look at her. She's not going to sit down and roll over when I tell her."

But there was something doglike about the way the Revenant tipped her head to one side, as if wondering what they were talking about. Tamzin thought of the Daunt, of how its doggish character had lingered even inside all that armor and mad science. Was there some trace of Eve still, trapped inside this looming thing? If there was, she surely wouldn't be happy about what she had become.

The crowd was growing bored. Mortmain, through a second microphone mounted in his box, said teasingly, "Ladies! A little less chitchat, if you please. Let's get down to business. Chop-chop!"

The Revenant looked upward, not sure where the amplified voice was coming from.

"That's Mortmain," said Tamzin. "You want revenge? Mortmain's your man. He's why we're here. He's the one who made you like this. Mortmain's the one who makes us fight."

"Why?"

Tamzin shrugged. "It's show business."

"Mortmain," said the Revenant. The green light behind its goggles grew brighter, as if the boos from the crowd were fueling it.

"That's good!" said Max. "If you can just keep it occupied for another twenty seconds, there's going to be —"

The deck under Tamzin's feet flinched like a fly-stung horse. An ominous rumble echoed through the Arcade, louder than the crowd. Dust sifted down through the spotlight beams, and the microphone on its long cable swung to and fro. A woman in the cheap seats screamed. Somebody shouted, "An explosion!" Someone else yelled, "flames," but Tamzin could see no fire.

"Or maybe sooner," said Max. "The clock must be slow . . ."

Tamzin had no idea what he was on about. Mortmain was on his feet again, calling for calm, but no one could hear him amid the growing panic.

"Revenge," said the Revenant suddenly, lashing out. Tamzin saw the blow coming from the corner of her eye, a flash of light on chrome and blue metal. She ducked and let out a squeak of terror, but the big, blue-armored hand passed harmlessly above her and snatched the microphone as it swung past. Crushed in an iron fist, the microphone burst with a crackle and a sudden, loud-seeming silence. The Revenant reached up its other hand and seized the cable.

Tamzin turned and fled, shouting for Max to follow her as she ran to the stage door. Nobby Murk opened it and let them into the backstage area, which was full of milling bodies.

"An explosion!" someone said. "The starboard-side paddle wheel blew up! There's fire . . ."

"It's all right," Max told Tamzin. "It was part of the plan. Posie's octopuses placed a bomb, just big enough to cause a distraction while we got off the town . . ."

"Posie's here?" Tamzin shook her head, dazed with it all.

"Of course," said Max, trying his best to sound nonchalant and capable. "You got me out of the Oubliette, didn't you? I'm returning the favor."

"What is that Revenant doing?" asked Skip Recap suddenly, grabbing Tamzin by both shoulders and turning her so she could see out through the viewing window into the arena.

The Revenant was climbing the microphone cable. Up, up, hand over armored hand, swinging through the stage lights, in wider and wider arcs, while the steep rows of seating swarmed like a kicked ants' nest with people desperate to escape the imaginary fire and others desperate to escape the all-too-real Revenant.

The cable must have been very strongly tethered, or Mortmain would never have trusted it to hoist him up and down. But under the weight of the Revenant something up above gave way. Debris fell, adding to the stampede. The cable whipped across the arena. The Revenant flew into the lowest row of seats, throwing up more debris. After a few seconds, Tamzin caught the green glow of its eyes as it unfolded itself from the wreckage and started to make its way to Mortmain's box.

"It wants revenge," said Tamzin. She started to laugh, mostly out of surprise that she was still alive to watch all this. "It's going after Mortmain!"

They spilled out into the arena: Tamzin, Max, the other fighters, the guards, the stagehands, all one now in their amazement. The world seemed upside down: The fighters standing on the sawdust had become spectators; the action and the violence were happening above. People scrambled over the seats and over each other to reach the exit doors. The guards stationed around Mortmain's box were firing pistols at the Revenant. Their bullets missed it, or ricocheted off its armor adding to the panic of the crowd. The Revenant lumbered on. If anyone got in its way, it shoved them aside, or tossed them casually over the parapet into the arena. Some were so keen to escape it that they just jumped. The guards threw down their guns and fled.

"We should help her!" yelled one of the fighters.

The others looked uncertain, but a few ran forward. Tamzin and Max went with them. One of their guards raised his gun, but Nobby Murk knocked him sprawling. The others made no effort to stop the fighters as they ran across the arena to swarm up the loops of microphone cable that trailed from the wrecked section of seating.

It was a hard climb. Tamzin almost did not make it, but as she neared the top Skip Recap reached down over the shattered balcony where the Revenant had landed, gripped her hand, and hauled her up to join him. She was too startled to thank him. Max came after her, and they all moved together along the curve of the seating over trampled bodies, lost shoes, spilled cartons of popcorn, until they reached the splintered ruin of the box. The Revenant had not bothered with the door, simply walked straight through the wall, leaving a Revenant-shaped hole.

The other fighters hung back when they heard the noises coming from inside. Tamzin edged forward and peeked in through ripped velvet curtains.

The lights had gone out by then, but into the shoulder-pieces of the Revenant's armor Mortmain had set twin headlamps in chrome housings, and they lit up the dreadful scene well enough. Bodies and upturned chairs lay strewn about like toys flung down by a toddler in a tantrum. The mayor cowered behind a drinks trolley. Miss Margate was screaming. Mortmain was backed up against the far wall.

"Revenge," the Revenant said.

Bathed in the glare of its shoulder lamps, Mortmain gaped up at his creation like a deer caught in the lights of an oncoming suburb. "Yes, yes," he whimpered. "Revenge! You shall have it! But on Tamzin Pook, not me! She's the one who killed you, Vespertine! Not me! Not me! I brought you back! I made you as you are now. Look at what you have become! So strong, so beautiful . . ."

The Revenant seemed to consider this. It shrugged and sheathed the bloody blade that lived inside its arm. Mortmain, with a flicker of his old confidence, started to say something more. But, before he could finish, the Revenant picked him up and, although he was a big man, whirled him twice around its head and flung him through the glass window of the box. His flailing hand grabbed hold of its long red hair as he fell, but the hair was only a wig; it tore easily from the Revenant's head. Mortmain went through the shattering glass with a terrified shriek, and fell with a nasty thud into the sawdust below, where so many of his slaves had died.

The Revenant turned away. Its blood-slick blue armor had been dented in several places by bullets. Its bare scalp was grayish and crisscrossed with scars where Mortmain had opened it to insert his contraptions. A few devices that had been too big to fit inside Eve Vespertine's skull protruded slightly through holes rimmed with scar tissue. Tamzin, meeting the thing's marsh-gas gaze, felt suddenly and awfully sorry for it.

"Revenge," the Revenant said, but it did not sound any longer like a threat. It just seemed a bit disappointed that slaughtering Mortmain and his hangers-on had not brought it satisfaction.

"He's dead," said Tamzin, going to the window and looking down at Mortmain, spread-eagled in the sawdust like a broken toy. "It's over." But she had a nasty feeling it was not just Mortmain on whom Eve Vespertine's Revenant wanted revenge, but the person who had caused her death as well. And she felt a sudden, suicidal urge to tell it, It was me; it was my fault. I'm the one you want.

Someone tugged at Tamzin's arm. It was Skip Recap. "Come on, Pook. Before it kills us too. The others are heading outside. You heard that bang earlier? There's been an explosion . . . Whole town's sinking."

"No, no, it was only a small bomb," Max protested. "It was just a diversion, part of Doom's plan. We're here to rescue you all . . ."

Tamzin glanced back. The Revenant just stood there, looking at her, as if it were waiting for her to tell it what to do next. Tamzin did not know what she should say to it, and before she could think of anything it turned and smashed a way for itself through the wall, vanishing into the shadows beyond. Tamzin watched it go. Then, with Max at her side, she hurried after Skip and the others, out into sunlight and the smell of burning.

37

TROUBLED WATERS

It was always strange to emerge from the darkness of the Arcade after a show and find it still daylight outside. It was stranger still today, with gray smoke billowing across Margate's decks and panic and confusion everywhere. Tamzin stayed close to Max, afraid that she might lose him in the swirling crowds. Above the smoke, the sky was full of airships and balloons carrying visitors from other towns home to safety. But the danger was past, it seemed; the mysterious explosion that had reduced the starboard paddle wheel to twisted wreckage had set fire to its wooden housing too, but the Margate fire brigade had already doused the flames. Groups of onlookers stood exchanging the latest rumors as they watched hoses play over the ruins.

"It was a raiding party from the Anti-Traction League. Three of them tried to get to the Arcade slaves in the paddock earlier — they caught two, but one escaped. He must have let off that bomb . . ."

Max, hearing this as he passed, doubled back and grabbed the man who'd spoken. "Where are they? The two who were caught?"

❊

They were penned in a locked-up shed near the rear entrance to the Arcade. Mortmain's guards had thrown them in there before the show began, and they had been forgotten in the confusion. Tamzin found a wrench in a nearby workshop and smashed the padlock off.

Trubshawe was the first to recover the power of speech. "Miss Pook! You're alive!"

"Reckon so," said Tamzin, looking down at herself to check, "but it's hard to tell. There are people wandering around this town who aren't. Not Mortmain, though — he's dead and gone, and good riddance." She hesitated, not sure how to deal with the love and gratitude she felt. "You came. All this way. You came to rescue me . . ."

"We meant to free you before you got to the arena," said Max, "but Mr. Doom was taken ill . . ."

"It was a passing thing," growled Doom, who looked about as healthy as Eve Vespertine. "It would not have mattered if you had used those wire cutters with a bit more gusto . . ."

"Nobody could have cut those wires in time!"

"I could," snarled Doom. "It is only that you went at it like a milksop, and gave the townsfolk time to catch us." He scowled. He was ashamed of himself, which was making him lash out at Max, which he knew was unfair, which was making him feel more ashamed, which was making him lash out more — it was a vicious circle.

"The explosion was supposed to go off when we'd got you and your teammates down to the lower deck," said Max. "It was meant to provide confusion and draw everyone's attention to the starboard side so Captain Kardos could come in close on the port side and take us off. But of course we fluffed our part of the plan, so . . ."

"It did provide confusion," admitted Tamzin. "You rescued me."

"But we were planning to rescue all the Arcade fighters," said Max. "We thought they might fight for us, in Thorbury."

"You could still ask them," said Tamzin.

They walked together through the town. There was a mingled sense of shock and carnival about the place. Margate's main source of income lay in ruins, the Master of Amusements was dead, and the rogue Revenant who had murdered him was still on the loose. Some prankster had popped the Bouncy Castle. Its colorful towers were wilting slowly with a sound like a choir of mournful whoopee cushions. But on the plus side, those members of the audience who had survived the stampede would have quite a story to tell, and the Arcade fighters were being carried shoulder high around the top deck by their fans.

When Max put his proposal to them, they considered it, then shook their heads. Some were already looking for air-traders who could carry them to the homelands from which they'd been taken; others, like Skip Recap, had no intention of going anywhere.

"You think we'd give up all this?" he asked, and, looking around at the crowd of fans and well-wishers, Tamzin had to admit life aboard Margate might well be more attractive than a journey to Thorbury with a battle at the end of it.

Ultra-Violent Violet had found the mayor, and was leading him around by his gold chain of office like a dog on a leash. "We're going to get the Arcade up and running again, but on better terms this time. We'll be free fighters now, with a full share of the profits."

"And no Revenants?" asked Tamzin.

"Mortmain's assistants will keep the old ones running," said the mayor, looking sly.

In truth, he was hoping Mortmain himself might keep the

Revenants in business. After all, if Mortmain had brought Eve Vespertine back to life, might not Mortmain's assistants know how to do the same with Mortmain? But when he sent his people down to salvage Mortmain's body later they found a Mortmain-shaped depression in the sawdust where he had fallen, and a trail of blood leading from there to the nearest exit, but no Mortmain. The doctor had survived Eve Vespertine's revenge, it seemed. But where he had gone, no one knew.

By that time, the sun was dipping westward, and Tamzin and her rescuers were on their way to rendezvous with the *Haile Maryam*. Rather than shove their way back through the crowds on the top deck, they went forward to the bows, where a broad staircase descended to the lower decks. At its top, among a scattering of coin-operated telescopes and I-speak-your-weight machines, the thing that had been Eve Vespertine stood like an unsightly figurehead, gazing out to sea.

It did not look around when they came upon it. It did not seem to notice them at all as they edged past it and went quickly and quietly down the stairs. But before they reached the middle deck Tamzin's conscience got the better of her, and she turned back. She thought she understood how the new Revenant must feel, adrift for the first time in the wide, confusing world outside the Arcade. Perhaps helping it was the only way she could atone for what had happened to Eve Vespertine.

She laid her hand on the chromium exhaust grille in the Revenant's back and it turned its dead face to her, its eyes like two jellyfish in a dim aquarium. "If you're looking for another battle," said Tamzin, "you could stay here and play-fight with Skip and that lot in the Arcade. Or you could come with us."

"I want revenge," said Vespertine. "Killing the loud man

Mortmain was not enough. The feeling is still in me."

It is me, thought Tamzin. It is me she needs to kill before she can be at peace. And she reflected on just how dangerous it would be if she took the Revenant with her and it worked that out. But at the same time, she had to consider how useful a Revenant would be to Max and Miss Torpenhow when they got back to Thorbury.

"Max wants revenge too," she said. "You can help him get it. He has a whole city to capture, and all he has to help him are Mr. Doom, who gets drunk, and Mr. Trubshawe, who's an artist, and Miss T, and me. So you'd be a big help, Vespertine. You were a good fighter when you were alive, and you're even better now. You're like a one-person army."

She ran back down to join the others, who were waiting on the deck below, and after a moment heard the heavy tread of the Revenant coming down behind her.

"Are you sure this is wise?" asked Doom.

"I don't think anything I've done since Miss T first got me out of the Arcade has been exactly wise," said Tamzin. "But if we're really going to take Thorbury, and if what you did today was an example of your brilliant planning, well, I'd rather have that thing with us than not."

They went aft. The streets, which were quiet anyway down on those lower decks, emptied entirely when people saw the Revenant tramping behind them. At the slipway, Max remembered that the flare he had been given to summon the Haile Maryam had been in the pocket of the jacket he had abandoned, but he waved his arms and jumped up and down, and out there in the gray waves a watchful periscope must have been turned his way, because it was not long before the submarine surfaced. The Squid Squad symbol on her conning tower had been painted out so that the League could deny any involvement with the events on Margate. The men who rowed the boat across to pick up their passengers wore no uniforms. They were unhappy at bringing a Revenant aboard their boat, shaking their heads and making the sign against evil, but they were too scared of her to argue.

Captain Kardos, though, was made of stronger stuff. "That ungodly thing is not coming aboard the Haile Maryam," he said firmly. So Vespertine stayed outside, clinging to handholds on the submarine's hull while it powered away from the raft town and turned toward the west.

38

Six Against a City

There were numerous rugged little islands where the Anglish
Sea widened into the Atlantic. On one of the largest, Oak
Island, was a merchant air base, and there Miss Torpenhow was
waiting with the *Fire's Astonishment*. The *Haile Maryam* anchored in
the rocky cove below the airship hangars. That evening as the sun
went down and the sheep called plaintively among the heathered
hills, her crew and their passengers lit a fire on the beach. They
cooked chicken pieces on long skewers, gave thanks to their various gods, and toasted the success of their mission.

"But not with wine, Mr. Doom," said Miss Torpenhow sternly,
when he held out his mug for Trubshawe to fill it from the bottle
they had brought from Djebel Tarik. "You made a great fool of
yourself last night. I am surprised at you. What were you thinking? It is not just your own self you endangered."

Doom started to grow angry, but turned sad instead. "I was
thinking I was still young," he said. "When I was a young man, I
could drink all night, and still be fighting fit come daybreak."

"Well," said Miss Torpenhow, softening a little, "those days are over. And we shall say no more about it. But you will take no more strong drink while you are part of this company."

"Yes, ma'am," said Doom, making a low bow that Miss Torpenhow thought was meant to mock her. But he truly was sorry to have disappointed her, and very glad of her forgiveness.

❀

Down where the little waves were breaking and the wet sand shone, Posie Naphtali was walking in the shallows with Max at her side. She said, "It was very brave, what you did. And quite romantic."

"Romantic?" said Max uneasily, wary of the larger waves that rolled in sometimes, and nervous of the crabs and sharks he imagined lurking among the offshore rocks.

"Yes. Going so far and risking so much to save Miss Pook."

"But it wasn't *romantic*," protested Max. "I didn't go because — I'm not . . . It is just that Tamzin Pook is part of my company, and a comrade. When you are fighting a war, you cannot let your comrades down. Tamzin would have done the same for me. And done it better, I expect, for we made a dreadful mess of things."

"Well, I think you and Tamzin Pook would fit very well together," said Posie. She was partly teasing, but only partly.

Max considered saying something forward like, "I would rather fit together with you," or something mysterious like, "But I love another," or telling her he had dreamed of her last night, which was sort of true. But nothing seemed quite right, so he said nothing, and the waves rolled in and tangled weed around their ankles, and Posie found an interesting sea snail to explain to him, and the moment passed.

But later, as they walked back together to the fire, she said, "One day, when your city is safe, you should come and find me again aboard the Haile Maryam, and I will show you the deep places of the sea."

❀

Tamzin sat at the top of the beach where the breeze hissed sibilants in the marram grass. She felt strangely content, despite the terrors of the day. She had never been to this island before, or even heard of it, yet she felt she was at home. She watched Max, and Miss Torpenhow, and Doom, and Trubshawe, grateful that she was with them in this place, and in this moment, whatever came next. They were all quite annoying in their various ways, but she was so glad of them. They made her feel better and braver than she was. They made her feel happy.

All that spoiled it was the Revenant, who had followed Tamzin from the submarine and now waited nearby like her personal angel of death. When Miss Torpenhow came limping over to join her, Tamzin jerked her head toward the motionless giant and said, "I don't know if I should offer her a chicken skewer or a fuel top-up."

The Revenant, as if it knew they were talking about it, swung its head toward them. Miss Torpenhow said, "Miss Vespertine, may I ask if you remember anything from when you were — well, from before you became as you are now?"

Vespertine seemed for a time not to have heard. Then it said, "I remember nothing before the Arcade, and Mortmain's trainers, with their electric whips."

"Well," said Miss Torpenhow encouragingly, "you are quite new in this steel body of yours. Your memories of your former life may yet come back to you."

Gods, I hope not, thought Tamzin. *Because if she remembers who she was and who I am and what I did to her* . . . And she wondered again what foolish impulse had made her bring the Revenant with her from Margate.

❈

Later, when night had fallen, they sat around the dying fire and spoke of what to do next.

"For we are no closer to finding an army, or anyone to help us take back our city," said Max. "I thought one of the Arcade fighters would join us, at least."

"One did," said Tamzin, nodding to where Vespertine stood like a green-eyed idol in the dark. "You remember General Kleinhammer telling us we'd need heavy weapons to take on the Boethius Brigade and the Scrap Metal Seven? Well, Vespertine is a heavy weapon."

"But we will still need soldiers," said Max.

"Not necessarily," said Doom. He had been thinking hard while his hangover faded. "I reckon we could do it without."

"You mean — just us? Five of us, against a city?"

"Six against a city," said Trubshawe. "I will come with you. Thorbury Reconquered sounds the ideal subject for a painting — it could be the making of my career. Of course, I cannot help with any of the actual fighting. A man of my genius has a duty to the world to keep himself out of harm's way. But I may still be able to make myself useful. And, anyway, we have an airship, so perhaps there is no need for any fighting? Couldn't we just fly over Thorbury and drop a bomb on Strega or something?"

"No!" said Miss Torpenhow and Max together, thinking of the danger to their fellow citizens, the damage to the lovely old buildings.

"No," said Doom. "Airships are no use in battle. Too big, too slow, too good a target for Strega's gunners. But if we could get the six of us aboard Thorbury we might soon find there's more than six of us, if you take my meaning. If folks there are being treated as bad as Hilly's friends say, they'll be itching to fight back. They're scared because they don't have the weapons or the leadership. But we could give them those things. Unleash our friendly local Revenant, grab some guns from the nomads. We'd soon be in a position to dictate terms to Strega and his clowns."

"Well said, Mr. Doom," said Miss Torpenhow. "We have wandered long enough. We have seen action once, and, although our operation in Margate did not go quite as smoothly as we might have hoped, we were victorious in the end, and we shall learn from our mistakes. Let's waste no more time trying to find other cities to help us. If Thorbury is to be saved, we must save it ourselves. What do you say, Mr. Mayor?"

There was a long silence, until Max remembered she was talking to him. He thought of how quickly and completely things had gone wrong that morning at the paddock. He wanted to say no, no, it is too dangerous. He wanted to stay safe here in the west, with these people he had come to care about, and well away from Thorbury and its woes. But a tide seemed to have turned, and it was pulling him homeward now, toward his duty and his destiny, and, even though he felt far too young and frightened to face those things, he knew he must.

"We should go," he said.

"Hear, hear," said Trubshawe.

"Good," said Miss Torpenhow. "Thorbury was heading

northeast when that sky-train captain met it. If it has continued on the same course, we ought to find it somewhere in the Sculpture Garden."

"We fly at first light," said Oddington Doom.

"What's the Sculpture Garden?" asked Tamzin.

39

THE LAVA FIELDS

Long, long ago, something terrible had happened to the country northwest of the Rustwater Marshes. Perhaps it was the same eruption that had raised the Tannhauser Mountains, whose smoldering summits marched along the northern skyline like a cavalcade of dragons. Or perhaps some dreadful weapon of the Ancients had struck the Earth there. Whatever it was, it had opened a great rent in the skin of the world. Lava had come boiling out, and flowed, and cooled, and flowed again until it formed an ugly scab two hundred miles across. A landscape of dark and twisted rock, thinly flocked with gray-green lichens, it looked like a sea that had turned to stone in the middle of a wild storm. In places, huge bubbles had formed and burst, leaving strange hollow hemispheres like ruined domes. Spires and pillars of lava had been whittled by the wind into shapes that looked half human, like statues carved by a madman. The Sculpture Garden, the old Nomad Empires called it, and they had shunned the place, believing it the abode of trolls and Scriven.

The planning departments aboard modern Traction Cities had no time for such fairy tales, but they mostly agreed that the lava fields were not worth venturing into. London had crossed them once, on its way east in 786 TE, bulldozing a broad pathway through the lava of which other towns had sometimes made use since, the so-called London Road. Opening off from this thoroughfare were countless wriggly little canyons and valleys, a maze too narrow and winding for predators to hunt in, but full of good sheltering places for weak or damaged towns, and small clearings in the lava where semi-static farming platforms stopped for years on end to plant their crops.

Now into this remote and stony place terror had come. Thorbury was plowing a path of its own through the heart of the Sculpture Garden, moving rapidly northeast beneath a cloud of engine smoke and powdered basalt. Towns that had come to rest and refit in the lava fields scrambled to get out of its path as it came bursting through the walls of the canyons where they lay hidden. Farmers herded their animals into the holds of their timber traction villages and fired up engines that had not been used for years. The smuts and old birds' nests they blasted from their chimneys let Thorbury's spotters know exactly where to find them.

At first, each time the city caught a town, the others stopped running and relaxed. A city of Thorbury's size could get by on one meal every few months; now that it had eaten, they assumed there would be a reprieve while it stopped to digest its catch. But Thorbury kept coming. At night, the pale glare of oxyacetylene torches could be seen flickering in its Gut as the unlucky towns it had consumed were pulled apart on the move. Rickety new watchtowers began to sprout from its upper decks, allowing its spotters to sight even more prey. Sometimes, if a town looked likely to escape, big guns mounted up there would thunder out, targeting the prey's wheels and engines, but often hitting homes instead.

The new master of Thorbury, people said, did not care if the towns he caught were reduced to wrecks before they were dragged inside his city. All he wanted was their raw material, the iron and fuel and timber that would make his city faster, stronger.

So the towns fled, and Thorbury followed them. Some of the smaller ones doubled back and found convoluted routes through the lava that took them past the pursuing city and away to safety. The rest stampeded eastward, hunting for an escape route but never finding one, until they realized that Thorbury was driving them into a trap.

The Sculpture Garden narrowed at its eastward end. On its northern edge lay a long spur of the Tannhauser Mountains, sheer and impassable. To the south, the lush green levels of the Rustwater Marshes seemed to promise safety, but swallowed any town that ventured there. And to the east the way was barred by the mighty Wassermauer River, a torrent of meltwater spilling from the edge of the Ice Wastes. The Wassermauer had carved its own way through lava long ago, plunging over cataract after cataract. It was too broad, too deep, and too fast flowing to be forded. So the towns gathered, helpless, on its western banks, or squirreled their way into whatever crannies and hiding holes they could find among the old lava flows, and waited. And the new master of Thorbury, realizing he had them cornered, allowed his city to slow a little, and moved east at leisure, gobbling them up one by one.

❈

In the long light of a evening, the *Fire's Astonishment* swept low over the lava fields, and Tamzin saw the Wassermauer shining like spilled lead in its gorge. At a dozen points along the shore the smoke of trapped towns rose. Among the rapids in midstream was a tangle of wreckage and sodden timbers where one desperate townlet had tried to escape aboard a makeshift raft, and been swamped. In the west, a backlit haze of engine fumes and powdered stone announced the coming of Thorbury.

The *Fire's Astonishment* was far from the only airship in the sky. News of the Madness of Thorbury was spreading quickly along the Bird Roads, and ships were arriving hourly to take on refugees. The people trapped on the western bank of the Wassermauer were prepared to pay almost anything to get away, for the rumors said Thorbury did not let the inhabitants of the towns it ate join its own population, as cities were supposed to. Some claimed they were being killed out of hand by Strega's men, others that they were simply left to fend for themselves on the bare earth. To most townspeople, the two things amounted to much the same. The ones who could afford it fought for a place aboard the airships. The ones who could not, if they were brave enough, packed whatever belongings they could carry and set off on foot into the lava fields, hoping other towns would pick them up. The rest stood helplessly upon the upperworks of their towns, watching Thorbury make its relentless approach, and praying that it would be stopped. But how?

❁

But how? was the question that had been echoing around the gondola of the *Fire's Astonishment* for the five days it had taken the little airship to fly there from Oak Island. We must stop Thorbury — but how? We must get rid of Strega — but how? We must get on board the city — but how? They had approached the problem from a dozen different angles, considered and rejected scores of plans. Doom had described old battles, using spoons and salt cellars to represent the opposing forces, in case the strategies that had led him to victory before might somehow be of use again. Miss Torpenhow had offered examples from history of times when smaller forces, by luck or trickery, had triumphed against overwhelming odds. Trubshawe had conceived of cunning ruses, such as painting Vespertine to look like a statue and delivering her to Strega's quarters as a gift, so she could spring to life and cut off his head when he was least expecting it.

Vespertine had offered no suggestions of her own, although her eyes flared slightly when the chopping off of heads was mooted. Max stayed mostly silent too; he kept inventing plans in his head, but he could see for himself that they would not work, so there seemed no point in explaining them to the others so they could point out all the flaws to him.

Tamzin also kept quiet, though for a different reason. All this talk reminded her too much of the Amusement Arcade and the way the fighters there would make their plans before a show began. But those plans had seldom lasted more than a few seconds in the face of whatever horror Dr. Mortmain had devised for them. She believed it was better not to plan. Wait and see, was her way, and when you saw what you were up against, and which way the wind was blowing, improvise desperately.

And that afternoon, while the Fire's Astonishment flew past Thorbury and then ahead of it to where the trapped towns cowered, the answer had come to her. A merchant town called Shilpit (its name painted in big letters on its town-hall roof) had stuck tight in the canyon through which it had been hoping to escape. As the Fire's Astonishment passed overhead, Tamzin had seen the last refugees scrambling away from it on foot, leaving it deserted. And a plan had arrived in her head like a gift.

"We can get aboard Thorbury the same way Strega did," she said. "That stuck-tight little town down there will be Thorbury's next meal, and at the speed Thorbury is moving I don't think they'll be stopping to check if anyone's home before they scoff it."

"So you think we should hide ourselves aboard it, and burst out with guns blazing once it's in the Gut?" asked Trubshawe nervously. "That's the same trick Strega used to get his mercenaries onto Thorbury in the first place — he'll be expecting it."

"No," said Miss Torpenhow, looking thoughtfully at Tamzin. "No, he won't. Gabriel Strega prides himself on being cleverer than the rest of us. He thinks we're all stick-in-the-muds and he's the only one who dares break the rules. It is Strega's trick, and that's precisely why he won't expect it to be used against him." She smiled at Tamzin. "Very good, Tamzin."

"And we won't be bursting out with guns blazing," said Doom. "There's no future in that. We'll get in without being spotted, if we can. Sneak about and see if the citizens are ready to help us take on Strega and his nomads."

"Sneak about . . ." said Max, looking at Vespertine, trying to imagine her sneaking anywhere.

"And we'll keep Strega distracted while we're doing it," Doom went on. "Someone will have to visit him on the Command Deck. Someone who poses no threat, and who he will want to talk to. It can't be me, as I'm needed in the Gut, and it can't be Max or Hilly because they'll be recognized, and Vespertine isn't suited for that kind of undercover work. But I'm thinking maybe if an artist arrived, impressed by tales of Gabriel Strega's brilliance and keen to paint his portrait, so that all the Hunting Ground may see the great man's likeness . . ."

"Oh, yes!" chuckled Trubshawe, and then, realizing where this was going, "Oh no!"

"It has to be you, Trubshawe," said Doom. "You just need to talk artistic flannel long enough and loud enough to take Strega's mind off any odd reports that might start coming up from the Gut."

"What about me?" asked Tamzin.

Doom grinned at her. "A traveling artist needs an assistant," he said. "Someone who can give him a bit of moral support, and stop him chickening out. And someone who, if she gets a chance and the need arises, can stick a knife between Gabriel Strega's ribs."

40

SHILPIT

$\mathcal{S}$hilpit had two tiers of barns and houses, squatting on a chassis built from bolted-together nomad traction forts. Above the base tier, everything was made of wood or lacquered paper. The big engines at the stern had been powerful enough to shove it halfway through the winding canyon, knocking down buttresses of soft volcanic rock that barred its way. But then it had met a reef of basalt, and it had tried to turn around but wedged fast; canted over at an angle, like a sinking ship. By the time the *Fire's Astonishment* set down on its tiny air dock that evening, it was entirely deserted. The lava for several miles around was littered with overstuffed bags and bits of furniture the townsfolk had abandoned as they fled.

Doom led the way from the air dock up to Shilpit's old command tier. From the slanting deck outside the town hall they could see Thorbury coming: a mountain veiled by clouds of smoke, rising dark against the gaudy banners of the sunset. The wind, gusting from the west, carried the steady thunder of its engines and the endless, grating snarl of its tracks grinding over or through the lava flows. Pillars of basalt toppled before it like the statues of deposed tyrants. On the air intakes, which reared up like the business ends of brass-band instruments from the edges of the engine district, gangs of tiny figures could be seen frantically clearing powdered stone from the dust filters.

"It is like a Revenant Engine," said Vespertine in her graveyard whisper. "Like in the Arcade. It is like a giant Revenant Engine."

Tamzin looked sharply at her. It was the first time she had heard Vespertine speak of the Arcade like that, as if she remembered fighting Revenants herself back when she had still been Eve Vespertine. If her memories of the Arcade were coming back to her, how long would it be before she uncovered the memory of what Tamzin had done there?

But Vespertine showed no further sign of remembering. She seemed as innocent as a child, and despite her fears Tamzin felt a big-sisterish desire to keep her safe. There was an antiques and old-tech shop nearby that had not been completely looted, and in its window she saw an empty Stalker's head: a battered iron bucket with the wheeled skull of some lost nomad empire stenciled on it. She climbed in through the broken shop window to fetch it, and handed it to Vespertine. "I thought it would make a helmet for you," she said. "Just because I was too polite to stab you in your face doesn't mean Strega's men won't try it."

Vespertine looked down at the helmet. She put it on her head, and her green eyes looked out at Tamzin through the narrow eye slit. "You are good," she said.

Tamzin patted her on her armored chest for luck, right where Mortmain's porcupine had speared her. "I'm not," she said. "But I wish I was, and maybe that counts for something."

They split into three groups and started moving quickly through the empty town, turning on the lights in every building they could get into. In their haste to abandon Shilpit, the town's engineers had not fully shut down its engines, and with Vespertine's help Doom opened them up again and got a good plume of smoke rising from the exhaust stacks. He was afraid that if Shilpit looked *too* dead Thorbury might bypass it and go after the towns clustered on the riverbank first.

By the time they gathered at the air harbor, it was fully dark. A big moon was rising above the Sculpture Garden, making the spires of lava look even more like twisted statues. In the west, clouds blotted out the stars. The oncoming city blazed with lights beneath its shroud of dust. Engine noise rolled through the canyons. Max remembered that Thorbury meant Thunder City. He had never stopped to wonder why it had been given that name, but then he had never heard it until now as its prey heard it. It really did sound as if a great storm were rumbling above the lava fields, and drawing ever nearer.

Trubshawe went aboard the *Fire's Astonishment* and started warming up the engines. The others stood awkwardly at the foot of the gangplank.

"The watchers on Thorbury will see you take off," Max warned.

"All to the good," said Miss Torpenhow. "Airships often take flight before a town is eaten. It will make this poor old place look a bit less deserted."

"Good luck," said Doom, shaking Tamzin's hand. "We'll see you in Thorbury's town hall."

"Good luck yourself," Max told her. He felt he should hug her, but lost his nerve and gave her a wan smile instead.

"You too," said Tamzin. "You too, Mr. Doom. Good luck, Miss T. Good luck, Vespertine."

Miss Torpenhow hugged her. Vespertine stood like an iron

statue and said nothing, but Tamzin was pleased to see she was wearing her new helmet. She felt a wild, helpless love for all of them, the sort of love she had never let herself feel for her fellow fighters back in the Arcade. She was truly part of a team for the first time, and for the first time felt that might bring her good luck instead of bad. She couldn't put the feeling into words, though, so she just looked at them for a second or so, fixing the moment in her memory, then ran up the airship's gangplank, heaved it in after her, and closed the gondola hatch.

"You're sure you know what you are doing?" she asked as the airship lifted into the air and the wind caught it.

"Absolutely!" replied Trubshawe in his usual, carefree way. "I flew her halfway from Margate, didn't I? I mean," he added, sounding slightly less carefree, as one of Shilpit's exhaust stacks seemed to lean across the sky ahead. "I watched very closely as Doom and Angmering flew her, and they let me take the controls several times . . ."

A dreadful lurch, a sickening swerve. Then the exhaust stack was behind them, and the stricken town was dwindling below, too far below for Tamzin to tell if her friends were still watching from the air dock.

"Er . . . oops," said Trubshawe to himself, not very reassuringly.

The Fire's Astonishment turned uncertainly in the sky, and flew toward the oncoming mass of Thorbury.

❇

Max stood on the dock until the sound of aëro-engines had faded into the bass rumble of the approaching city. He felt lonely, and guilty, and afraid. It seemed wrong to be sending Tamzin and Trubshawe ahead of him. This was not their fight. He loved them for choosing to fight it anyway, and felt ashamed that he needed them to do so.

I will give them the freedom of the city when Thorbury is mine again, he vowed. *I will make them heroes.*

But he did not really believe he would see them again. They had flown into danger, and here he stood waiting for danger to come and find him, and it seemed too much to hope that all of them would survive.

He turned back toward the town hall and a small, dark something darted out from beneath a pile of ropes on the dock nearby, startling him out of his gloomy thoughts. It was a tiny cat, black with white mittens. It must have been left behind when its owners fled. It ran ahead of Max along the dock.

In the shadows at the dock's end, where the stairs went up to the top tier and the town hall, Vespertine was waiting. He wondered if the Revenant had watched the airship leave too, and stayed hidden because she could not think of what to say either. She was wearing the old Stalker helmet that Tamzin had given her, and he could see nothing of her face, only the glow of her eyes shining through a slit in its visor. The cat's eyes flashed green reflections as she looked down at it.

"Don't hurt it!" said Max, afraid that the creature's sudden movement would make Vespertine strike. But she only stood watching while the cat twined itself around her big, armored legs. Then, with a kind of clumsy gentleness, she stooped and picked it up.

"It is a small cat," she said.

The cat seemed comfortable in her huge metal gauntlet. She patted it carefully with her other hand, and it rubbed its head against her fingers. The light of her eyes flickered softly. "I wanted a cat when I was the person before I became the person I am now," she said.

Max went nearer. "You remember that?"

"Not everything," said Vespertine, very intent on the cat. The thick visor muffled her voice. "But I remember wanting a cat," she said. "I like this cat."

The cat meowed loudly, and Vespertine actually jumped. Max laughed. "It's hungry," he said. "We could probably find it some food, if we looked around."

"Then we should do that," said Vespertine. "I think I will keep this small cat. I think I shall call it 'Small Cat.'"

Small Cat ran up the Revenant's arm and sat on her shoulder as they climbed the stairs.

Max said, "Do you remember what happened to Eve Vespertine? In the Arcade?"

The Revenant did not answer, but he saw the light flare fiercely in her eyes.

I must keep her away from Tamzin, he thought. But perhaps she will be destroyed in the fighting, and it will not matter. Or perhaps we will all be killed, and then nothing will matter anymore . . .

❀

In the empty council chamber of Shilpit's town hall, Doom was giving Miss Torpenhow a lesson in the handling of weapons. He showed her how to open his pistol, empty out spent cartridges, and put in new ones. He showed her how to clear it if it jammed. He pointed at the portraits of Shilpit's former mayors and mayoresses on the chamber walls, and suggested that she use them as targets.

"But it feels wrong," Miss Torpenhow protested. "Those are works of art."

"They ain't very good ones. They're all cross-eyed and have peculiar expressions."

"Maybe the people they portray *were* all cross-eyed and *did* have peculiar expressions, Mr. Doom. I am sure somebody loved them all the same. It feels quite wrong to shoot at them. I might be shooting at someone's father, or someone's beloved aunt."

"Yes," agreed Doom, standing behind her and adjusting her grip on the pistol. "And the folks you might have to shoot at in Thorbury soon are likely someone's dad or auntie too. The only difference between them and these painted bozos is they'll shoot you first if they get a chance. So best get some practice in while you can, eh?"

Miss Torpenhow had to admit that there was some sense in what he said. She took aim and fired, missing the portrait on which she had sighted by several yards. But it was only because the recoil of the gun had thrown her off; her next shot smashed into the picture frame, the third shattered the glass, and she was shooting holes smack through the middle of mayoral foreheads by the time Max shouted from the outside that Thorbury was almost upon them.

"Thank you, Mr. Doom," she said, holding out the pistol to him. "That was most instructive, and really quite easy once one gets the hang of it."

"You keep it, Hilly," said Doom, unbuckling his gun belt and wrapping it around her narrow waist.

"But you must have a weapon, Mr. Doom."

"I'm better off with my sword," he told her, patting the hilt of the cutlass Kush Tundurbai had given him in Djebel Tarik. "If I need a gun, I can always take one from one of Strega's blokes, I reckon." Max was calling to them again. Doom started to the door, then stopped, looked back at her, and said, "You take care of yourself now, Hilly, you understand? No silly risks. Let me take those. You've got to come through this in one piece. That kid ain't up to running his own city yet. He's going to need you to help him."

"Of course, Mr. Doom," said Miss Torpenhow, slightly startled by the earnest way he was looking at her. And then, because he had called her Hilly, she said, "Of course, Oddington." And then she felt a curious but very intense urge to kiss him, but she was not sure how one went about such things, or what he would think of her if she did. And while she stood there wondering, the whole town suddenly shook with a series of tremendous impacts as the harpoons of Thorbury came slamming down on it.

41

THE ARCHITECT ENTERTAINS

It does not look at all how Max and Miss T described it," said Tamzin.

The Fire's Astonishment was circling the upper tiers of Thorbury. If there were people with big guns and suspicious minds down there, Trubshawe wanted to give them time to see that the airship was unarmed before he attempted to dock. Tamzin peered through the gondola windows, hoping for a closer look at the city she had heard her friends talk of so often, for it had been too far off and too wrapped in its own smoke and dust to make out much detail when they flew past earlier. The smoke had cleared now, blown away on the rising wind, but she was surprised to find no sign on Thorbury's top tier of the grand and beautiful old buildings Max and Miss Torpenhow had described. It was just a flat plain of metal, with here and there a hut, and here and there a few bare girders jutting up like dead trees. There was a domed building dead center, which she took to be an elevator terminus, and off to one side a large, boxlike structure apparently clad in sheets of tin.

"Are we sure this is Thorbury?" she asked, suddenly fearful that they had found the wrong city.

"It looks as if our friend Strega has been making some changes," said Trubshawe. "If we didn't already know he was a wrong 'un, this would prove it. Thorbury's Command Deck was one of the glories of the age, and he has knocked it all down, the blighter. Lots of changes going on below too, by the look of it. The poor old place looks more like an industrial platform now."

Tamzin felt sad on her friends' behalf, and also for herself. Max and Miss T had spoken so fondly of their city, she had almost started to feel she knew it. She had been looking forward to seeing the place where Max had grown up. She scanned the upper tiers again as the airship circled. "Someone is flashing a light at us," she said.

The light was as green as a Revenant's eye. It came from a lantern, which was being swung meaningfully to and fro by a man who stood on one of the gantries of the air dock. It seemed safe to assume it meant permission to land. Trubshawe steered the Fire's Astonishment toward the gantry, but in his nervousness he cut the engines too soon, and rather than gliding elegantly in to dock, the airship was caught by the wind and buffeted away. They had to circle the city again before they could get close enough for the airdock crew to catch her mooring ropes and make them fast.

"Neat landing," said the harbormaster, when Trubshawe and Tamzin finally stepped out onto the quay. This master of sarcasm was one of Strega's mercenaries, Tamzin guessed, a bulky, scar-faced brute with patterns of silver studs on his leather coat and a big sword at his side. Behind him stood a gang of guards, equally burly, all sniggering at the Fire's Astonishment's clumsy maneuverings.

"I am not used to your docking arrangements," said Trubshawe. "Anyway, I am not an aviator by profession, but an artist. I wish to see your mayor, Mr. Gabriel Strega."

"What do you want with the Architect?" growled the man. "Why should he waste his time on you?"

"Because I am here to make a likeness of him, and record the great events that are unfolding aboard his city."

The big man came closer, peering at Trubshawe, then at Tamzin. "Who's the boy?"

"Tamzin is my assistant. In the portfolio she is carrying you may see samples of my work."

Tamzin opened the portfolio. The wind fluttered the edges of the papers inside it. The harbor guards crowded forward to look as Trubshawe held up drawings he had made on the journey from Margate. There were views of passing cities, portraits of imaginary potentates, a sketch of the poor towns huddled on the bank of the Wassermauer.

"He's good," said one of the guards.

"Reckon you could draw me?" asked another.

"Look at that one. The eyes sort of follow you around . . ."

"Quiet," growled the harbormaster. He did not appear to be a man who had much time for art, but the drawing of the Wassermauer interested him. He held it up into the light. "You been out to them prey towns?"

"I was there this very afternoon. I have been gathering material for a great painting of Thorbury's triumphant hunt. The picturesque setting here among the lava fields, the majesty of your city and the pitiable state of the prey as they wait to be devoured will make for a most affecting work —"

"Shut it," said the man. He thrust the drawing at Tamzin, who stuffed it back inside the portfolio. "The Architect don't care about paintings," he said, "but if you've got intel on the prey he'll want to hear it."

"By all means!" said Trubshawe, beaming. "I shall be happy to tell him all I know."

❋

Three guards went with them, one leading the way up the metal steps to the Command Deck, the other two following behind. They held their automatic rifles in a way that let Tamzin and Trubshawe know they would be quite happy to use them. There was rain in the air now, the wind gusting strongly from the west. Lightning flickered in that black bank of clouds behind the city, and above the steady rumble of the engines Tamzin thought she heard real thunder growl.

The Command Deck when they reached it was as empty as it had looked from the air; powdered pumice, had piled up in drifts like gray snow against the few remaining walls. A line of ornamental lamps that must once have lined a pretty street now stood incongruous and alone, lighting the way to the square metal building that stood in the center of the tier. More guards were stationed at its doorway, and there Tamzin and Trubshawe met the first of Strega's Revenants. It stood silently watching them, immense and very old. The plates of its armor were crusted with rust and the faded symbols of all the war bands and cities that had claimed it over the centuries since it was reanimated. Now the grinning white skull of the Boethius Brigade was painted on the front of its faceless head. Through the round eyeholes of the skull, its own eyes looked out, just as round, and flaring sickly green.

"Good gods!" muttered Trubshawe. "I suppose that chap is one of the Scrap Metal Seven. He is twice as broad as our friend Vespertine, and half again as high, and Vespertine is not exactly petite . . ."

Tamzin, out of habit, was already gauging the Revenant's weak points. There was a gap in the armor where the body met the head through which she thought an electro-knife might fit. But she did not have an electro-knife, and, even if she had, she doubted the Rev would let her get close enough to use it. In its massive hand it held a weapon for which she did not know a name: a thick metal pole with blades jutting from each end.

"Come," said one of the guards. The door was opened, and Tamzin and Trubshawe were led past the watching Revenant into Thorbury's new town hall.

Which turned out, once they were inside, to be the old town hall, with its outer walls sheathed in metal and its inner ones stripped of all their finery. The corridors through which the visitors were led had been hung with paintings once, but now there were only bare walls, with hooks marking the places where pictures of past mayors and past glories had once hung. The big reception room into which they were shown had been decorated with elaborate murals, but they were being whitewashed over, and all that remained was a plump, pink person painted on the high dome of the ceiling, who represented the Spirit of Municipal Darwinism. She seemed to be looking with alarm at the approaching tide of whitewash, which had already swallowed up her attendant cherubim.

"What is Strega thinking of?" Trubshawe wondered aloud, standing in the center of the room and turning around and around. Here and there, through thinner patches in the whitewash, a ghostly face gazed down. "Why would anyone cover up all this art, all this beauty?"

Tamzin did not have an answer for that. But someone did. Neither of them had noticed a small man enter the room, dressed all in black, insignificant-looking among the guards who waited by the door.

Now he walked forward, his slippers making no sound at all

upon the polished floor, and said, "Strega is thinking of the future, my friend. And he understands that there will be no place in it for such sentimental distractions as art and beauty."

They turned. Trubshawe bowed, and Tamzin copied him. When she straightened up, she found Gabriel Strega watching her.

She had heard so much about this man over the past few weeks that she had come to imagine him as a sort of ogre, huge and menacing and evil. But Strega in the flesh looked utterly ordinary, even pleasant, the sort of mild-natured little clerk or mid-tier manager you might pass in any street on any town and never even glance at. He had a very pale round face with a high forehead, a small nose, a neat little beard. His only remarkable features were his eyes. They were large and very dark, and they seemed to glitter with inward laughter as he studied Tamzin.

She mumbled something about being honored to meet him, and Strega lost interest in her and turned to Trubshawe. "They tell me you are an artist," he said. "As you can see, the new Thorbury has evolved beyond the need for art."

"Ah," said Trubshawe. "But other cities have not. In London, in Paris, in Dortmund, in Peripatetiapolis, they absolutely love the stuff. And at present they are all talking of nothing but Gabriel Strega. So I thought I should come here and paint a portrait of the great man, so that I might tour those cities with it and let all the art lovers there see for themselves the features of the man who is transforming Thorbury."

"And you would make a pretty profit for yourself selling prints and copies of this portrait, no doubt," said Strega mildly. "But what would be in it for me?"

"Fame!" said Trubshawe. "A great man should be known by a great painting. When we talk of Nikolas Quirke, the image of him

261

that we conjure in our minds is as he appears in Walmart Strange's masterpiece, *Quirke Overseeing the Rebuilding of London*. Soon, whenever the name of Gabriel Strega is spoken, people everywhere shall picture *Strega Guiding Thorbury Through the Sculpture Garden*, by Giotto Trubshawe. Allow me to paint you, sir, and I shall ensure that the whole Hunting Ground knows your face."

Half smiling, Strega considered all this, then dismissed it with a little shake of his head. "They will know my face soon enough anyway," he said. "When Thorbury has eaten enough of these paltry little prey towns to equip itself with bigger jaws and engines, I shall turn it west to hunt bigger game. No, I do not require a portrait. But my men at the air harbor tell me you have information that may be of use. You have seen the towns that wait for us along the Wassermauer? Drawings of those might serve some purpose."

Trubshawe made blustering noises. It pained him to hear his art dismissed as something that was only of use for helping a city catch its prey, as if he were no better than a mapmaker.

But Tamzin said, "We flew over those places earlier. We can tell you exactly what they are, and Signor Trubshawe can make drawings for you."

"Excellent!" said Strega happily. "When so much prey is spread out before us, it becomes important to know which morsel we should seize on first, and which we can risk letting escape. Come through to my private chambers: we can eat, and you can tell me everything you have . . ." He paused, listening, as the floor trembled and a faint noise came echoing up through the city. It sounded like a huge storm raging far away. "Ah," he said, "we have begun eating Shilpit."

42

THE DISMANTLING YARDS

It was an unpleasant experience, having your town eaten under you. Max had never realized quite how unpleasant until it happened to him. Generally, when Thorbury had eaten towns in the past, it had appeared to be a rather leisurely affair. Usually the towns were happy to be eaten, and drove into the city's Gut of their own accord. Even when a lively one had to be harpooned and dragged aboard, there had been little sense of violence. Max had gone down to the Gut sometimes to watch, and the captive towns had come up the well-oiled ramps of the Jaws as neat as anything. But, now that he thought about it, there had always been a lot of preparation first. Warning shots had always been fired before the harpoons, and afterward the city would stop and angle itself correctly, and salvage teams would go out and attach extra tow lines to the prey, and the big winches in the Gut would turn slowly, slowly, while foremen bellowed instructions through megaphones to make sure the catch was brought in with as little damage as possible.

Thorbury now seemed to have no time for such pleasantries.

The city had barely loomed into view above the rim of the canyon where Shilpit lay trapped before the harpoons came slamming down. Standing on the deck outside the town hall, Max thought for a moment they were coming straight at him. But they dropped among the engine stacks, and the huge outer housings of the town's tracks. The town shuddered as they struck, then shuddered again as their barbs extended, getting a firm grip on the hull and chassis. There was a terrifying lurch as the heavy cables went taut, and suddenly the town was moving, tipping sideways, almost turning turtle as it was dragged backward up the canyon side and through collapsing spires of lava toward the Jaws of Thorbury.

Max lost his footing, rolled across the deck, hit the front of the town hall hard, and scrambled along it on all fours until he found a door to drop through. The whole town was filled with the din of things falling and breaking, and stressed girders moaning, and the screech and scrape of metal against rock. One of the harpoon cables snapped with a sound like a thunderclap, and the loose end went whipping across the town, smashing the bell towers off the Temple of Peripatetia. The bells tumbled through the near-vertical streets, adding their great bronze voices to the chaos.

"He's mad!" shouted Max, tumbling into the council chamber where Doom and Miss Torpenhow were cowering. "Strega's mad! This place will be in ruins by the time he gets it into the Gut!"

"No doubt he thinks that will save his dismantling crews some time," Miss Torpenhow shouted back.

"Why don't you both stop yabbering and get under here," shouted Doom from beneath a table that was bolted to the floor. They scrambled to join him as broken glass and plaster dust cascaded down into the chamber. Through the downpour came

Vespertine, holding Small Cat in one hand and sheltering him from the debris with the other.

"What is happening?" she asked, while shards of ceiling bounced off her helmet.

"We're being dragged into the city's Gut," said Doom. "From the feel of it, we're being hauled up the maxillary ramps now."

Vespertine nodded. "This was the plan."

"It was," said Max, "but I didn't realize it would be quite so . . ."

One last lurch. A chandelier that had been dancing happily enough on its fixings until then came crashing down and smashed like a dropped iceberg. Then there was silence. And then, dimly, from somewhere outside, voices shouting orders, and the grumble of big machinery.

"We're in the Gut," said Doom. "Get ready."

"Meow," said the cat.

"Shhh," Vespertine told it, putting it on her shoulder.

The floor was almost level again. They left the chamber and crept through wrenched and sagging hallways to the door. Outside, the sky had been replaced by the steel vaultings of Thorbury's Dismantling Yards. Work lights set in the high roof blazed down like hard new stars.

Already cranes and hydraulic arms were swinging into position above the captured town. A circular saw blade as high as a three-story house was lowered over the engine section. Jets of water from high-pressure hoses were played on it to cool it as it started to spin. The spray came drifting across the ruined upper tier, damping Max and the others as they crept through the shadows to a stairway and started down.

They found their way into the town's chassis, and from there to a hatchway in the track housings. Shilpit had been so twisted out of shape during its capture that the hatch would not open, but Vespertine kicked her way through it, and on the other side was a spindly stairway leading down, and a ladder at the bottom that could be lowered all the way to the deck between the town's tracks. Doom lowered it, and the companions climbed down the greasy rungs and jumped the last few feet to land upon the deckplates of Thorbury.

"Home," said Max, not quite believing it.

"Welcome back to your city, Mayor Angmering," Miss Torpenhow told him.

"It's not yours yet," said Doom, and at that moment the giant saw cut through the deckplates a few hundred yards from where they stood. They covered their ears against the noise of it. The cascading sparks lit up their faces, and made silhouettes of the men who had just stepped in between the town's wheels, not two yards away.

There were three of them. One carried a lantern and wore the gray overalls of a salvage worker; the other two held guns and had white cartoon skulls painted on their grimy body armor. Max guessed the salvageman had come to check the condition of Shilpit's chassis prior to dismantling, and the gunmen had come with him to look for loot or survivors. But, by the time he had worked that out, it was all over. Doom, without hesitating or saying a word, strode up to the nearest of the armed men and ran his sword through him, snatching the gun from his hand as he fell. The other raised his own gun, but was distracted from shooting Doom by the sight of Vespertine lurching out of the shadows. He shot her instead, and the gun yammered, and the bullets pummeled the Revenant's armor and whined off in all directions,

266

making Max and Miss Torpenhow duck for cover. Then Vespertine reached him and the saw-light glinted on the blade springing from her forearm and there was a splash of sudden red and only the salvageman was left, gawping at the bodies on the deck.

"No!" Miss Torpenhow shouted, as Vespertine turned toward the man, lighting his scared face sickly green with the glow of her gaze.

"We can't let him go, Hilly," warned Doom. "This ain't that sort of fight."

"He's not one of Strega's mercenaries," Miss Torpenhow said. "He's a Thorbury man. He's one of the people we've come to save. Isn't he, Max?"

Max didn't know. He supposed there must be plenty of people aboard Thorbury who were happy enough with Strega. Maybe this poor, cringing salvageman was one of them. But he held up his hands and went closer to the man and said, "I'm Max Angmering. I'm here to take the city back. Will you help us?"

The man was too much in awe of Vespertine to answer. He stood staring at the Revenant, his face all freckled with the blood of his companions.

"How many of these blokes has Strega got down here?" asked Doom.

The man seemed to come to his senses. He shrugged. "Forty, fifty . . . I don't know. More at the guard posts on the stairs."

"And how many of her sort?" asked Doom, pointing at Vespertine.

"Three. They stay at the elevator station mostly. There's four more he keeps up top somewhere."

It was hard to hear him. The saw was still working, and huge hammers seemed to be playing Shilpit's superstructure like a xylophone. Doom picked up the second dead man's gun and threw it to Max.

"This is a Bugharin automatic rifle, known in the trade as a Boogie," he said. He unbuckled a belt of circular leather ammunition drums, which the dead man wore, and tossed that to Max too. "If you're not a natural marksman like Hilly here, a Boogie is the gun for you. It ain't accurate, but it'll make anyone with any sense keep their heads down."

Max strapped on the belt, tested the weight of the gun in his hands. It felt heavy and purposeful, entirely unlike the rifles he and his friends had used to shoot clay pigeons in the parks of Paris. He started to let himself think this thing might work. They were aboard the city; they had guns, and a plan, and a new ally. He turned to ask the salvageman his name.

But the man was gone. A fresh burst of sparks from the saw showed him, twenty yards away and running hard. Doom raised his gun, then lowered it. The man had already disappeared behind the wheels on the far side of the town.

"Off to warn Strega," said Doom disgustedly.

"Maybe not," said Miss Torpenhow. "Maybe his nerve just failed him. Not everyone is as brave as you, Oddington."

"And not everyone is as trusting as you, Hilly," grumbled Doom. "Let's get going, before that little rat sends all the bigger rats to find us."

43

A Slight Awkwardness at Dinner

The big old rooms of the town hall had been divided and partitioned in strange new ways. The dining room in Strega's private quarters had been part of something larger once. The ceiling was the giveaway; half the ornate plaster decorations were hidden by a new wall.

"We are using the space more efficiently," said Strega. "The men who built these cities brought too much of the muck and clutter of the old world with them. We can do without all that."

He sat down at the head of the table. A servant standing behind his chair snapped a crisp white napkin open and laid it on his lap. Trubshawe, who was used to fancy dinners (although in his opinion he was not invited to enough of them), sat down too. Tamzin took the seat opposite him, feeling wary and out of place. She had imagined all sorts of dire things waiting for her in Thorbury, but she had not expected dinner.

"No doubt you know my story, Signor Trubshawe?" Strega asked. "I was not always the Architect of Thorbury. I came from nothing. I grew up parentless aboard a little nowheresville that was swallowed by this city when I was knee-high to a gnat. Despite the grip the old Angmering family and their cronies had upon the place, I was able to rise as far as the Planning Department. But there my career stalled."

"The mayor did not appreciate you?" ventured Trubshawe, looking at the bottle of wine another servant had brought in the way a man lost in the desert might look at an oasis.

The servant poured a little wine into Strega's glass. He tasted it, nodded, and gestured for the woman to fill the glasses of his guests. "The mayor did not like my plans," he said. "None of them did, the old ninnies who ran this city in those days. 'Unsuitable,' they called me to my face. 'Unhinged,' they whispered when my back was turned. I ask you, Trubshawe — do I seem unhinged to you?"

"Er . . ."

"But I showed them. And now I am putting all my proposals into action. Thorbury is to be the first and greatest of a new type of predator city: modern, efficient, and ruthless."

"Most, um. Most, ah," said Trubshawe.

"Impressive," said Tamzin.

"Thank you, Miss Pook," said Trubshawe, raising his glass to her. "Impressive, that is the very word."

"Pook?" said Strega, and his eyes found Tamzin's again, and something was going on behind them, as if some intricate machine had been set in motion. "That is a most unusual name."

Tamzin thought she would like to strangle Trubshawe, but the table was too wide to reach across. She contented herself with glowering at him in a way that made it clear she would strangle him as soon as circumstances permitted. "It isn't unusual where I come from," she said.

"Oh, no? And where is that?" asked Strega pleasantly.

Tamzin couldn't think. She looked down at the bowl of soup a servant had just set in front of her, as if she hoped to find an answer in its depths. *Not Margate. Don't say Margate. If you say Margate, he will put two and two together and ask himself why a famous Revenant fighter would be here, in his city, where he is guarded by all his Revenants. Say another city. Say . . .*

"Paris!" she blurted out. But at the same instant Trubshawe, growing alarmed at her silence, said, "Manchester!"

Strega looked from one to the other of them, still with that pleasant smile, as if he were waiting to have the joke explained to him.

"That is, Mr. Trubshawe met me in Paris," said Tamzin, improvising frantically. "But Manchester is where I'm from originally."

"Manchester?" Strega sipped his soup, watching Tamzin all the while. "A fine city. I spent some time there, in my years of exile. You know the Great Northern Hotel on Tier Four, behind the air harbor?"

Tamzin tried to look as if she did. "I heard of it," she said. "I'm from Tier Five," she added, and then wondered if that was higher or lower than Tier Four, in Manchester.

"Ah," said Strega. "The jewelry quarter."

"Yes," agreed Tamzin.

Strega beamed at her. His curiosity seemed satisfied. He turned to Trubshawe with some remark about the soup. He motioned for a servant, and murmured something, and the man bowed and left the room. Then he turned back to Tamzin, whose own attention had been taken up entirely by trying to eat her soup without making slurping sounds.

"Miss Pook," he said, "the strange thing is, when I was in

Manchester, the Great Northern Hotel was on Tier Two, and there was no jewelry quarter at all. How do you explain that?"

"Tamzin was just being polite!" said Trubshawe hastily. "She knew you had it wrong, but she is too polite to say so, being a guest under your roof and so forth."

Strega nodded, apparently accepting the explanation. "Tamzin Pook," he said. "A very uncommon name."

The door opened. The servant Strega had sent out a moment before returned. With him came a big man wearing a gorgeous red velvet coat over battered body armor. The newcomer's hair was a stiff red crest running down the middle of his scalp. The rest of his head, his face, and the whole of his body as far as Tamzin could see was covered with tattooed lines in the shape of jigsaw-puzzle pieces.

"Captain Boethius," said Strega, dabbing his mouth with his napkin and standing to introduce his guests. "This is Signor Trubshawe. The young lady is Miss Tamzin Pook. Miss Pook is the escaped Arcade slave who arrived on Bad Luftgarten with Max Angmering a few weeks ago. My agents there assured us that they had disposed of her and the rest of the Angmering gang by setting them adrift in a burning airhouse. What do you think of that?"

Boethius scratched the back of his neck and looked from Tamzin to Trubshawe, from Trubshawe to Tamzin.

"I think your agents must have been mistaken, Architect," he said.

Strega snapped his fingers. "That is exactly what I thought, Boethius! And, you know, if these two escaped from the airborne bonfire, it seems to me we should assume Max Angmering got out too. I wouldn't be surprised if he sent them here as a distraction while he creeps aboard Thorbury and tries to . . ."

He fell silent, his eyes on Tamzin still, watching her as if he thought he could find the whole plan written in her face.

"I'll tell the boys at the air dock to check over that airship again," said Boethius.

"No," said Strega. "These two were alone aboard the airship. The others will have come another way . . ." He laughed and clapped his hands together, delighted to have solved the puzzle. "Of course, they were aboard that town we just ate!" Reaching out quickly, he helped himself to one of the pistols from Boethius's gun belt and pointed it at Trubshawe. "How many men does Angmering have with him?" he asked.

"Um, er . . ." said Trubshawe.

Strega swung the pistol to point at Tamzin. "How many, Mr. Trubshawe, or your young friend here will never get any older."

"Only four," said Trubshawe. "But —"

"Four?" Strega laughed again and returned the pistol to its owner. "Do you hear that, Boethius? There are four fools creeping around in this city's Gut. I expect they have shooting implements, and some half-baked plan to rouse the populace. Kindly take a squad of your best men and kill them all."

44

BOOGIE WONDERLAND

Max had never spent much time in his city's Base Tier. His father had always encouraged him to get down there, meet the engineers, and watch the dismantling crews at their work, but it was a hot, dark, noisy, smoky, smelly place, and Max had found every excuse he could to stay in the fresh air on the upper tiers.

So he had no idea where he was when the Boethius Brigade came down on him.

He, Miss Torpenhow, Oddington Doom, and Vespertine had left the Dismantling Yards and found their way along walkways and narrow corridors, the noise of Shilpit's demolition fading slightly as they moved deeper into the city. The corridors they crept along were tubular like huge pipes, with a spaghetti of smaller pipes running along the roof and walls, even along the floor sometimes. The air was hot and stale, and filled with a haze of smoke. Through this the liberators stumbled, Doom in the lead, Vespertine bringing up the rear with her cat perched contentedly on her shoulder. Once a gang of workers crossed their path, marching noisily down an intersecting corridor. Some glanced at the strangers, but Thorbury had been full of strangers since Strega took control, and a lot of the strangers had guns, and a few were Revenants, so the workers sensed nothing amiss.

The group of nomads they met when they turned a corner shortly after that *did* sense something amiss, but Doom's Bugharin was barking at them before the penny dropped.

"These noises scare Small Cat," said Vespertine conversationally, and Max glanced back and saw her standing there, lit up by the stuttering glare of Doom's gun, with her hands clasped protectively around the cat and its bright, frightened eyes peeking out between her fingers.

The gunfire ended. Doom glanced back at the others, grinned and walked on, vanishing into the shroud of smoke that swayed above the nomads' bodies. He was enjoying himself.

The corridor led to a series of large holds, through which the group moved cautiously, keeping to the shadows. Luckily, there were plenty of shadows to keep to, for the holds were stuffed with material taken from the towns Thorbury had eaten on its sortie through the Sculpture Garden. There were bales of fabric, stacks of girders, iron in sheets and bars and ingots, rolls of wire, pipes of various sizes, wheeled hoppers full of nuts, bolts, roofing tiles. All of it seemed to have been warehoused in a hurry, crammed into the big, echoey spaces any old how, and through the aisles between it Max and his companions found their way.

"If I recall correctly," said Miss Torpenhow, "the last of these storerooms opens onto Lateral Street, and beyond that the engine district begins."

But in the last of the holds the Boethius Brigade was waiting for them.

Doom sensed something as they made their way between the decking timbers that were stored there in house-high stacks. He slowed, held up one hand to warn the others, then yelled, "Down!" and flung himself sideways into the lee of a timber stack as a dozen Boogies opened fire at once. Max and Miss Torpenhow dove for cover too; Vespertine, trusting in her armor, lumbered into shelter with ricochets pinging off her battered breastplate. Max heard her promising the cat that she would keep him safe.

For a nasty few seconds — it felt much longer to Max — they found themselves pinned behind one of the stacks. From time to time, he would lean out and squeeze the trigger of the gun Doom had given him, and it would make hammering noises and jar his elbows while it pumped bullets randomly into the smoke and shadow at the far side of the warehouse. Once or twice, he saw scurrying figures there, and shot at them, but he never knew if he hit them, and he had never fired for long before someone fired back and the timber he was hiding behind started to dissolve in clouds of flying splinters and an awful drumming sound, as if flocks of invisible woodpeckers were attacking it. Doom and Miss Torpenhow were sheltering behind a neighboring stack. He could not see Vespertine, until suddenly there was a flash of light in the corner and there she was, breaking cover and striding in her dogged way toward the guns, with their muzzle flash reflecting from her armor and the bullets that hit her striking little sprays of sparks sometimes. Max stayed behind his timber stack and she passed out of sight, but he knew she had reached the enemy because he heard men yelling, and someone shouting in panic, "Jaeger! Jaeger!"

The gunfire grew raggedy and fell silent. Then Doom was calling to him to move forward and he moved, through the smoke, over a deck littered with spent shell casings, to where the Boethius men lay in wet heaps. It was a messy sight, and Max wished he had not seen it. Vespertine stood among the bodies, looking down at them, her nice blue armor red and dripping now, a dent in the front of her helmet giving her a grumpy look.

"They were scaring Small Cat," she said.

"There will be more of them," warned Doom, and, indeed, more could be heard, beyond the big sliding door at the far end of the hold. They were shouting orders and warnings out there, running to and fro in their heavy boots.

"Well, we're stuck here now," said Doom.

"I am sorry," said Miss Torpenhow. She touched his arm. "If I had not brought you here . . ."

"If you hadn't brought me, I'd still be staring into a beer mug in Bad Luftgarten," said Doom. There was a lightness about him, she thought; he was like a big old animal freed after a long captivity. "This is the way I always wanted to go out," he said. "A good cause, overwhelming odds. Stuff of stories, ain't it? Only I don't want you and Max going out with me. When the next wave start their nonsense, you make yourselves scarce. An old coot and a kid, you'll blend in easy enough with the Gut workers till you can get off this town and safe away."

"I am not an old coot, Mr. Doom!"

"You're my favorite old coot," he said, and something hit him in the side and sent him sprawling.

"Oddington!" wailed Miss Torpenhow, crouching over him.

Bullets were flicking past; Max could not see them, but he could feel them somewhere, and knew that the air around him was full of fast-moving pieces of hot lead, and that it was just blind luck that none had found him yet. The door was still shut: The gunfire was coming from the far end of the warehouse.

"They're behind us!" he shouted.

"Must have worked their way round through those same corridors we came down," said Doom, trying to rise, failing.

Max fired a burst in the vague direction of the enemy and then helped Miss Torpenhow drag Doom into the lee of a hopper full of flanges. He looked around for Vespertine, hoping she could help, but the Revenant had troubles of her own. Something was trying to wrench the hold door open, and it was taking all Vespertine's strength to keep it closed.

"They are coming from both sides!" Max shouted.

Miss Torpenhow was kneeling beside Doom, trying to bandage the wound in his side. Her hands were red and shining with the blood that kept pumping out of him. Max leaned out and fired another burst, just in time to fell two nomads who had been rushing toward him through the passages between the timber piles. He knew he'd hit them; he saw them fall; he felt nothing. Their friends, hidden among the stacks, started shooting back. He ducked behind the hopper, listening to the bullets make dull music as they slammed into it. He felt nothing. His hands were shaking, so it was difficult to do what needed to be done: unclipping the empty leather magazine from his Bugharin, taking a full one from his belt, clipping it into place. He felt nothing.

"Oddington," Miss Torpenhow was saying on the floor.

He could hear running boots again: more nomads, dodging from stack to stack, closer and closer to his hiding place while their friends kept shooting, so he dared not stick his head out to see how many they were or where.

Vespertine at the door gave a cry of frustration as the handle was wrenched out of her grip. The door rattled open, revealing the answer to a problem that had been dimly troubling Max.

Q: Who could be strong enough to open a door a Revenant was trying to hold shut?

A: Another Revenant, of course. Two more, in fact; no, three! Their gnarly, saurian armor slithered with dim reflections as they lumbered into the hold.

They were taller than Vespertine, and also wider. They were so encrusted with spikes and spines they reminded her of the porcupine that had killed her the first time around. And suddenly the vague itchy desire for revenge that had been driving her ever since she woke in Mortmain's lab found its focus. It was not soft once-born on whom she wanted revenge, but things like this: these clumsy, clanking parodies of life. They were so stupid, so contemptible, so ugly, and so like herself. She hated them.

She drove her blade into the throat of one, spraying sparks and gouts of oil. A second caught her from behind, held her by both arms so his undamaged comrade could finish her. But she discovered that there were secondary spikes concealed inside her forearms that jutted out behind her when the need arose; it had — they did. They punched through the Revenant's armor into whatever gumbo of mummified innards and arcane machinery lay beneath.

The Revenant howled with fury. Vespertine twisted free. The one who had been aiming a killing blow at her hit the one who had been holding her instead, crushing his head like a tin can. So that was one down and two to go. The one whose throat she had punctured was still stumbling around leaking black smoke so it was easy enough for her to collar him and rip his head clean off, her Arcade training coming in useful now, the head clanging on the deck like a dropped pan. This was what she had been built for, and she was enjoying herself.

But Revenant three was still undamaged, and only angered by the trick she'd played to make him brain his comrade. As she turned from the headless one, the third swung his polearm into her visor, and when she staggered back under the blow he seized her bladed arm and, twisting hard, ripped it from its roots and flung it away.

Vespertine watched it go, amazed. She looked down at the place where it had been: her armless shoulder joint jutting bone and multi-colored wires, the small sparks spitting. She looked up, and the polearm struck her again across the front of her helmet, and then again, and then again, and then again, and then she was on her knees, not quite sure how she'd gotten there, and the Revenant was swinging his polearm back for a last blow and she wondered what had become of Small Cat, and then the blow fell.

"Vespertine!" screamed Max.

But the green glow faded from her eyes, and she toppled backward like the wrecked machine she was, and lay there.

"No!" shouted Max, and emptied most of the new magazine at the Revenant who had struck her down, but the Revenant didn't seem to notice, and suddenly there were men emerging from the stacks all around him, and more coming in through the open door. Max threw his gun down and raised his hands, and someone hit him so hard in the side of the face he went away for a moment and woke up on the floor.

Miss Torpenhow was sobbing somewhere nearby. Smoke swirled and eddied under the electric lamps that swung on their long flexes from the warehouse ceiling. A man stood looking down at Max. He was a big man, wearing a red velvet coat over his armor. His face was tattooed to make him look like a jigsaw puzzle, though why anyone would want to complete a jigsaw of a face so ugly Max could not imagine.

"Angmering?" he asked.

Max nodded.

The man shrugged and drew his sword. "Kill the others too," he said to one of the men behind him, and then something curious happened to his head, as if one of the pieces of the jigsaw had suddenly been taken away. The man seemed to find it curious too, because he lowered his sword and put his hand up to the place, and a look of slow surprise crept across his face, and then he slumped sideways and Max did not see him again.

There was more gunfire happening. Max forced himself half upright, thinking vaguely about taking cover. The hold was filling with new people, not nomad mercenaries but men and women in ordinary clothes, or in the overalls of Gut workers. Some of them carried guns, and some were using crowbars and other tools of the salvage business, and they had taken the mercenaries by surprise. The Revenant who had struck poor Vespertine down came storming at the workers, but one of the fallen mercenaries had been carrying a huge gun, like a handheld cannon, and Miss Torpenhow — the same Miss Torpenhow who had once taught Max history and geometry and complained about his grammar — sprang forward, lifted the big gun up, and pulled the trigger. The recoil flung her backward, and the shot blew the Revenant's head apart. It blundered away toward the back of the warehouse somewhere and fell over.

"We must move!" people were shouting. "Move out! Move out! There will be more!"

Max made an effort, and got himself upright. Two men in gray overalls were carrying Doom away. He thought one of them was the same salvageman they had surprised under Shilpit when they first came aboard. It was all very confusing. And it was about to get more so.

One of the newcomers stopped in front of him and pulled off the welder's mask she had been wearing, and underneath was a girl. She had smudges of dirt on her long, delicate face, and her golden hair had been cut short, but there was no mistaking her.

"Helen?" he said.

"Max, you flaming idiot," said his sister. "What in the name of all the gods do you think you're doing here?"

45

THE PUDDING COURSE

When Strega worked out who she was, Tamzin was sure he would kill her, or at least throw her into a prison where she would wait to be killed. But Thorbury's Architect was a man who worked hard, rising before dawn each day to spend long hours in chart-strewn planning sessions and smoky engine rooms. He needed little sleep; he had no wife or family; he disliked art and music. Good food was his one pleasure, and he was not about to interrupt his dinner over a paltry little attempted coup. The soup bowls were cleared away, a main course of roasted duck was brought in, and Strega went on chatting happily to his guests, as if nothing had happened.

"I guessed who you were at once, of course," he said. "Did you think I would not have eyes in the skies above the Sculpture Garden? My people watched your little airship fly in from the west. They thought you must be scavengers, but I thought, maybe not, maybe here is young Angmering, trying some trick to win his city back. But I wasn't sure, and I imagined, if it was Angmering, he would arrive here on the Command Deck by airship, not sneak in from below. I must admit that threw me, as I'm sure it was intended to. He is cleverer than I had imagined, the Angmering boy. Do try the duck — it is superb."

Tamzin looked at the plate in front of her. It was a large plate, decorated with the crest of Max's family, and filled almost to the edges with creamy mashed potato, roasted carrots, greens, and slabs of duck, cooked rare. On the far side of the table, Trubshawe poked disconsolately at his own meal, but Tamzin could not even bring herself to pick up the heavy silver cutlery. The sight of the food made her stomach turn over. She wondered what was happening to Max and the others, down in the city's Gut. She listened for gunfire, or explosions, but the city's engines were still running, driving it on through the night toward the river. Their steady rumbling swallowed any other sounds.

A knock at the dining-room door. The two mercenaries who stood guard there stepped aside, and a third entered: a woman, with the same crested hairstyle as Boethius.

Strega nodded at her. "Captain Wommba. Is our problem downstairs sorted out?"

"A word in private, Architect?"

Strega laughed. "Please, Wommba, my guests are as eager as I am to hear your news."

"In private," said the woman, scowling. Strega, with a show of irritation, pushed back his chair, threw down his napkin, and went outside with her. Just for a moment, as she listened to their low, inaudible conversation on the far side of the door, Tamzin felt hopeful. Was it possible things were not going Strega's way down on Base Tier? Was it possible that Max, Hilly, and Doom were safe? But a moment later, when Strega returned to his seat, he seemed as smug as ever.

"So . . ." he said, pausing to savor a mouthful of duck.

"So . . . the question which arises now is, what shall we do with you both? The Angmering boy must be killed. We can't have people getting the idea they can attack my city and get away with it. Anyone who is down there with him must die too — they are probably already dead, of course. But you two . . . An artist is no harm to me. Perhaps I shall keep you around, Trubshawe. Perhaps I will consider letting you paint your great portrait of me. Or was that just a ruse to distract me from what your friends were planning downstairs?"

Trubshawe looked miserable and said nothing. Strega ate some more, then turned his friendly smile on Tamzin. "And you, Miss Pook. I am sure there is a place for you aboard the new Thorbury. What were you thinking of, throwing in your lot with Max Angmering and his friends? You come from nothing, just as I did. What have people of Angmering's class ever done for you, except make you risk your neck for their amusement?"

Tamzin did not know what she had been thinking. She did not even know what she was thinking at that moment. It was hard to think at all with his dark eyes on her, and that dark intelligence glittering behind them, ready to twist any answer she made and turn it back against her. He was playing with her. It reminded her of how Mortmain's Revenants had sometimes toyed with the less able Arcade fighters, mocking them, goading them, leading them on, letting them reveal their weaknesses before the Revenant grew weary of them and dealt the killing blow.

The room jolted as the city went too fast over some crumbling reef of rock. The glassware on the table jangled. One of the servants cried out in alarm, and Tamzin remembered that Strega was not a Revenant. Thorbury itself was the machine she had to fight. *It is like a giant Revenant Engine,* Vespertine had said. Down in its depths, Max and the rest of her team were doing their best to distract and disable it, but it could not be defeated until its brain was destroyed, and its brain was Strega, and she was the only one in position to strike him down.

"So, Miss Pook?" he said, pushing his empty plate aside, taking a sip of water. "Do take your time. You have gone a little pale. The motion of the city is unsettling you, perhaps? But you'll get used to it."

A servant took Tamzin's untouched main course away. Another set dessert in front of her — a dome-shaped, glistening pudding of some sort, with the red of raspberries oozing from beneath it. They took away the knife and fork she had not used to eat her main course, and left behind a smaller fork and a spoon from which her own distorted reflection looked up at her like a trapped genie. She considered the fork, and wondered how deep into Strega's eye she would have to drive it to kill him, but the thought of doing that, and the wobbling of the wet white pudding, and the red that seeped and mingled so glutinously with the grease around it, made her so sure she was going to be sick that she half stood, shoving her chair back, hand to her mouth . . .

And at that moment, without warning, the city stopped.

46

THE HIDEOUT

They had gone, by unnerving little tight companionways and the tubular passages that snaked across the city's underbelly, into a deep and rusty trough behind an axle housing where Helen Angmering and her friends had made a lair. There were lanterns swaying from the metal roof, crates and blankets to serve as furniture, someone brewing tea on a paraffin stove. Oddington Doom lay on a stained camp bed, while a fussy, nervous old man pulled bullets out of him and dropped them, one by one, into a dish his assistant held ready.

"Will he be all right, doctor?" asked Max, when the gory work was done.

"I'm not a doctor, young man. I'm a vet. Minding the livestock on the agricultural levels is more in my line. But I don't think anything serious has been punctured. I think, with luck . . ." He patted Max's arm, understanding that Max was worried for his friend, and needed to help in some way. "You'll find a small shrine to the gods of healing over there, beyond the pantry. Ask them to do what they can for him. You're wounded yourself, so they will look favorably on your prayers."

Max went in search of the shrine. Little plastic figures of the gods stood there and a lot of ribbons and coins had been placed in front of them. As he tried to find the words to pray, he fingered the dressing on his cheek. He kept forgetting he was wounded. It was just a graze. It was just a small cut and a bit of bruising; the dull pain of it seemed the least of his worries. His sister had dressed the wound herself, kneeling beside him, her rifle slung across her shoulder. He had asked her where she'd learned to use guns and tend wounds.

"I've been learning all sorts of things, Max," she said, before she was called away to see to someone else.

He mumbled some brief prayers, and went in search of Miss Torpenhow. She was near the stove, helping to hand out tea in tin mugs. She had come unscathed through all the gunfire, but that hand cannon she had turned on the Stalker had strained her arm so badly with its recoil that she wore a sling, and bruised her ribs so much when it knocked her backward that she winced each time she moved.

"What's happening?" asked Max, hoping the rough, serious-looking men and women who milled around the tea station had told her something.

"A lot of debate, I think," said Miss Torpenhow. "These good people are a sort of secret society who have been preparing to try to oust Strega ever since he took over. Apparently, there are several hideouts like this where they store weapons and supplies. They were not yet ready to move, but our arrival forced them to act. Now they are trying to decide what happens next."

"What happens next," said Helen Angmering, appearing just then to claim her own mug of tea, "is that Strega's mercenaries

288

sweep through Base Tier, and find us, and we have to fight them, even though we have not enough people, or enough guns, or enough time to prepare. If we'd had another month to get ready, we might have stood a chance. So thanks for that, Max."

"I'm sorry," said Max. "I didn't know . . ."

"You thought you were the only one who wanted Strega gone? You thought we needed you to swoop in like some sort of hero and save us all? It never occurred to you that good people here would be busy trying to get rid of him as well?"

She went to sit down on one of the packing crates that stood about. A young man followed her, and spoke quietly to her, then both of them looked at Max.

Helen smiled and shook her head. "It's all right," she said. "It's all right, Max. I'm glad you're here. Something would have sparked a fight sooner or later. I'm glad it was you. I'm glad you brought that Revenant with you. They say it took out two of Strega's before they got it. That will make things a lot easier."

"Her name was Vespertine," said Max, feeling suddenly appalled that he had just let them leave poor Vespertine lying there on the battlefield like a bit of broken machinery. And what about her cat? What had become of her little cat?

"I didn't know those awful things had names," said Helen. She reached out to the man behind her, took his hand, and drew him into the light of the lantern that swung to and fro above her. "Max, this is Raoul. I've been staying here on Base Tier with Raoul's family. Most people down here are too scared to make a stand against the nomads, but they all hate Strega. We thought if we could just get enough weapons together and wait for the right moment . . ."

"But the right moment never comes," said Raoul. Helen was still holding his hand. He withdrew it gently from her, and held it out for Max to shake. He was a long, lean person, and he spoke with the accent of Base Tier. "I am glad to meet you, Max Angmering. I'm glad something's happening at last. We killed a lot of them in the holds. They're saying we killed Boethius himself. Everyone in Thorbury must know the fight has started now. Maybe they'll come and help."

"I wouldn't count on that," said another man, older, pushing past Max. "Helen, Raoul, we just had word from our people on Upper Residential. Strega's sending more nomads. They're coming down all the stairways, and the spinal elevator. If we wait here for them, we'll die like rats in a trap."

"Well, I don't fancy that much," said Helen. "We should do what we discussed."

The man grinned. So did Raoul.

"What did you discuss?" asked Max.

"We're going to take the main engine control room," said Helen. "If we can hold that, we'll have something to bargain with."

Her words, already hard to hear beneath the thunder of their city, were drowned out entirely by the activity that had already begun around her. People were pulling on makeshift armor and making ready to move out. Those lucky enough to have stolen nomad guns were checking them over and slipping ammunition into the pockets of their overalls; others were grabbing the crowbars and shovels that would serve them as weapons.

Miss Torpenhow handed Max the pistol she had been given by Oddington Doom. "Not much use to me with my arm out of action," she said.

"What will you do?" he asked.

Orders were being shouted. Helen and the others were making their way toward the exit. Max wanted to go with them, but lingered, waiting for Miss Torpenhow's answer.

She shook her head. "I will stay here with the wounded," she said. "Someone has to explain the situation to Mr. Doom when he wakes from his nap."

47

SMALL CAT

All through the battle in the warehouse Small Cat had stayed hidden in the coil of rope where Vespertine had hidden him. But when the gunfire and the shouting died away he grew bored and climbed out. He stepped fastidiously around the spilled blood, played for a while with some of the shiny cartridge casings that were scattered everywhere, and found his way eventually to where Vespertine lay among the wreckage of the other fallen Stalkers. Climbing up onto her battered armor, he sat on her chest and let out a small, plaintive meow.

Vespertine, deep in dreams she was not entirely sure were her own, heard the sound, and dimly recognized it. The strange devices inside her sparked and jolted back into life. She rose through ghostly veils of memory into the hard light from the warehouse lamps.

Her helmet had been so beaten out of shape that she could barely raise her head, or see out of the eyeholes when she did. She reached up with her left hand and, after great difficulty, succeeded in removing it. Only then did she remember that her right arm was missing.

The cat jumped down off her armor and walked away toward the door with his tail sticking straight up.

"Small Cat," warned Vespertine, "it may be dangerous out there. You should come back."

The cat did not come back. So Vespertine heaved herself upright and went limping after him.

Outside the door was a street. It looked very like any street on the base tier of any city or large town in that particular period of the Traction Era: a metal pavement, a metal ceiling and a forest of fat supporting pillars holding the two apart. Along the sides of the street were the entrances to other warehouses, but they were all shut. Posters stuck to the pillars showed the round, pale face of a bearded man with the word "Strega" printed above him. Vespertine remembered Tamzin and the others talking about this man before she came into the city. She was more interested in her cat, though.

"Small Cat!" she called, and was answered by a faint *meow* from the end of the street.

She went in the direction of the sound, her left leg dragging slightly. Around the corner was a kind of square, and a shallow flight of metal steps leading up into a brightly lit covered area with more posters of Strega and other things upon the walls, and large doors concealed behind a concertina gate at the back. A lot of people stood around in the brightly lit area, as if waiting for something. Her cat was running up the steps. Vespertine, afraid the people might harm him, called out again and started after it. She ignored the people, who screamed when they saw her climbing the steps and ran this way and that with shouts of, "Stalker!"

A man with a peaked cap and brass buttons on his coat stood in front of her and said, "You can't come in here! You clear off now!"

But Vespertine raised her one remaining hand, and he cleared off himself.

Small Cat, alarmed by all the noise, scurried behind a large, rectangular machine that stood against one of the walls.

"Come out," said Vespertine.

Small Cat did not come out.

The machine was called SNAX. It was a glass-fronted box, in which lots of food was on display. Vespertine crouched beside it and tried to reach her hand into the narrow space where Small Cat was cowering, but her hand was too big. She stood up again, and started to move the machine, but that was difficult with only one arm. While she was trying, a bell chimed, and the doors at the back of the area slid open. There was another small room behind them, and the people inside it opened the concertina gate and came hurrying out. Humans with skulls on their armor and guns in their hands, and behind them one who was not human at all.

"Quick, boys," the man in charge was shouting. "Form up. We'll meet with Wommba's team at the central port axle housing and push forward from there, shooting anyone who tries to stop us. Kulkin's lads'll be doing the same on the starboard side."

"But is it true they've got their own Stalkers, Sarge?" asked a worried voice.

"It is not true they've got their own Stalkers, soldier. That is a fib what is being put about by villains to frighten idiots like you."

"Then what's that, Sarge? Over there, behind the snacks machine . . ."

The machine, which Vespertine had been starting to lever away from the wall when the elevator descended, chose that moment to fall. The crash echoed around the station. The mercenaries who had emerged from the elevator reacted to Vespertine's appearance in several different ways. Some ran out into the street, screaming as loudly as the people earlier had done. Some drew weapons and started to fire them at her, until Vespertine swatted them aside. Some turned and fled back into the elevator, only to be swatted aside themselves by the clanking black metal Stalker that had traveled down with them from the upper tiers. It raised its arms, and fearsome-looking blades slid out of slots in its armor.

"I used to have one of those," said Vespertine, "but it has fallen off."

The Stalker swung a bladed fist at her. Ducking, she noticed that men were busy on the steps outside, setting up some kind of heavy weapon on a tripod. Small Cat, meanwhile, fled across the station and into the elevator.

Vespertine sighed. She did not have time for this. "You are frightening Small Cat," she told the Stalker. She grabbed him by the next fist he flailed at her and swung him so that he was between her and the weapon on the steps outside. The weapon's first shot punched him in the back so hard that he cannoned into Vespertine and almost knocked her over. The green light died out of his eyes as if a switch had been thrown. Vespertine gave a shove that sent the wreckage of him reeling backward to scatter the weapons team while she stomped into the elevator.

Small Cat sat in the corner, licking his paws. A single terrified mercenary was whimpering prayers to the gods of war as he punched desperately at the controls. Vespertine picked him up and threw him out.

"Never use elevators during a battle," she called after him, remembering something that her friend Oddington Doom had told her.

That made her wonder what had happened to Oddington

Doom, and to Max and Miss Torpenhow. She scooped her cat up and kissed him on the top of his head — she did not know why, but that seemed like something one should do to cats.

"Come along, Small Cat," she said. "We must go and find the others."

But the elevator doors had already slid shut, and a sudden lurch told her that the elevator had begun moving upward at speed. It gave her a strange sensation, as if she had left her stomach behind. But she did not think she owned a stomach. She watched the moving arrow above the door, and wondered where the elevator was taking her.

48

STOP THE CITY!

They were a strange bunch, the rebel band who went swarming through the streets of Base Tier that night. Some were workers from the Deep Gut, faces kippered by furnace smoke and ingrained with dirt. Others were clerks and housewives from the middle tiers who had fallen foul of Strega and his nomads and been sent to the warrens below as punishment. A few, like Max and Helen, had come from even higher up the city. In days gone by, each group would have grumbled loudly about the others. In days to come, no doubt, they would again. But for that night they were united. They had one aim, and one hope. They would have died for each other, and knew they might yet have to.

The warehouse district was a labyrinth, and Strega's nomads could not guard every street and alleyway. The rebels went aft without meeting any resistance, only a few nightshift workers — some who ran from them, some who cheered them on, and a few who joined them. They hurried along walkways between the hot, thundering blocks that housed the city's engines. They had still not fired a shot by the time they arrived at the main control room.

It was a drum-shaped building, with a single door set high up at the top of a spindly outside stairway. Beyond it lay the open apron at the city's stern, where the exhaust stacks towered up into night and rain. After the heat of the warrens, the air smelled clean. Max caught a scent of hay and wet earth from the farming terraces on the tier above.

They crouched low and ran along wet metal catwalks through the rain and the shadows of vast ducts until they were clattering up the stairway to the control-room door. For a moment, Max thought they would make it all the way to the top unseen, but then the sky tore open high above the city and a sudden blue-white flash of lightning revealed them to the nomad sentry at the stairs' top. He managed to get out one warning shout before a lady named Dindy Wibs who used to practice archery every Tuesday morning in Bellevue Park raised her bow and put an arrow through his throat. He gurgled, toppled over the handrail, and fell, but Max never heard him hit the ground because by then other nomads were rushing out and there were popping sounds, shouts, the quick stuttering light of gunfire, more bodies falling down the stairs and off the stairs, and the lightning flashed again and showed Max that the men who had been leading the desperate attack were gone and he, Max, was somehow in the front of the assault, or near the front.

They fought their way to the door, and through it, and on through offices where glass shattered and blinds jangled as the bullets flew. And then they were standing on the circular balcony that ran around the control room, and the last few nomads who had taken shelter there were throwing down their guns and putting up their hands, and the engineers who kept the city running were rising from their stations at the control panels, wondering what to do.

Max's sister found him in the confusion. She told him

298

something, but he was too busy staring at the wet red badge pinned on the shoulder of her overalls to understand. "You've been shot!"

"I'm fine," said Helen. She didn't look it; she was as white as an unwritten page, and swaying slightly. "I said, there are more nomads coming. A whole crowd of them, moving through the engine district behind us. We have to let Strega know we're here."

Max thought of what she had said about holding the control room so they had something to bargain with. Here, now, with half of them dead and a much bigger force closing in on them, it did not seem like quite such a foolproof plan. But he supposed he had to try. He ran down the stairs, looking for a phone or vacuum tube that he could use to contact the Command Deck. Then he had a better idea. A group of engineers stood watching him, waiting to see what he would do. He wasn't certain if they were Thorbury men or Strega's hirelings, so he pointed Doom's gun at them and said, "Stop the engines."

"What, all of them? It's a complex process. It takes hours to make the necessary —"

"There is an emergency brake, isn't there?" (Max was pretty sure there was — Miss T had covered it in his lessons when he was a kid. Or had he imagined it? How he wished he had paid more attention now!) "Just do it!" he shouted, waving his gun at the men. They fled to their stations, started pulling levers, turning dials, shouting, "Full astern all!" down intercom trumpets, while Max, to encourage them, fired his gun into the air and shouted, "Stop the city!"

❋

The city stopped. The plates and glasses on Strega's table, slow to get the message, kept moving, flinging themselves enthusiastically off the table's edge to smash upon the floor. Strega's pudding landed with a squelch in the middle of his chest. A servant entering with a tray of glasses lost her footing and went crashing into the mercenary who stood guard inside the door. They went down in a heap, glasses shattering, the mercenary grunting guttural nomad swear words as he shoved the girl off him and scrambled up . . .

. . . only to find that the gun he'd dropped as he fell had found its way into the hands of Tamzin Pook, who thumbed off the safety catch, and discovered within herself again that cool detachment that had served her so well in the Amusement Arcade.

Strega, irritably trying to wipe dessert off his coat, sensed the atmosphere in the room shift, looked up, and grew very still and thoughtful. Tamzin swung the gun between him and the mercenary, who was frozen in a curious position, half risen from the floor.

"She will not use it," said Strega. "If she was the sort of person who could shoot us in cold blood, she would have done so by now. Take it back."

The mercenary unfroze, and took a step toward Tamzin, reaching out for the gun. But Trubshawe, who had held on tight to his pudding plate during the jolt, suddenly saw a use for it and, jumping forward, smashed it down on the man's shaven head. The blow was not hard enough to knock the nomad out, but it dazed him, and as he staggered and looked round to see who had hit him, the girl he'd sworn at slammed the heavy wooden drinks tray into his head from the other side, and he went sprawling.

"Trubshawe, take his sword!" shouted Tamzin.

The sword was a nomad kindjal. It was short, ugly, and dangerous-looking, much like its owner. Trubshawe tugged it from its sheath and stood up, holding it, looking as if he were posing for the figure of a warrior in one of his own paintings. The servant girl, trembling, clutched her tray like a shield. The other servants shifted and said nothing, waiting to see which way things went. The man on the floor groaned. Tamzin looked down at him, but he showed no immediate interest in getting up again. She turned back at Strega. His chair was empty.

"Where is he?" she asked.

The servants shrugged, shook their heads. She could not know if they were on Strega's side, or if, like her, they had been too distracted to notice him leave.

"He will come back now with more of his hooligans, and we shall all be killed," said the girl with the tray, not sounding too scared about it, just slightly surprised, as if she had not expected her evening to turn out this way.

"Why didn't you shoot him when you had the chance, Tamzin?" asked Trubshawe.

Tamzin had no answer for him, so she went gun in hand to the door and through it, hoping to stop Strega before he found his reinforcements. Trubshawe, the tray girl, and two of the other servants came with her, hurrying across the echoey, whitewashed council chamber, down the stairs and across the lobby.

"Where are all the guards?" asked Trubshawe nervously.

"Gone down to deal with Max and Doom and Miss T," Tamzin guessed.

"What, all of them?"

"There's fighting in the Gut," said the tray girl. "I heard Mr. Strega talking to that Wommba woman while I was waiting to bring your pudding in. She said there was a battle going on, and not going any too well by the sound of it, and he got angry and said she was to send everybody down, and she said 'Everybody?' and he said, 'Everybody.'"

"Not everybody," said Tamzin.

They had reached the entrance, where all the guards had been earlier. The guard post was empty now, but Strega had not left the city's Command Deck undefended. Of course he hadn't.

Out on the open expanse of the deck, where rain was blowing under the streetlamps, the Architect was waiting. Between him and Tamzin stood three of the Scrap Metal Seven.

49

SCRAP METAL

Trubshawe and the others started to edge slowly backward, as if they hoped the Revenants might not have noticed them. The Revenants stood motionless. But Tamzin had seen the six green eyes in those three blank metal faces brighten the way they always did when a Revenant acquired its target. They would be fast, these things, she thought. If you ran from them, they would run faster. If you shot at them, the bullets would bounce off.

"Sword," she told Trubshawe, stretching out her hand for it.

"But, Tamzin —"

"Give me the sword," she said, "and go. Get back to the airship, if you can."

She passed him the gun, and took the sword. It was heavy, but well balanced. The leather-wrapped hilt felt good in her hand. It was not electric, but, even so, if she could jam it into a weak point on those machines she reckoned it might do some damage. If she could only avoid the blades they would be swinging at her for long enough to get close . . .

"But, Tamzin," said Trubshawe.

"Go!" she said. "Go find the others, if they're living still. And if

303

they aren't, then fly away and paint a picture of us, so people will know how well we fought."

Lightning flashed, painting the spiky shadows of the Revenants across the deckplates. Tamzin kept her eyes on them. After a moment, she felt Trubshawe's hand rest for a second on her shoulder, and then heard the footsteps as he and the servants backed away, slowly at first and then starting to hurry.

"Where are you going?" called Strega, out of the darkness beyond the reach of the streetlamps. "Stay! Miss Pook is supposed to be a bit of an expert at this sort of thing. I'd say she has a fair chance. I'm looking forward to watching her pit her skills against these three. Take your seats for the big fight! Place your bets!"

He was moving as he spoke, making his way toward the elevator station. A brief trip would take him to the tier below. The men guarding the air dock could come with him down to Base Tier, where he would find out why Boethius was taking so long to bring things under control. He was sorry to miss Tamzin's last stand; he genuinely did believe she might be able to bring down one of the Scrap Metal Seven before they killed her, and he would have liked to see that. But if he lingered on the Command Deck there was always the danger that Trubshawe might find the nerve to take a potshot at him, so he strode into the station, just as the bell above the doors chimed to announce that the elevator had arrived.

There were no staff on duty. Strega slid the concertina gate open himself. The doors behind it opened with a sigh. A haze of smoke hung in the elevator car. The hot metal aroma of the city's bowels came out of it, along with a scent that might have been gun smoke. Green eyes found Strega's face and bathed it in their eerie glow.

"What are you doing up here?" he asked sharply, assuming this was another of Boethius's Revenants. "You're needed in the — "

Thunder broke above the city, and white light briefly flooded the elevator station as Vespertine stepped out of the smoke. Her armor had been battered by bullets, her armless shoulder dribbled dark fluids, her dead face was helmetless and without expression. From its perch upon her good shoulder a small black cat looked down at Strega. It bared sharp little teeth at him, and hissed.

"Who the —?" Strega started to say.

Vespertine's huge hand slammed him aside. He hit the station wall like a flung doll, slid down it, and lay still. The lightning flared again as Vespertine stomped past him, out into the rain.

The three Stalkers were closing in on Tamzin. One hefted a double-ended axe no human could have lifted. One fired up a sputtering, diesel-powered battle strimmer. The third just shrugged and sprouted six-inch spikes from its arms and upper torso, like a metal cactus. They were all intent on Tamzin, but they all sensed Vespertine arrive. Their big heads swung like turrets as she came through the rain toward them.

"More of you," said Vespertine. "Old dead things. Old rusty tins of angry pickles. I hate your sort."

The long-ago technomancers who reanimated the Scrap Metal Seven had not built them to talk. They had no voices. There were not even mouths in their flat steel faces. Their eyes flickered when Vespertine spoke. Tamzin had the feeling they disapproved of this upstart, with her fancy modern armor and her fancy modern ways. They turned to face her, forgetting Tamzin. Tamzin wondered for a moment if she might make it out of this alive after all, and then thought not, because even Vespertine couldn't take on all three of these old horrors, especially while she was missing an arm, and especially while the arm she was missing was the one with her main weapon attached to it.

So I must try to even up the odds a bit, thought Tamzin, and found before the thought was done that she was already sprinting toward the broad back of the nearest Stalker, the one with the axe. A roll of thunder masked her footfalls. A white tree of lightning spread across the sky. She scrambled up the Stalker's back as if it were a wall. Just as she had hoped, it turned out that he could not bring the axe to bear on her when she was sitting astride his huge shoulders and, just as she had hoped, her sword fitted in through the gaps of his armor. She jammed it downward into complicated workings and was rewarded with sparks, grinding noises, and a small electric shock. The Stalker shambled sideways and almost fell, and she tumbled off his shoulders and hit the deckplates. The dust was turning quickly to mud under the rain; she slithered as she tried to rise. The Stalker, still spraying sparks from his neck, swung his axe at her, missed, raised it for another swing, and caught Vespertine's massive foot in his chest. All her weight was behind the kick, and it sent him clanging down. Before he could rise again, Vespertine had snatched up the axe and slammed it through him, pinning him to the deck. She wheeled toward Tamzin, and Tamzin felt a sleek, writhing bundle of wet fur and sharp little claws pressed into her hands.

"Please look after this small cat," said Vespertine, and turned away to deal with the second Stalker as he came at her with his battle strimmer.

Tamzin slithered away through the mud, the cat struggling in her hands. Trubshawe and a couple of the servants had lingered to watch the fight, or had come back when Vespertine arrived — Tamzin did not know why they were standing there, but she was glad of them. "Please look after this small cat," she said, pushing the animal at Trubshawe, and then turned back into the fight.

The whirling, bladed chains of the battle strimmer were designed for mowing ranks of nomad infantry, not for use against the armor of a Revenant. They made sparks and a tremendous din as they flailed against Vespertine's chest, but she reached past them, grabbed the strimmer's shaft, snapped it off short, and rammed the jagged end through the Stalker's eye. His head exploded in greenish flames, and Vespertine turned her attention to his spiky friend, who was attacking simultaneously.

The cactus-spiked one's battle plan was simple, and involved bear hugs. He would have made short work of any human he folded into that pincushion embrace. But, again, his tactics were no use against Vespertine's armor. Did the Stalkers think she was human, Tamzin wondered, circling at a safe-ish distance while the cactus wrapped his huge arms around Vespertine and squeezed. Vespertine jabbed at him with her one remaining elbow spur, worked her arm free, and reached up. She groped her way across his visor and crammed a finger in through each of his eye sockets until she was holding his metal head like a bowling ball. For a long few seconds, they stood frozen like that, the Stalker's spikes grinding against Vespertine's armor, Vespertine straining with all the hydraulic muscles of her single arm. Then in a spray of oil or something nastier the head was off and Vespertine was holding it aloft, the way Arcade fighters sometimes did to let the cheering crowds applaud their triumph.

The headless Stalker fell over. The one with the axe stuck through him lay still, like a big beetle pinned in a display. The third, with his head on fire, came back for more. His visor had melted or fallen off and you could see the skull beneath, wrapped in green flames, but still the dark machinery inside him drove him on. He was holding the heavy engine of the battle strimmer by its snapped-off shaft, and swinging it like a club at Vespertine's unprotected head.

"Eve!" shouted Tamzin, and again she was moving without thought, using the body of the skewered Stalker as a step to launch off, hewing with her flimsy sword at the burning one's arm.

The sword broke. Vespertine, alerted by Tamzin's warning cry, dodged the blow. The Stalker swung again, blindly, and hit Tamzin.

It felt like being struck by a speeding city. Even before she hit the deck, she knew bones were broken and maybe worse. She landed hard, slid three feet or so in the mud, tried to rise, and found she couldn't move. There was blood in her mouth. She spat out pinkish foam. Pain like an immense dark wave reared over her. The last thing she saw as the wave came crashing down was the Stalker collapsing to his knees, still feebly swinging the broken strimmer. Then Vespertine knocked him down and stamped his skull flat, and the last green embers burning there went out, and there was only darkness.

50

SURRENDER

It was weirdly quiet in the control room. The thunder was growing less frequent as the storm moved away. The captured mercenaries squatted in a corner, guarded by Raoul's father and Dindy Wibs, the archery lady. Helen was having the hole in her shoulder bandaged by the vet. The engineers stood or sat in nervous little groups at their stations, with nothing to do now the engines were shut down. Max left them there and went upstairs and through the shattered offices to the doorway, where Raoul and a dozen other survivors waited for the next assault.

"There's movement out there," reported a girl with binoculars, positioned in a darkened office off the small lobby. "They're hanging back still, out under the ducts."

"What are they waiting for?" someone groaned.

"Bringing up Stalkers maybe?" wondered Raoul.

"No sign of any," said the girl.

Broken glass squeaked and grated as people moved around, crouching, looking for better vantage points from which to fire when the nomads launched their attack.

"Someone coming," called the girl. "Hold up . . . It's just one. He's on his own. On *her own* — it's Wommba."

"Who's Wommba?" Max asked Raoul.

"Jex Wommba, Boethius's second-in-command," Raoul said. "What trick is she trying?" He shouted to the girl with the binoculars, "What do you see, Etta?"

"She's got a white flag," the girl called back. "She's waving it."

"It's a trick," someone said.

From outside, faintly, came a new voice. "Max Angmering!" it shouted. "Is Max Angmering in there?"

"Why is she asking for me?" Max wondered.

"She thinks you're our leader," said Raoul. "It makes sense. You're Mayor Angmering's son, you come aboard tonight, all this kicks off."

"But I'm not in charge. That's you, or your dad, or Helen . . ."

"Max Angmering!" the Wommba woman shouted, out there in the rain.

"She wants to talk," said Max. "That's better than fighting, isn't it?"

He started to go toward the door, but Raoul pulled him back. "No, Max! They might have someone ready to shoot you as soon as you go outside."

"But they might not," said Max. "She might really want to strike a bargain."

"I'll go," said Raoul.

"No," said Max. "Because if it is a trick, and they do shoot me, well, you're more use to Thorbury than me. You, and Helen, and all the rest of you. I'm nobody really. All I've got is a name. So I may as well use it."

Before Raoul could protest, he went to the door and opened it. No shots rang out. He stepped outside. Rain was blowing into the city. The huge ducts of the exhaust path gleamed coldly in the first light of a new day. Down below him, at the bottom of the staircase he had fought his way up half an hour ago, a woman with a white-blonde crest of hair stood looking at him. The flag she held up was a dirty sheet. It flapped wetly in the wind that gusted between the exhaust stacks.

"Max Angmering," she said.

"Captain Wommba," said Max.

She glanced behind her, into the complicated shadows of the engine district. Max imagined all the other nomads waiting there, watching him, fingering the triggers of their guns.

Then Wommba looked up at him again and said, "We had a message from the Command Deck. There's been a change of power. A man called Trubshawe is in charge up there now. Says Strega is his captive."

"Trubshawe?" said Max.

"Thing is," Wommba went on, before Max could ask her about Tamzin, or what had happened up there, "according to our contract, my people and me are supposed to go and rescue Strega now. But we've wasted a lot of blood already in this city. Too much for what Strega's paying us. We've had a pretty good offer from the Mayor of Hamburg, who's off on some mad adventure out east . . ."

"I heard about that," said Max.

"So if you send our wounded out and any prisoners you've got, we might take a rain check on this little war. Get in our airships and push off. How does that sound?"

Max started to giggle with relief, then remembered that he was

Mayor of Thorbury now, and giggling was beneath him. He drew himself up as straight as he could and said, "You have our permission to gather your people and depart."

Jex Wommba gave him an ironic little salute. "If you run into any trouble in the future, Mr. Mayor," she said, "just give us a call. We'll be trading as the Wommba Brigade from now on. Our rates are very reasonable."

"What about Tamzin?" Max shouted as she turned away. "Is Tamzin Pook alive?"

The woman shrugged, and kept walking. Her voice came back at him through the rain. "Who knows?"

51

THE GATES OF THE SUNLESS COUNTRY

There was a white ceiling, and a patch of sunlight on it some-times, and sometimes the sunlight slipped from the ceiling down the wall beyond, and there were the moving shadows of clouds.

For a long while that was all that Tamzin knew, except that faces sometimes appeared, looking down at her: Max Angmering's face, or Miss Torpenhow's, or Trubshawe's, or other faces that she did not know. There were voices too, coming and going, mingling with her dreams.

A nasty blow; the arm is broken; a lot of cracked ribs; internal injuries . . .

Were they talking about her? Washed in and out on tides of pain-killing medicine, she did not *feel* as if she had broken bones, internal injuries.

But there came an evening when the sunlight on the ceiling was an evening color, and the face leaning over her was Vespertine's. The shock of that jolted Tamzin far enough awake that she remem-bered what had happened to her, and could guess where she must be: a hospital in Thorbury.

Which meant she must have won, she supposed.

Vespertine's eyes looked down unblinkingly. More memories came back to Tamzin.

"You smashed those old Revenant Engines up all right," she said, and was surprised by how thin and far away her own voice sounded.

"They were frightening Small Cat," said Vespertine, and scooped up the cat, which had been sharpening his claws on Tamzin's bed-clothes. (Cats were not permitted in the hospital, but no one had felt like pointing that out to Vespertine.)

She stood holding the cat and looking down at Tamzin. Her battered armor had been retouched with paint that was not quite the same shade of blue, and the bullet holes were patched with neat little disks of brass, pinked at the edges, like stars. Her expression was so unreadable that Tamzin started to read things of her own into it. She started to think that maybe fighting those Revenants had brought back all Vespertine's memories of Margate.

"Do you remember being Eve?" she said.

Vespertine nodded solemnly. "I have all her memories. I have had them since we left Margate. But they are not my memories. They are Eve's, and she is dead, and I am someone new."

"She is dead and I'm what killed her," said Tamzin in her small new voice. "Do you remember that day in the Arcade?"

"I remember Eve's memory of it."

"I should have warned her. I could have warned her. I didn't mean it to happen, but I sort of hoped it might. I thought it would serve her right. Have you come to get revenge for her?"

Vespertine put the cat on her shoulder. It walked over her head and down onto the other shoulder, where it started playing with the wires that jutted from where her arm had been. "It was a

Revenant that killed Eve Vespertine," she said, "and I have avenged her by destroying six of them. So that is over. I came to see if you were awake, Tamzin Pook, and you are. I shall tell the others. They will be glad. I am glad too. We make a hot team, you and me."

❀

When Miss Torpenhow returned at last to her own little apartment, she found it unchanged. On her travels, she had imagined all sorts of disasters — it might have been demolished, or looted, or turned into quarters for mercenaries. Busy nursing poor Oddington, she found excuses not to come and visit it, for several days, because she was afraid of what she would find. But when she summoned up the courage, it was all just as she had left it, except that the dust lay a little more thickly on the windowsills and the tops of the piano. Mr. and Mrs. Werner had popped in a few times to water her plants and gather the letters that had piled up on the doormat. There was a musty, shut-up feeling about the place, and Miss Torpenhow busied herself for a while throwing open windows to let the fresh air in.

But something had happened to the apartment after all, because when she sat down in her own armchair and looked about she could not help but think, Did I really live here all those years? Is all this stuff really mine? It seemed so curious, the shelves of books, the roses on the wallpaper, the dowdy clothes hanging on the rail in the bedroom. It was like the stage set for a play that had ended. It did not feel like home at all.

❀

Wherever Max went during the heady few weeks that followed the battle, people would greet him as if it were he alone who had saved them from Strega.

"Angmering! Angmering!" bystanders shouted happily when he passed, as if having a member of the old ruling family in charge again could somehow undo all the change that Strega's time had wrought. The new council had far more members from the lower tiers, but even they seemed to assume that, when elections were held in the autumn, it would be Max Angmering who would be voted in as mayor.

Meanwhile, Thorbury was reversing slowly and carefully back along the path it had carved for itself through the Sculpture Garden. It stopped each evening so that the refugees from the towns it had so rudely eaten could come aboard if they wished. Plenty did, and where they were all to live was becoming a problem. At the first meeting of the new council it was decided that plans to rebuild the Command Deck just as it has always been were premature. Max and some of the old councillors argued as hard as they could, but his sister, and Raoul, and the other new delegates all agreed that with the population increasing so suddenly, Strega's schemes for enlarging the lower tiers were too sensible to abandon.

Even Strega himself might be of help, said Helen. Trubshawe and the town hall servants had found him lying unconscious in the upper elevator station on the night of the battle, and now he was kept under heavy guard in the prison's deepest cell, awaiting execution. Perhaps, if they reduced his sentence to life imprisonment, he might consult on the improvements.

It all gave Max the feeling that Strega had won. Perhaps it had never been Strega who was the problem, but a dark idea that had used him as a vessel. The idea was out in the world now, ready to shape it in sinister new ways. He supposed Helen and the others would want to go ahead with Strega's improvements to the engines too;

they would have to, if Thorbury were to carry so much more weight. And what about the Jaws? He had glimpsed the blueprints Strega had drawn up for a whole new set of civic mandibles, capable of swallowing larger prey than Thorbury had ever hunted before. Would those be built too?

"Angmering! Angmering!" people shouted as he walked around the Command Deck. Flapping banners tried to give an air of gaiety to the shanty town of temporary offices that had sprung up around the town hall. Outside the elevator station, a mound of wreaths marked the spot where Max's father had been killed. There were plans to erect a permanent memorial. But the rooftops Max had scrambled over as a boy, the streets he had walked, the parks he had played in, the town hall where he had lived, all were gone, as if they had never been.

Max waved at his well-wishers. But this was not his city. The Thorbury he loved lived only in his memory now, and he thought he might remember it better if he went far away.

❋

As for Oddington Doom, he had come "almost to the gates of the Sunless Country" as people said in those days, and it had taken a long, long time for him to find his way back. While he lay there in the hospital, in a room a few doors down from Tamzin's, Miss Torpenhow sat by his bed and read to him from books she fetched from her apartment, not caring whether he was awake or not. So what he remembered of his illness, when he began to feel well again, was her voice, and her face looking down at him, like an angel sitting guard. And if she was a rather old and bony angel, Doom did not care; he had come to love every line on her face, and every one of her persnickety mannerisms.

Whether she felt the same way about him, he was not sure. The fact that she had devoted so much time to him suggested that she might. She would talk for hours, and sometimes, when he did not want to talk, she would sit in silence, holding his hand in hers. But perhaps she would have done those things for any of her friends if they were injured? So Doom kept his love to himself, and it made him feel as melancholy in his own way as Max.

❋

Of the six of them, only Giotto Trubshawe was entirely happy during those weeks. To everyone's surprise, including his own, he had acted bravely and resourcefully after Vespertine finished off the Stalkers. He had rallied the town hall servants into a sort of militia, secured the elevator station, and captured Strega — and while it was true that Strega had been unconscious at the time, that was hardly Trubshawe's fault, and while it was also true that the battle had been over by then and the elevator station hadn't really needed securing, Trubshawe had not known that at the time. So he was a hero of the city, which he liked, and he was painting again, which he liked even more.

Although the Command Deck was not to be returned to its former glory, the stark white walls of the council chamber were an affront even to the most hardheaded members of the Emergency Council. Trubshawe had been put in charge of restoring the murals there, and teams of students under his command were carefully brushing and wiping and peeling away the whitewash until the figures of gods and goddesses and long-dead Angmerings emerged, looking somehow transformed by their experiences, like everyone else aboard Thorbury.

52

HOME

There came a day — a late summer day of sunshine and high white clouds, with the city moving south at a gentle pace — when all of them were finally well enough and free enough to meet up at one of the cafés that were now reopening in Bellevue Park. There they sat around a table set with tea and coffee pots and plates of the pastries for which Thorbury's cafés were famed, and talked about the things they had been through together. Then Max felt he had come home at last. It was not the city that was his home now, he thought; it was these people. He looked across the table at Tamzin, while the others were laughing at some tale Trubshawe was telling, and her eyes met his, and he guessed she felt the same way. More tea and coffee pots arrived to take the places of the empty ones. The mountain of pastries dwindled to a molehill. Vespertine, who had no need of pastries herself, fed pieces of them to Small Cat, who sat in his favorite place on her shoulder. And at last the talk turned to what they would do next.

"I shall be working for at least another year on the town hall," declared Trubshawe. "I am designing a great mural commemorating the battle, and after that the city may have other commissions for me. I am having the contents of my studio shipped here from Bad Luftgarten."

"I suppose I shall go back to tutoring," said Miss Torpenhow, trying to sound cheerful about it. "Though, I confess, making history has been a great deal more exciting than teaching it ever was."

"What about you, Tamzin?" asked Max.

"I don't know, do I?" said Tamzin. Her injuries were mostly mended, but she felt useless and restless without any more battles to fight. "It's easy for you," she told Max. You'll be mayor. Me, I don't know if I should stay here, or go somewhere else, or what. All I know how to do is fight Revenants, and there's not much call for that now."

"I will not be mayor," said Max.

They all gawped at him. "But everyone says ——"

"Everyone says wrong, then. I won't be putting my name forward for the election when it comes. I don't want it. I don't think I'd be any good at it."

"You need only be a sort of figurehead until you get the hang of it," said Miss Torpenhow. "The council can make all the important decisions, but I know people would like an Angmering in the town hall again."

"They will have an Angmering," said Max. "They will have my sister, Helen. She was much braver than me in the battle, and she's much closer to the people on the lower tiers. She stayed with them and fought with them all through Strega's time. Helen belongs here. I don't, not anymore."

"It is true that the city has changed a great deal," said Miss Torpenhow. "Or perhaps it is we who have changed a great deal. Something is certainly different."

Vespertine looked at them each in turn. "I shall go north," she said. "No one in this city knows how to reattach my arm, and I liked having two arms. It was more symmetrical. Hilly says there are nomad technomancers in the Ice Wastes who still understand such matters."

"I said there *may* be," said Miss Torpenhow.

"We still have the *Fire's Astonishment*," said Oddington Doom. "I had thought of taking off in her and seeing what jobs I could scrounge up, but I'm too old to be out there alone."

"I would come with you, Oddington!" said Miss Torpenhow very quickly, and then, more shyly, "I mean, if you would like me to."

"I'd like nothing more," said Doom.

"And me," said Vespertine. "And Small Cat."

"Me too," said Tamzin.

"What sort of jobs?" asked Max.

Doom shrugged. The movement made him wince, for his wounds were still not quite fully healed. "I don't know," he said. "Nothing too dangerous. I'm not as young as I was. But it seems to me that a small band of experienced adventurers, with their own airship, and their own Revenant . . . Well, there must be stacks of cities with the sort of problems they might hire a bunch of ne'er-do-wells like that to sort out for them."

"I should certainly like to see more of the world," said Miss Torpenhow. "There is so much I've only read about in books — Arkangel cruising the Ice Wastes on its iron runners, and Kaiju-Tokyo striding on its mighty legs along the shores of the Pacific . . ."

"I'd like to see the Middle Sea again," said Max.

"See Posie Naphtali again, you mean," Tamzin said.

"There must be a thousand cities out there," said Doom. "No sense in spending all your time on this one."

"Well, I shall stay here," said Trubshawe, thinking of the cozy new house he had just rented in the pastry-makers' quarter. "I shall stay here, and when you're not all too busy risking your necks in foreign parts, you must come back and tell me of your adventures, and I shall make great paintings of them."

"But where shall we begin?" asked Miss Torpenhow.

"With the arm people," urged Vespertine.

"The Middle Sea," said Max.

They fell to arguing. Tamzin half listened, and fingered the brass sun pendant that still hung around her neck. She wondered if somewhere out there in the wide world she might one day meet the person who had scratched her name on it. But it was only a passing thought. She had found her family, and they were sitting around this table in the sunshine. Wherever they decided to go, she would be happy to go with them.

The others were still arguing. Quietly and carefully, using all the skill and cunning that her life in the Arcade had taught her, she helped herself to the last of the pastries.

ACKNOWLEDGMENTS

This book is dedicated to Jeremy Levett, and he's definitely earned it. We worked together on *The Illustrated World of Mortal Engines* a few years ago, which means it's now almost impossible to write about the Traction Era without incorporating something he has either invented or improved upon — Oddington Doom's account of life in Oztralia is full of Jeremy's creations. Even when I'm not drawing on the products of his mighty brain, I'm often thinking, "What would Jeremy do?" It's unlikely that this book would exist without him.

Nor would it have got very far without my brilliant agent, Philippa Milnes Smith; my editors at Scholastic: Lauren Fortune, Wendy Shakespeare, and Samantha Stewart in the UK; Emily Seife, Mary Kate Garmire, and Starr Baer in the USA; and Scholastic UK's senior design manager, Jamie Gregory. Ian McQue is probably the best science fiction artist of our age and I'm delighted he has found time to create another wonderful cover illustration. *Fire's Astonishment* is the title of a novel by the great Geraldine McCaughrean: a truly astonishing book, and the spark that set me writing *Mortal Engines*. It's sadly out of print, but if you can't find it, read some of her others, they are all superb.

Thank you to Sam and Sarah Reeve for putting up with me, and Sarah McIntyre for chivvying me along.

And finally, and most importantly, thank you to everyone who has read the Mortal Engines books over the past twenty-three years, and especially to those who asked for more — I'm sorry it's been such a long wait.

ABOUT THE AUTHOR

PHILIP REEVE lives in Devon, England, with his wife and son. His first novel, *Mortal Engines*, was published in the UK in 2001. Three sequels followed, the last of which, *A Darkling Plain*, won both the Guardian Children's Fiction Prize and the Los Angeles Times Book Award. Philip later wrote three prequels to the Mortal Engines Quartet—*Fever Crumb*, *A Web of Air*, and *Scrivener's Moon*.

He has also written a novel set in dark age Britain called *Here Lies Arthur*, which won the Carnegie Medal, a stand-alone novel called *No Such Thing as Dragons*, many illustrated younger fiction books with illustrator Sarah McIntyre, and a YA trilogy, *Railhead*. He is the coauthor, with Brian Mitchell, of two stage musicals, *The Ministry of Biscuits* and *Lord God*. He has also made a short film called *Gwenevere*, which you can find on YouTube.

Learn more at philipreeve.com.

EXPLORE THE WORLD OF
MORTAL ENGINES!

THE ORIGINAL SERIES!

THE PREQUEL SERIES!